The Johnson Project

April 4, 2016

Libertyville, IL

"You know, Mrs. Buckman, you need a license to buy a dog, or drive a car. Hell, you need a license to catch a fish! But they'll let any butt-reaming asshole be a father."

-*Parenthood*. Dir. Ron Howard. Perf. Keanu Reeves, Universal Pictures, 1989.

Dr. Cathy Radio Broadcast – Syndicated

Dr. Cathy: *Kids. Don't have 'em if you're not gonna raise 'em. Why is that so hard to understand? Callers, maybe you can explain why a woman would get naked with a man, let him penetrate her vagina with his penis and then be surprised by a pregnancy. Hello! Ever heard of birds and bees? We all know how it works yet every single day someone calls me in tears about a "surprise" pregnancy and wonders what to do. Really? Could you maybe have thought about that before you screwed around?*

Chapter 1 - Joey Is Six Weeks Old

<u>News Nine Investigates with Mickey Bruce – Chicago</u>
According to staff here at the Michigan Avenue Planned Parenthood, fewer women have requested abortions in the last two weeks. Perhaps a result of zealous demonstrators scaring away patients or maybe a sign of the times. Still another theory speculates that fewer women are actually pregnant. Sources in Europe have reported a downturn in pregnancies which would logically mean fewer abortions. American experts initially scoffed at the

assertion although this reporter is beginning to see some truth to that possibility. One thing's for sure. Business here is way down. This is Mickey Bruce, Investigative Reporting from the Loop. Back to you, Micah.

"Are you hearing this?" Ted asked his wife who was next to him in bed, engrossed in her book.

"No, why?" She mumbled.

Ted lowered the volume and turned to his wife. "Mickey Bruce claims that fewer women are having abortions. Huh."

Audrey made a face. "That's good, right? Maybe abortion rates are down because of better contraception and education and all that."

Ted considered. "Nah, that can't be it. He's saying that abortions are down because fewer women are getting pregnant. Ha! Crack reporter Mickey Bruce wouldn't make up crazy stuff just to get ratings."

Audrey rolled her eyes. "Tell that to the mayor and every Chicago alderman he's ever sunk his teeth into." She went back to reading.

"Your six-week is tomorrow, right?" Ted asked.

"Yes, but you're not invited." Audrey answered, not looking up from her book.

Ted let his phone fall to his side and feigned surprise. "I might just have a few questions for the good doctors at Lake Forest OB-GYN."

Audrey rolled her eyes. "Like what?"

"For one, I'd like to get the green light on the sex thing." He wiggled his eyebrows in what he thought was a seductive manner.

"Like we need their permission? Ted, my doctor will tell you we can get back at it tomorrow, I'll tell you to wait until next month but the reality is, it'll be eighteen years before we get any time to ourselves. Let's be real."

"I suppose you're right. Still, I want to go so I can observe their methods. See their stuff. Take some notes. Bwahahahaha."

"Don't, Ted. You make them all nervous with your strange IVF ways. Besides, you ask too many questions. They all think you're... well, odd."

"Oh, now, they love me over at Lake Forest OB. I take all the complicated, tedious pregnancies in this town and let them have the easy deliveries. They should be thanking me. They should probably send me a gift basket of that edible arrangement stuff, really. The cookies not the fruit."

Audrey turned to her husband. "Please. You know darn well you don't have time to sit around while they make me wait an hour past my appointment time just to show me how busy they are. I'll be lucky to get in by four."

Ted grabbed his phone and scrolled through to his schedule. "Never mind. We have a big staff meeting tomorrow afternoon. You're on your own."

Ted pretended to be put out. "Actually, we have some weighty matters to discuss. Important medical... thingies."

"Like new company cars for the entire staff? Oh, wait. You already did that."

"We work hard. We play hard. I'm sorry I can't sit with you and hold your hand in that hormonally charged waiting room full of weepy, tired women."

"It's okay, dear. You have your own waiting room full of weepy, tired women. I understand." She set her book down and turned her head. "Uh-oh, is that Joey? I think I hear Joey."

Ted popped out of bed and headed for the door of their master suite. "Never fear, son. Daddy is on the way!"

Ted didn't waste any time scurrying through the sitting room that led to the nursery. He treasured these moments. Both of his kids would grow up all too soon. Ted picked up his little bundle and shushed him until he stopped crying. "That's my brave little man." He kissed Joey's bald head and savored the softness of his peach fuzz. He crossed the hall to Allie's princess suite to peek in and hear her breathe. Knowing that his family was safely settled for the night was the most peaceful, fulfilling feeling a man could ever possibly enjoy. He whispered to his son, "Come on, pal. Mama's the feed bag, I'm just the transport."

Chapter 2

Dr. Rafael Johnson looked into the dilated pupils of a very pregnant teen. Part of his job as a liaison Psychiatrist to the Chicago Public School System was to make counsel available to young girls who were "in trouble" as his mother's generation used to say. Rafael arranged open house events and personally met with youngsters who needed guidance.

"I shouldn't have to make a choice about keeping my baby. Why you even tell me somethin' like that?" The teenager slurred her words.

Rafael knew his overused speech was falling on deaf ears but he had to take a shot. "You already have a baby and you're living in a shelter. Your boyfriend is in prison for at least eight years. You don't have a high school diploma… Please consider the life this child will have."

"There's programs that will pay for everything. I just need you to sign me up for all that. I'm gonna need a place, too. Can you get me my own place? With Wi-Fi? Near where I can see my crew?"

"I will absolutely do everything in my power to see that your children have what they need but it's going to be very difficult for you especially when you start working…"

"Working? I'm a homemaker. I can't work."

"How can you be a homemaker if you don't have a home?" Rafael didn't mean to lose his temper but the absurdity was breathtaking.

"Get me a place from, like, the county or the state. I know lots of girls who get to move out when they have a baby. An apartment, food stamps, a check for, like four hunnert dollars a month. Don't give me no bullshit. Jus' get me signed up. That's the only reason I came here for."

"It doesn't work like that." But Rafael could tell she didn't want to hear it. "We need to consider options for this child."

The pregnant teen stood up and wrapped her too small coat around her bulging tummy. "You're supposed to make me feel better about having my baby. I don't need *options*. Fuck you, stupid spic." She grabbed a bunch of bananas and stormed off dramatically until she bumped into a chair and almost fell. Rafael jumped up to help her but she sneered at him and exited while holding her middle finger over her head.

The ancient gymnasium was empty. The seats were arranged to hold at least one hundred girls but, at best, fifteen had sauntered in, took some food and left. Rafael noted they were all repeat customers looking for a day out and free food.

His phone chirped three times before he looked down to see that his brother was on the line. He already knew what the call was about. At least he wouldn't have to argue with a teenager although talking to Ted wasn't a far cry.

"Hello, Ted."

"Raf! You *are* alive. I was beginning to think the worst."

"I received your messages regarding the family weekend at Mother's, I just don't know if I can make it up there Friday. I have paperwork and I have to prepare for a school board meeting next week…"

"Of course you can make it up here. You need a break and Allie is insisting she see Uncle Raf. And think about Joey! He barely knows you!"

"Well... Honestly, I could use some family time. In fact, I desperately need it. I want to see Joey, of course. Count me in and tell Allie we will continue our discussion on squirrels."

Ted laughed. "And expect her to sleep at night?"

"Funny, Ted. I'm sorry I've been so out of it lately. I've been busy with the open house and just couldn't..."

"How'd it go?" Ted asked in serious mode.

Rafael looked around the empty room. "It was an epic fail as the kids say. I'm not reaching them anymore. I couldn't even fill the house."

Ted considered his brother's statement. "It's hard to spread the word to pregnant teens. They keep their secret or go into denial. Your audience is a tough crowd. Hard to even pinpoint let alone talk some sense into."

"I've posted at every Chicago public high school, through social media and actually old fashioned word of mouth brings them in. But not this time.

"Maybe your message is getting across and there just aren't as many pregnant teens. Maybe all your hard work has paid off. Did you ever think of that?"

Rafael made a doubtful face. "If only it were true. Sadly, no, these girls will get pregnant no matter what and I need to be here to keep them healthy and hopefully get them on a better track."

"Yeah. Hey, I'll see you Friday night at the manse. Try to get there while Nora is still sober, okay?"

Rafael smiled for the first time that day. What were the chances his sister would stay sober on a Friday night?

Chapter 3

Nora Johnson Berger approached the witness stand where a terrified five year old boy couldn't stop his lower lip from trembling. His whole body was shaking in fear. Nora was focused on the hideous, ragged cut on his cheek, the result of a beating with a tree branch complicated and infected because of delayed treatment. The wounds on his back and buttocks weren't visible but Nora knew they were there. She'd read the hospital records. Saw the history of fractured bones, untreated burns and savage whip marks. She was furious but kept her voice gentle for the boy.

"You've been terrific, Billy. Just one more question, honey. Do you want to live with your mother?"

He looked hopefully at the defense table where an unsmiling, though stylish-looking mother narrowed her eyes, waiting for the response. She tried to nod to the boy without looking like she was coaching.

"I d-d-dooo, but she doesn't want me there." Billy sobbed.

"What makes you say that, Billy?" Nora strained to keep her voice even and stood in the line of sight between him and his mother.

Billy wiped his eyes and tried to give the right answer. "She said that I have to say I want to live with her but Ron will have to hide if the people come. I have to say Ron won't be there. But he'll be there and it's all my fault."

Nora looked from the bereft boy to the judge. "Approach the bench, your honor!"

The judge motioned for Nora and the defense attorney to approach. Nora's teeth and fists were clenched. The judge turned to Nora's adversary. "It seems your client has been fibbing, Mr. Norelli. Do you have anything to say?"

Tony Norelli was confident. "The kid is, what? Five years old? He doesn't know what he's talking about..."

Nora burst but kept her diatribe to a fierce whisper. "How dare you? Your client is a disgrace to motherhood and obviously still consorting with that animal she's married to. Believe it or not, he's out on bail after torturing a five-year-old. You'd think your client would cut him loose, maybe even get a restraining order to keep him away from her son. No, not this mother-of-the-year. And the shiner she's carefully concealed under a thick paste of make-up tells me he's back at home cutting switches, ready to strike again. He's not even the biological father but your client chose him over her own child."

The judge was on her side but didn't need the drama. "That's enough, Mrs. Berger. Step back, both of you."

The case would have the same outcome as a hundred other cases on any given day in any given courtroom in any given U.S. county. The judge tapped his gavel and ruled by rote. "The child will remain in foster care until his mother can comply with this court's requirement to cease a relationship with her husband." With another tap, the judge was gone. Norelli whispered an explanation to his dumbstruck client. Nora jammed papers into her briefcase while she watched a confused and miserable Billy take his backpack and walk toward the downtrodden foster mother who mechanically helped him with his coat and guided him to the door of the courtroom. Billy looked helplessly at Nora with the same expression of anguish she had seen too many times in her life. He wasn't looking to his mother, he was looking to her because he needed help and so far, the world had failed him.

That look broke Nora's heart and she vented every bit of angry frustration at the immediate target: the idiotic mother who couldn't believe she was losing custody of her son. Again. "Do you have any idea how many childless couples out there would love to adopt your son? Who would love to give him a home and give him a life? Let Billy go while he still has a chance to bond with a loving family! What the *fuck* is the matter with you?"

The defiant mother, still genuinely shocked by the court's decision was spoiling for a fight. "What the hell do you know? You may be black but everyone knows you're the daughter of Mary Johnson. You grew up with a silver spoon in your mouth and you dare tell me I shouldn't keep my own child? These accusations are way overblown and you know it. My husband is a good man with a good job and he's good to me. Maybe if all of you would leave us alone, he wouldn't get so angry. I'm gonna get my boy back and keep my family together!"

Nora knew the bitch was right. That's what killed her every time she came to court. Eventually, Billy would return to a horrible situation with this punching bag and have a miserable, abusive childhood. His mom would just get better at hiding it. Sure, he lived in a nice neighborhood but the horror he would experience over and over and over... Maybe, she prayed, he would escape early and get the peace he deserved in his adulthood. Except that rarely happened. This would not be her last court date with Billy. She would continue to expose the horrible abuse, the sadistic punishments and the mental cruelty but the judge would have to consider the fact that Billy had a roof over his head, a yard to play in and really, was the foster alternative better? Something about this kid, though, brought out her claws.

"You need to know something!" Nora angrily wiped a tear from her cheek and turned on the mother. "I have just made it my life's mission to stalk your ass until Billy can take care of himself. Every time you turn around I'll be there! You haven't see the last of me."

Tony Norelli just wanted to meet his pals for a drink but for some reason felt the need to defend his client. "Hey, Nora, you're crossing a line, here. Really, your conduct is kind of unprofessional. You don't know what this woman has been through."

"I know what Billy's been through. Did you see that cut on his face? This...this... woman stood by while her... husband beat a child with a tree branch and then locked him in a closet for two days before getting him to a hospital. The boy sat in his own waste, while bleeding, crying, starving and begging for two days! God, Tony, don't you see she's a monster?"

"My client is also a victim. She's getting the counseling she needs..." Tony tried to mean it.

"This is the fourth time in court! The fourth time in the hospital! How many beatings and terrified nights has Billy gone through that we don't even know about?"

The woman glared. "I refuse to let her treat me like this. Can this... this... *African American* treat me like this?" Tony hoped this would be over soon so he could forget about this day and get right to his favorite barstool. There was never a happy ending in family court. Never. Nora left the courtroom quickly. It was that or she would start using her fists. God, she wanted to break that woman's face. Maybe it was time to move into real estate law. Wills, contracts, anything but this.

Chapter 4

Mary Johnson watched the city of Chicago from the board room of her high rise office. Her late husband had purchased the building back in the sixties when the power couple formed their philanthropic foundation with the intention of making the world a better place. Dr. Oliver Johnson didn't live to see all the good that came from their generosity, but Mary always thought of him after an especially good day and somehow knew that he was guiding her to make the right decisions. She also knew that he would be proud of his children, although he never got to meet them. Actually, he died before any of them officially became Johnsons.

Mary had encouraged Ted to pursue a medical career but it was Ted who went into reproductive health to honor his late father. Nora and Rafael also chose fields that Oliver would have championed, both in the care of children. She felt comfort in the fact that Rafael and Nora were somewhat close to her right now, both worked in the Loop and often dropped by the office for lunch or coffee. Ted's practice was in Lake Forest, just up the North Shore. He and Audrey lived within a few miles of Mary's estate so she got to see them frequently. Life was peaceful in her golden years. Two grandchildren, hopefully more in the future. Yet the rest of the children of the world needed her.

She waited for her assistant, Burke, to bring in her next challenge. She was happy to meet with the reps from IPAT and greatly appreciated their progress in the fight against child trafficking but the men visiting today were old school and tended to patronize. Still they were dogged in their approach to ending the filthy crimes against children so she would endure the pomposity as long as the end result was productive. The walnut double doors opened and Mary mentally prepared herself as Burke led her three guests into her office. She noticed Burke stayed put, probably worried about leaving her alone with the aggressive bunch.

After the customary rounds of handshakes and small talk, the Moroccan leader got down to business. "Mrs. Johnson, your last donation was more than generous and completely unexpected." His gratitude was sincere at least.

Mary smiled graciously. "I believe in your cause, Mr. Kabli, and I know you are devoted to the mission."

He maintained the obsequious expression but his eyes lit up as he dared a glance at his associates to let them know the trip to Chicago would be worth it. "I do worry about your situation, Mrs. Johnson. You are unmarried, a widow. How generous of you to carve out your savings for our quest. I hope your late husband has provided well for you."

"He has, indeed. And the money he left has been invested wisely, leaving me very comfortable and quite willing to help the causes that will best benefit the children of the world." Her net worth was somewhere in the high-billions and well documented. Mr. Kabli must have known that but Mary would go through the paces.

"I am so relieved to hear this and it pains me and my associates here to even ask for more but we must. As you know, the lion's share of your last donation was spent in Eastern Europe where it brought relief for a short time. Now we find a pressing need in many African nations. Can we impose upon you again so that the African children will be relieved of their suffering?"

"Of course, Mr. Kabli." She reached for her check ledger as the men let out a collective breath of relief only to inhale again once Mary added, "However, I have some concerns."

Kabli kept the smile on his face but only because he half expected a conditional donation so he was not unprepared. Why this woman couldn't retire happily in her big house and rock her grandchildren and pet her cats was beyond his ken. American women, even the older ones, were far too independent for their own good. "I agree that we should expand our resources to Africa. In fact, I have just returned from there."

"But of course, I read of your generosity during the Mosul Refugee crisis in Iraq. So many poor souls in makeshift tents with no food, no water. Your efforts were heroic! I am told you brought over four million water bottles to the many families in transition. So generous!" Kabli was pleased to show Mary that he knew of her other recent donations while complimenting her magnanimous gesture. He had done his homework.

"It was my pleasure, Mr. Kabli. The government tried to hide the catastrophe but I have sources over there who told me we were headed for human tragedy if desperate measures weren't taken soon. We were able to rush the water and medical supplies by private plane in a matter of hours thankfully because the foundation has a warehouse in Egypt. It took some negotiating with the Federation Council and the Prime Minister but..."

"Of course, of course. You were the angel of mercy in this case. You were there handing out water bottles and in doing so brought hope. I applaud your courage for entering such a dangerous part of the world." His condescension filled the room.

"As I've said before, I have a wonderful team that takes care of all the logistics and they also take care of me. I owe everything to my capable staff."

"I hope you will consider IPAT just as capable and trust in our judgement."

"My point is, while in Egypt I spoke with the deputy Prime Minister and he..."

"Of course, Mrs. Johnson. Your diplomatic efforts are important and you made excellent headway with your visit."

Mary was careful. "I'm concerned that we are abandoning Eastern Europe. There's still so much..."

Kabli took Mary's hand and interrupted again. "You are a kind-hearted woman, Mrs. Johnson, and it hurts me that you even know about the unmentionable crimes against children. I hope you can understand that we are not abandoning the children of Eastern Europe, we are simply compromising with Mr. Putin. It is all part of diplomacy and knowing when we have met our match. I will explain this to you: Mr. Putin would rather we not expose some of Russia's, let's say, dirty laundry, and we have agreed to stay out of his way. The African officials in certain nations are slightly more open to negotiation as long as we are careful not to offend their pride. We must walk a very fine line in our work. It is not ideal, of course, but we must make this agreement in order to help children elsewhere. Do you understand?"

Mary smiled benevolently at the men. "I do. Yes, I do." She knew that her attempts at diplomacy were seen as ceremonial before the male negotiators stepped in to make firm deals. She also knew that some of the IPAT staff were being threatened in Eastern Europe. So when it came right down to it, volunteers getting killed wouldn't help anybody, certainly not the children. There would always be gut wrenching decisions to make and children who would be left behind. Now these old-fashioned, well-meaning men wanted her money but not her opinion and, they were about to get both wishes granted. Mary reached for her chirping cell phone. It was the family cell, Ted called it the 'Bat Phone,' the only one that stayed charged and on call 24/7.

"Excuse me, gentlemen. It's my daughter-in-law, Audrey. I won't be a minute."

They hastily excused themselves to the far end of the office to give her privacy while taking in the glorious view of the lake and the city. Mary spoke gently and, true to her word, the call lasted less than a minute. She stood and clasped her hands to address her audience. "Gentlemen, I never understand all of the political ramifications but I know you always make the right decisions. Please accept a donation of five million dollars to get started on your venture in Africa. Eastern Europe will have to take a back seat but I know the money will be well spent. Godspeed."

They were expecting only three million and far more maternal input so they were pleased to be done so early with more money than they dared hope. Mary hastily scribbled out the check. "Now it seems my grandchildren need a babysitter this afternoon so I need to get back home." She made the rounds of good-byes and thankyous and hand kisses then nodded to Burke, a sign to bring the car around to the front door so she could head home to Lake Forest and cuddle with her grandbabies, Allie and Joey.

Chapter 5

Ted headed the meeting in the conference room at Johnson IVF. The office manager, Sybil sat at his side taking notes. His three partners showed concern.

"I don't get it," Ted said.

Dr. Zoe Lakey waved her hand in dismissal. "Ted, it would be hard to get if we were Joe Schmoe's Run-of-the-Mill OB, then there would be cause for concern, but we're not. Every pregnancy that we treat is high risk so we're going to have some good days and we're going to have some bad days."

Dr. Khan Patel did not agree. "It has been weeks, not days. When was our last successful IVF?"

Everyone looked down at their notes.

"It's been at least a month according to my records," answered Sybil with self-importance while unnecessarily, but with drama, checking her clipboard. Ted pulled the file he was looking for. "Yes. Mrs. Milliner was our last positive and that was... let's see... Crap! That was six weeks ago. What the hell?"

"You are correct." Khan confirmed. "Before that was my patient, Anna Rejke. She is now ten weeks pregnant. My last two procedures have not taken."

"That can't be right," Zoe suddenly looked worried. "Del, what about you?"

Dr. Roman Delgado sighed deeply. "I received bad news this morning from a patient that I was sure would be celebrating her success but instead she called me in tears."

Ted turned in shock to Roman. "The Rusches? Shoot. How many cycles has it been?"

"Fifteen. They're ready to quit. My most recent pregnancy was twelve weeks ago. What's going on, Ted? What are we doing wrong?"

"Nothing." Ted answered. "Something's off..." His words trailed off as his thoughts took an unusual turn.

After a moment of silence, Zoe shrugged. "We can't let word get out. We have to keep this in house. Our patients have to believe in us."

Khan murmured something about equipment. Ted paced. "Um. Did any of you catch Mickey Bruce on the news last night? He claims that abortion rates are suddenly way down all over the place. Kinda weird, don't you think?"

"I saw it," Zoe said, wondering where this was going. "The last thing our patients want is an abortion. So... what?"

"Does anyone take that guy seriously? When he's not hounding city workers, he's making crazy assumptions. He's looking for headlines." Del shrugged.

Khan nodded. "Some sources today say he is not incorrect. I saw a post from London this morning with some alarming numbers regarding pregnancy rates but what does this have to do with us?"

Ted shrugged. "Dunno. Just seems odd. All righty, let's call it a fluke and get busy making babies. We've got a full schedule this week and we're due for some good news."

They left quietly as Ted stayed by himself at the head of the table, deep in thought. He jumped when his ring tone erupted with "Be My Little Baby." A quick glance told him Audrey was on the line. He answered immediately.

"How'd it go?" He asked.

"Good. Everything's good. Doc says all my parts are still there."

"Excellent! Were the kids okay with my mom?"

"Of course. It's incredible that she can run a billion dollar foundation, yet drop everything when I need a sitter."

"That's mom." Ted smiled.

"Have you noticed she's repeating herself? Sometimes telling the same story twice in one conversation?"

"Yes. It's really annoying when the story was boring to begin with. Having to hear it twice is torture."

"Ted. I just think we need to watch out. She's getting older..."

"I hear you. She's not driving anymore and she's better about checking in. I don't think she's ready for one of those alert button necklace things yet."

"Agreed. Oh, by the way, she taught Allie how to play Go Fish so be ready for that when you get home."

"Let the Go Fish tournament begin!" Ted looked at his watch. "Hey, how'd you get home so fast?" He could hear Joey cooing in the background.

"Oh, that was weird. Usually the waiting room is packed and it's a fight to use the restroom. But today it was just me and a few mommies about to burst. I asked Elaine, you know, the office manager there, and she said, in complete confidence, mind you, that they're not getting any new patients. Maybe word got out about the long waits. They have to be worried."

26

"Hmmmm."

"What? Why are you hmmming...?"

Ted interrupted. "Hon, I gotta go."

"Okay. See you at dinner."

He found the remote and turned on the flat screen. He changed the channel to CNN and was immediately taken to New York City where a reporter talked about the sudden dip in pregnancy rates. He switched to Fox and got the same story. Even the local news in Chicago talked about the odd phenomenon that was suddenly getting serious attention. The ABC Eyewitness news reporter ended with, *"If you are newly pregnant, please send us a text. We'd like to speak with you!"*

Ted hit an international number on his phone as he headed to his office. It took a few minutes but a sleepy female answered. "C'est Lily. Bon jour."

"Lily, it's Ted. Wake up."

"Ted, I fell asleep at my desk. I've been up for forty-eight hours. I was going to call you tomorrow."

"So I'm not crazy? Same thing over there?"

"Nothing official but the media people are getting more rabid as they fact check. The docs are comparing notes. There is obviously a problem but no one knows to what extent."

"What about your practice?"

"We have had no conceptions in weeks. Not in Paris. Not in Hamburg. Not in Zurich. What about Chicago?"

"None in my office and Audrey went for a checkup here in Lake Forest which is a huge practice. At least twenty docs. Apparently, they aren't getting any new patients."

"There is most definitely a decrease in pregnancies."

"But there are some viable pregnancies, right?"

"I've had calls from WHO and CDC. Everything is off the record, of course, but the problem is real. We have found no recent pregnancies. None."

Ted was incredulous. "Seriously? This is a thing?"

"It could be just an anomaly, some kind of virus. I'm sure the CDC is checking it out in the States. There's a team over at Carrel studying the patterns. Pierre has kept me up to date."

"Wow. Keep me posted from your side of the world and I'll see what I can find out here."

"I will, Ted. Hug your babies for me. I want to meet them someday."

"Will do."

Ted started with a call to a colleague at UCLA then a friend at Johns Hopkins. While trying to make some sense of the situation, Sybil burst in on him several times with messages from more associates and random news sources including AP. By the end of the work day,

Ted was thoroughly discouraged. He asked Sybil to get the gang back together but this time the meeting would be at his house, after work, and they were asked to bring their spouses.

Chapter 6

In the comfort of Ted and Audrey's great room, the doctors from the practice and their spouses watched in silence as the story unfolded globally via television, internet, Twitter, Instagram, Facebook and every social medium in existence. A team at the Carrel Institute officially broke the news at 7:17pm Central Time Zone with a statement from Pierre Charbot, one of Ted's contemporaries in the field of high risk reproduction. There were no regularly scheduled programs to be watched that night. The whole world hung on the scraps of information that eked out slowly from the few knowledgeable sources. At some point, Ted excused himself to take a call while the others listened to the somber reporters all trying to break something new, reveal more detailed analysis than the other stations. Many reporters struggled for composure as they read from their Teleprompters after hearing from experts who offered little hope. Ted returned from his call and hit the mute button on the television. He stood and spoke with uncharacteristic gravitas. "That was Lily.

She's at Carrel with Pierre Charbot. It's been confirmed. We know for certain that no one, on this planet, has conceived artificially or naturally in the last six weeks."

"Is it everywhere? Worldwide?" Roman asked, his wife sat next to him with a dazed look.

"Yes." Ted confirmed. "All continents. Although parts of Europe haven't had a conception in at least eight weeks. Tracking it down to one area to find the cause is going to take some time if at all."

"So the virus is airborne?" Khan asked.

"Most definitely. The spread must have been immediate, within days as far as we know so far. It's a bug, an airborne viral infection. The CDC is calling it the Aqar297 virus. Anyway, everyone has succumbed to this Aqar bug. Every female has it, even young girls, and there are no side effects, no illness, no flu. The only lasting consequence is infertility."

Zoe was nearly out of her chair. Her husband held her hand. She was in tears. "So *I'm* infertile?! *Me*? There's a cure, right? Someone's going to figure out how to reverse the effects, right, Ted?"

Ted couldn't look his partner in the eye. "Lily got to take a look at a test patient they've been working with for the last few days and they've found an anomaly in her uterine lining. There's some kind of autoimmune disorder that is making the uterus reject fertilized eggs that try to attach. They aren't sure if the embryos have been affected by the virus or the just the uterine lining but either way, no one will be getting pregnant."

"What about the couples who have frozen embryos donated before the virus?" Zoe almost brightened at the thought.

"Lily said that's their next step. But I have a feeling if the uterine lining is compromised, well... I don't have to tell you..."

Khan thought he was being helpful when he said, "The doctors in this room should know that you cannot reverse this type of sterility." His wife, although not a physician, gave him a pained look telling him to shut up which kept him from speaking further.

There was silence except for the sound of Zoe Lakey weeping. Finally Roman made a grim statement. "So, you're telling us we no longer have careers."

Ted was astounded. "I'm telling you, Roman, that the end of the human race is imminent. I wasn't really thinking about our jobs."

Zoe's husband helped her up. Roman and his stunned wife also rose. "I get that, Ted, but I have a family to raise, a mortgage to pay and no more patients. Not all of us have a billionaire dynasty to fall back on."

Zoe turned on Roman. "Well at least you've already had your kids, Roman. We were waiting until the right time." She sobbed and left the room with her stunned husband trailing behind.

Roman and his wife followed out the door.

Ted turned to Khan and his wife. "We still have pregnant patients. I guess we should... I don't know."

Khan understood. "I will stay with you as long as we have patients. Of course."

Audrey, also stunned but trying to understand. "How is it that the pregnant women now are staying pregnant if they have this virus?"

Ted considered. "I don't know but there's been no upturn in miscarriages so hopefully, those moms will be okay. We have a lot of research to do. A lot of questions to answer."

Audrey calculated. "So in seven or eight months, the last babies on earth will be born?"

Ted took her hand. "Yes."

Khan and his wife had four children but the shock was still great. They stood to take their leave. "I'd like to help with your research, Ted, and I'll stay on to care for our pregnant patients."

The men shook hands. The women hugged.

Chapter 7

The public reaction in the States was peaceful and heartbreaking. People took to the streets looking for consolation, perhaps some justification. There was no rioting, no demonstrations, just sad souls contemplating the future and hoping for a solution. But there were no experts encouraging hope and everyone looked at their life and their world with a new perspective.

It only took one day for the stock market to react and the results were frightening. Plenty of experts appeared on the news to predict dire consequences and financial ruin but no one could say what form it would take because there was no one on the earth qualified to analyze the new turn of events. No precedent or history to learn from. Certainly, no game plan. Everyone had to wait and see.

Friday dinners at the Johnson estate were normally happy affairs but the uncertainty had everyone in a serious mood along with the rest of the world. Mary sat at the head of the table in her grand dining room with a view of a magnificent yard leading to the shores of Lake Michigan. No one noticed the scenery, though. Joey gurgled in a bassinet between Mary and Audrey. Ted sat to the right side of Mary with Rafael at his side. Allie was happily eating apple slices next to Uncle Raf. The adults were waiting for Lou and Nora before they would eat and discuss the topic that was being discussed everywhere. In the meantime, Allie told everyone about her best friend at school, girl-Jordan. Everyone smiled and listened patiently. Allie made it very clear that she was also friends with boy-Jordan, but girl-Jordan was her absolute bestie which was news to Ted who all along had been thinking that Lauren G. had achieved that status but apparently not.

They heard Lou and Nora come through the great hall and into the dining room where everyone rose to greet them. Allie was delighted to hug her aunt and uncle and loved it when Uncle Lou threw her into the air and caught her although it made her mom nervous.

Lou Berger was a decorated Chicago detective on the fast track to higher office. He and Nora met in a courtroom one day during a brutal custody hearing. They worked together on the case, both inspired by the other and managed to score a win for the children by placing them with the paternal grandmother. They stayed together from that point on and tied the knot within months. Both were devoted to their jobs and found in each other the perfect mate who understood eighteen hour days, night shifts and weekends spent at a computer. It was true love in the moments they shared during the tiny amounts of free time away from work. Lou held the chair for Nora to be seated and sat down himself, ready to eat.

"So what's new?" He joked without smiling.

Everyone appreciated the attempt but they waited until Allie went into the nearby playroom and engrossed herself in a fantasy story with a doll house and a new picture book before discussing the Aqar virus.

"Any way you look at it, it's a pandemic with no cure." Ted ventured. "Although Charbot has made it very clear that he will be the savior in this crisis and the press seems to agree. Pierre is just happy to have messianic light thrown his way. The guy's kooky but if anyone can run a lab to fix this, it's him."

"It should have been you, dear." Mary said.

Ted shrugged. "They got it covered. Yuan Chen is over there and Lily, of course. They got every top notch doc in fertility and beyond. If there is a solution and I'm not so sure there is, the best minds will be on the lookout. The thing is, they can't even properly categorize the pathogen as of yet." He looked around the table at his family. "We might not live to see the cure for this. Might not happen in our lifetime."

"Don't say that, Ted!" Audrey scolded. "I can't bear to think of Allie and Joey when the last...." She couldn't continue. No one wanted to think that far into the future.

Lou jabbed his fork into the air. "It will probably be one of those two kids who figure out a way to make things work. Watch 'em. Just like their pop."

Mary smiled at her son-in-law. "That's why we must soldier on and make sure every child on the planet is cared for and provided a top notch education. Fresh young minds can conquer the worst situations. They are the future."

"Or the whimper." Nora scowled in her usual pessimistic manner.

Rafael summed it up. "I suppose we all thought global warming or nuclear war would be the end of mankind. I never thought it would end with a virus."

"Really?" Ted answered, half serious. "I always did. I just thought the virus would kill us all. I'm a bit shocked at this infertility angle."

"I always thought zombies would somehow be involved." Lou said. It was a good attempt at lightening the mood and it made everyone smile a little.

"I'm still trying to wrap my head around it." Audrey sighed. "It seriously hasn't sunk in yet. I woke up this morning thinking everything's okay and then I thought, 'crap the world is coming to an end,' and I relived the shock of it. Then I drove through town taking Allie to school and nothing has changed. Yet everything has changed."

"It's crazy. We have terrorists everywhere trying to kill anybody who disagrees with them. Now nature quietly does the job. Huh." Nora opined.

Mary was more practical. "I firmly believe we have to make the most of the time we have left on this earth and figure out a way to keep our final bow on this planet a peaceful one. We still have work to do. The Johnson Foundation will serve the people, most especially the children, until the end."

"I agree, Mom. If we're gonna die out, let's keep it organized and painless and peaceful." Lou offered.

"This will sound horrible but there is some good coming out of the situation." Mary said. "Applications for foster children are through the roof! Everyone wants a foster child. Many think it's their last chance at parenthood."

"Remarkable," Audrey said. "At least there's a silver lining."

"The truly remarkable part is that we can finally be selective," Mary said happily. "Instead of choosing the least objectionable candidates to take in these poor darlings, we will have long lines of wonderful options. It's such a great relief."

"We'll be working overtime to get them through the courts," Nora added. "We're taking on temporary legal help just to keep up. Luckily, my latest contempt of court was thrown out so I can focus on the back log. Yay!"

"My darling, another contempt? What happened?" Mary asked, concerned.

Nora waved it away. "Nothing, Mom." Mary turned to Lou for the straight answer.

Lou looked around the table at his inquiring in-laws. "The usual Nora Anger-Management Show but we're good. There are more pressing matters on everyone's minds these days."

Everyone nodded in response.

"My job is done," Rafael announced. "No more pregnant teens. I don't need to counsel or persuade high school girls to make better choices because the reproduction choice has been made for them. Mother Nature has taken the wheel."

"Did you ever think that would happen?" Nora asked.

"No," Rafael countered. "But now we have to deal with a generation of young women who will never give birth or know the joy of motherhood."

"Will you stay on at CPS, sweetheart?" Mary asked Raf.

Raf shrugged. "I hope so as a guidance counselor. But this is the Chicago Public School system. We never know if our jobs are safe during normal times so now, with enrollment about to drop in the next few years, I expect to get my notice. On the other hand, many children will need counseling because of our sad situation. I have no idea. We're all waiting to find out what happens next."

Mary looked warily at her younger son. "Please don't go back to traveling all over. I just got used to having you near me and I hate to think of you back on the road. Maybe it's time you joined us at the foundation."

"I want to go where I can be of service. I still think the public school system needs all the help it can get right now. But if they do let me go, I will absolutely join you at the foundation. I suppose it was predestined."

"That's my boy. I know your father would be proud." Mary gushed.

Rafael blushed. It was nice to hear.

40

"It's just so weird to think that in a few years we won't see baby carriages in the park any more. We won't need preschools or daycare centers. It's crazy." Audrey marveled.

"Here's the crazy thing. There's going to be a big shift in the workforce over the next few years." Lou said. "All those teachers and babysitters and kid doctors will be looking for work. Even on the force, we're gonna need fewer cops because there'll be fewer people."

Audrey frowned. "This is going to cause an economic mess, isn't it?"

Nora agreed. "Like nothing we've ever seen before. You can't even compare it to the Depression. We're headed for serious instability but who knows where it will lead. I hope the government has a plan. I really do."

Mary smiled shyly. "I happen to know that the oval office has arranged for a task force to figure out a solution. They've asked top economists, sociologists and financial experts to analyze the future for America."

"How do you happen to know about this, Mom?" Ted asked, eyebrows raised.

She blushed. "I happen to know about it because I was asked to participate. I'm honored and humbled and hope I can offer some help."

The family responded enthusiastically. "I feel better knowing you're on the job, Mom." Ted said happily.

"I'm relieved they are taking a proactive approach," Nora added. "This is perfect for you, Mom."

"I will do the best I can."

"Who else is on the committee?" Audrey asked.

"Oh, dear, it's a who's who of business people, most of whom I've met. Warren and Bill, of course. Oh, and Susan, Whitney and Abigail. Some from the Wall Street crowd. No politicians whatsoever. It's all people who have been successful with money and Warren convinced them that my experience with the foundation might be of use."

"Makes sense." Nora said.

"We've been told in advance that the biggest government cuts will be on welfare and assistance programs. I have to say, and I don't mean to criticize, but I don't think the government did a very good job with it anyway. They've spent trillions over the years but they never could get it right. They got all caught up in the rules and exceptions and distribution and enforcement. I've always secretly thought they should stick to governing and let the private sector handle the social welfare of the people. We already have the infrastructure in place. Look at the churches, religious charities and NGOs who have mastered the art of assistance and they've done it on shoestring budgets. We get the job done, without the bureaucracy, by appealing to the kindness of humanity and common sense. Hopefully, we can gently take over the assistance programs which will free up money to be better distributed where it's needed."

"I love it!" Nora exclaimed. "But you'll have to fire half the government workers."

Mary nodded. "Yes. But the private sector will pick them up easily. We don't see any problems with employment in the near future."

"Really? I would think the opposite." Lou stated.

"I promise there will be plenty of jobs. And you will be secure, my dear, because the money we save will go toward police and fire fighters in all the areas that have been depleted due to budget cuts. We'll take a long hard look at the waste and hopefully have the power to make the correct cuts."

"Do you think you'll have that kind of authority?"

"We've been told the situation is dire and our recommendations will have to be honored. The task force members have been emailing each other all day. I think we're all leaning in the same direction."

"When do you get started?"

"I leave tomorrow for our first meeting in Washington. We've been told that time is of the essence."

"Is Burke going with you?" Audrey asked, concerned. Mary was in excellent physical health but the family worried about her traveling so much. At least this trip would keep her in the country.

"Of course. Burke will be by my side."

"I might have a few ideas for you, mom." Nora laughed. Mary sipped her coffee. "I'd love to hear what you think, honey. I'll be tongue-tied when I meet with all these giants tomorrow but I do want to make sure we take care of the children that we have left on the planet. I hope I can help."

Audrey smiled at Mary. "We can do a lot of good right now. Even if the world is going away, we still have to take care of the time we have left."

"I think so, too. But I also know that Ted will be busily looking at this horrible Aqar virus from every angle." Mary directed her statement to her older son. "Maybe you can come up with something to save the human race, dear."

Ted laughed. "No pressure there, Mom."

"And here's to great expectations." Rafael toasted with his wine glass. They all raised a glass in hope.

"Now let's just hope we can keep the crazies from rioting in the street." Lou added seriously.

"People are so scared." Mary said.

"The predictions are grim." Nora agreed.

Ted nodded. "Yeah, the pundits are going nuts."

Meet The Nation – NBS News

Andy O'Hern: *Nothing at first. Then certain jobs disappear. Daycare providers, obstetricians, pediatricians, social service jobs that involve children, eventually teachers...*

Ira Wainstein: *People die! No babies to replace them.*

Walter Safer: *Companies will fade away because there is less population to buy their products. A disaster of epic proportion!*

Ira Wainstein: *Seventy years from now, what's left of the population will have no younger people to take care of them. No one to run the government.*

Andy O'Hern: *No law enforcement, no courts, no prisons. Every man for himself.*

Walter Safer: *I won't be there to see the end of the world but I pray for those that make it that far.*

Ira Wainstein: *In the meantime, we have to act fast in order to stay strong as a nation. We can get through* this until the end but only if we capably handle the transition.

Andy O'Hern: *Let's see what the Task Force 200 comes up with. Wherever they're meeting right now, I'd like to be a fly on the wall. I have to believe they'll come up with a plan. I'll be very interested to hear their ideas.*

WLN News on the Street

Young Woman: *And who's gonna pay our share of social security? That's what I keep wondering. What are we supposed to live on when we're old, you know?*

Middle Aged Woman: *I knew it. My pastor knew it. I've said from day one we should have had the Ten Commandments posted in every school and maybe these kids would behave. God is punishing everybody for their evil. I would think it's the homosexuals who started this nightmare.*

Young Boy: *I think it's kinda' whack but I asked my mom if we still had to recycle our cans and newspapers and stuff and she said, no, why bother?*

Middle Aged Man: *Oh, this is just a phase. They put together an incredible team of doctors over there in Paris to fix the baby bug and they will. I hope so. I'd like to be a grandpa someday!*

Chapter 8 - Joey is Two Months Old

The UN, WHO and CDC quickly conceived, gave birth to and baptized The World Medical Association with Dr. Pierre Charbot as the primary guardian. He brought together experts from around the world and promised a breakthrough in the near future. He was given every available resource to solve the problem as quickly as possible including full use of the Carrel Institute. Donations poured in from around the globe, corporations sent billions. Many experts predicted that the economy would bounce back if the virus were cured thus everyone pinned their hopes on the brilliant man and his team. Charbot vowed to make the world whole again, which his team found difficult to believe given the amount of time he spent on the news being interviewed and the talk show circuit being lauded and the "business" dinners being fed at the best restaurants in Europe. The world looked to him as their only hope for the future and he gladly took the mantle while talking about it to every media outlet that clamored for his attention. Although he was married to his third wife, a former runway model who was half his age, he rarely saw her which worked quite well for both of them. In fact, part of his contract included a flat at the George Cinq where he met with his mistress two nights a week. It was no secret to anyone in the field that he had eyes for Dr. Lily Simone and came as no surprise when she was made a member of the research team. Lily assumed Ted would be joining them in Paris but Dr. Charbot didn't think Dr. Johnson would fit in with the group and did not extend an offer. The omission was noted by many in the field, some even questioning the irresponsibility of not bringing on Dr. Theodore Johnson, but the chosen leader had full control of the team and his decisions were sacrosanct. Charbot would have been shocked to learn that Ted would have turned down a place on the team, anyway. There was no way he was leaving his family. He didn't want to uproot them to move to Paris when Allie was just getting started in school. It didn't stop Ted, though, from doing his own research and sending his findings to Lily for consideration. No one could have stopped him. Khan helped with the day to day needs of the practice while Ted studied the virus.

Chapter 9

Germany was the first country to open its borders to any immigrant who could pass a background check. After an efficient and thorough analysis, Germany's parliament quickly assessed the need to bring in new people to keep the population stable and it turned out to be a sensible, sound decision which saved them from economic ruin. The United States soon followed suit on open immigration as did many other nations knowing that no new naturally born residents meant a huge dip in population and eventually the work force. Some worried that unskilled immigrants would drain resources but there were jobs aplenty, not necessarily desirable jobs, but there were employment opportunities and many immigrants were happy to accept any job as long as they could stay in America. The Democrats in office officially granted amnesty to all undocumented workers currently living in the States hoping to bring in more income tax and better assess the future. Anyone working in a field involving children or children's products knew they would be looking for work very soon but the opportunities in other fields grew. The president promised an aggressive and quick solution to the looming troubles ahead and for once, both parties agreed that drastic steps would need to be taken. The elite Task Force 200 worked tirelessly for weeks on a solution and kept the stock market afloat unlike other countries where financial collapses and government shut downs were happening all too frequently. Greece threw in the towel almost immediately. There was no money coming in, no structure and no law enforcement. Eventually, most residents moved to neighboring countries leaving the Greek Islands a wasteland of deserted buildings and homes. A beautiful, scenic country left to seed, inhabited by the stubborn few who refused to give up their homes. Without law enforcement, it also became a refuge for criminal fugitives and miscreants.

Brazil's economy came to a crashing halt within weeks of Greece's demise. The government stopped paying employees, crime took hold and the looting devastated every major city. Some communities pulled together to survive but it was basically every man for himself. When the murders and arson became commonplace, many people escaped to neighboring countries and up north to the States. There was no way to contain the chaos in the cities. Even the military gave up. Brazil became a no-man's land, much like Greece.

Russia experienced the same pattern as Brazil, and nearly at the same time. Sadly, a scattered government and harsh winter brought deadly results and disturbing photos from the few courageous reporters who covered the downfall. They aired footage of ghost towns and cities, picked clean by looters. Dead bodies decayed in the streets. The haunting images were a wake-up call to every other struggling country and many citizens knew it was only a matter of time before it would be their turn. Some people wondered why nobody came to the aid of the falling nations but every other country was in the same precarious position. American troops overseas were called home. Embassies closed. It was no longer safe to travel anywhere but the homeland. American businesses with workforces in other nations insisted that the U.S. government provide security for their factories and safety for their foreign workers. President Clinton made headlines when she suggested large corporations move their factories back to U.S. soil and help the employees migrate as well. *Impossible!* The corporations cried. The expense would be outrageous. Impractical. President Clinton claimed the expense to secure other nations for the purpose of maintaining a cheap work force was simply not going to happen. America was pulling out of most foreign countries and warned anyone visiting or doing business outside the U.S. that they were on their own.

One of the more vile results to emerge from the ruined countries was the cottage industry of selling kidnapped children. Human trafficking was brought to a new level. The NGOs stepped up to help and found their own ranks depleted because of the volume of need. Consequently, the people of the safe nations gave more donations to the humanitarian groups. The humanitarian groups recruited and hired more people and the work began. Thousands of people found meaningful jobs and experienced a new sense of fulfilment. The efforts brought communities together and established a sense of purpose that was never needed before Aqar. A new industry of human rights enforcement and awareness was born.

Chapter 10 - Joey is Five Months Old

Since Americans pinned their hopes on the Task Force 200 as their only solution, most were eager to follow the advice of the team because the devastation elsewhere served as a constant gloomy reminder. Nobody wanted a repeat of the fall of Greece, Russia or Brazil. Most of the population of the U.S. were willing to bear whatever extremes were necessary to prevent a catastrophe. The nightly news was full of horrible images of ruined countries and those on the brink. The U.S. and Canada were not going to allow the same but nobody expected the solution to be so simple or so quickly decided and announced. After only a few months, the details were hammered out and the rules were in place. The plan would shock the nation.

Mary told the family about the Task Force 200 plan the night before it was officially announced by the president. Her children were both flabbergasted and intrigued by the logic. They listened eagerly in the comfort of her great room as she relayed the new policy that would go into effect immediately.

"To begin with, all payroll contracts are null and void. It doesn't matter if you're with a little company, or you work at Taco Bell or you're the president of Boeing. If you have an employment contract with an American company, it is now null and void." Mary began.

"Interesting." Nora said. "I like where this is going." The others nodded their agreement.

Mary continued. "Now, the fun part. In every registered business in the United States, the lowest paid employee cannot earn less than twenty-five percent of the highest paid employee."

"What? Are you kidding, mom?" Ted asked.

"That's remarkable and so progressive!" Rafael marveled. "It's been talked about before but now it's really happening?"

"Just like Ben & Jerry's!" Audrey said.

"Precisely. We studied their model." Mary said.

"Babe, we're both getting a raise!" Lou said to Nora. They high fived.

"It's so simple yet it will solve so many issues, you can't imagine." Mary said. "Think of the possibilities! Add to it the fact that we have just added twelve million now-documented citizens to the work force who are now paying taxes and have health insurance. There will be less need for government assistance. There will be plenty of jobs as corporations move their manufacturing back to the States where they should have stayed to begin with."

Nora posed a hypothetical. "So, let's say the CEO of MegaCompany who makes thirty million a year has to pay the janitor of MegaCompany a little over one point two million per year? What, now?" Nora was doubtful.

"Of course not, honey. I wish that would happen but it won't. Instead, the CEO will have to take a pay cut. He'll have to downgrade to a salary of, say, five million per year in order to keep all of his or her employees."

Ted did the math. "The janitor gets a raise to two hundred grand per year?"

Mary nodded enthusiastically. "Yes! Isn't it wonderful?"

"How will this play out?" Audrey asked, genuinely perplexed.

"That's just it, sweetie. The plan forces a complete revamp of the payroll system which, in turn, solves the economic crisis. It forces the money to be more evenly distributed."

"Won't that drive up the price of consumer goods?" Audrey asked.

Mary shook her head. "Not at all. The companies aren't spending more on payroll, just changing the allocation of their profits."

"Wait. We're finally going to see everyone in the country earning a living wage?" Nora asked.

"It's time." Mary said.

Americans didn't even think it was constitutionally legal. But it was. Many wondered what the mandates had to do with infertility but it was worth a shot. Both parties agreed to it, the president made the new plan an Executive Order, congress unanimously passed it and nobody was happy about it, meaning it was the right call. The Task Force claimed it was the only solution for the looming problems. Simple as that. Corporations that paid their top executives twenty or thirty million dollars a year found this requirement intolerable. 'How can we pay our entry level college recruits a salary of seven to eight hundred thousand per year? That's ridiculous!' They argued. The Task Force suggested that they reduce the CEO's salary to a lower sum making it possible to pay more reasonable amounts to its employees. Members of the Task Force would not publicly advise companies how to manage the salary changes as the answers were fairly obvious: take your payroll budget and spread it out. The NFL, MLB and NBA at first thought their clubs would be exempt because they couldn't possibly pay low level employees twenty-five percent of their star athletes' salaries. The government suggested they lower the athletes' salaries in keeping with the new law. In the meantime, they needed to up the pay of the coaches, office staff and various members of the whole team including the towel boys. The same suggestion was made to a number of studios and production companies in California. They were encouraged to continue making fine movies, but perhaps it was time to reduce the salaries of the talent and the suits to keep production in compliance with the new law. It meant that every employee involved in the production would be compensated within a twenty-five percent range. No one could claim an employment contract as a reason for exclusion from the statute. Labor unions were disbanded. No exceptions. New contracts could be drawn up as long as the salaries were in keeping with the new law. There was also a stern stipulation that manipulations of the new plan would be dealt with harshly. Any company exploiting a loophole such as contracting certain employees in order to realign the salary schedule, would be heavily fined. The new law was not negotiable and any attempt to sneak pay under the table would result in jail time for the offenders starting with the company presidents and CEOs. Executives who didn't like it were free to move their corporation to another country. Greece, Brazil and

Russia were suggested to the sputtering, irate executives who at first refused to accept the policy. In any case, the IRS restructured its own work force to monitor the new system. In fact, the IRS added to its workforce and in keeping with the plan, many agents were given a raise. Oh, and another thing, the law added, corporate perks that were paid for by the corporation were still allowed; however, all perks must be made available to all employees. If the executives are allowed to use the corporate jet, *all* employees would be allowed to use the corporate jet. If executives are given cell phones, credit cards and company cars then *all* employees are given cell phones, credit cards and company cars. Basically, if the company is paying for it, every employee is entitled to it, otherwise, no one gets it. At least not paid for by the company. The president made it clear that companies wishing to do business in the United States or sell products in the United States would have to comply or be shut down. Jail time for the decision makers was promised to those that circumvented any portion of the law. The system would be in place for at least five years; then the economy could be reassessed or perhaps a new administration would make a change. There was simply no way around it. Canada followed suit. Australia was not far behind.

"It doesn't really affect the Johnson Foundation." Mary told the family at brunch. "My salary is a dollar per year, so I am not the highest paid employee."

"What is that after taxes, Mom? What's your take home?" Ted asked. Mary smiled back at her silly son.

"It's time you got a raise, Mom." Nora said.

Mary shrugged. "Perhaps I'll give myself two dollars a year going forward."

Lou had no idea so he asked. "Who *is* the highest paid employee at the foundation? Burke?" He chuckled at his own joke.

"Burke is well compensated, of course, but he's not an employee of the Johnson Foundation. That wouldn't be fair since he does so much personal work for me. I pay him out of my own finances. Anyway, his salary is not as high as Marilee Kozinski's, the CFO of the Johnson Foundation." Mary said. "She's in the stratosphere compared to most businesses, I realize that. She earns somewhere in the low seven figures. I have never begrudged her a penny because she's brilliant and kind and generous. She could probably make a lot more in a private corporation, at least back in the old days, but she believes in our cause and this is the work she loves to do. She has everything she could ever want and has provided for her family."

"Did you have to make any salary adjustments at the foundation?" Nora asked, curious.

"We have always paid well. Thank goodness I've had the resources to do so. I've always said my job is a breeze because I hire the right people. Our administrative assistants, why, even Marco who runs the mail room are all currently making six figures. So when the new law was announced I truly thought we were already in line with the parameters but I was surprised to learn that last year we hired on a messenger to run documents locally and he's such a sweetheart. He delivered a contract for me last year during the blizzard, oh my goodness, it was below zero and the winds, well, you remember. Anyway, Stan met the deadline that day and I shall never forget it. I just assumed his pay was commensurate with the rest of the support staff but I was just told recently that he only makes fifteen dollars an hour!"

"Whoa, this new raise must be nice for him." Audrey commented.

"Indeed. I'm sorry we didn't do it sooner. He has a family and lives in the city. Anyway, we could have gone the route of some corporations and lowered the executive salaries but I opted, instead to raise the salaries of those who fell outside the mandate although there weren't that many."

"I'm impressed, Ma. Personally, I got a fat raise and so did all the uniforms. It's nice to see cops getting paid what they're worth. I never thought twice about the chief's salary, but I always thought most of the rank and file were underpaid. Not anymore. You have no idea how it's boosted morale."

"It's the same for the teachers." Rafael added. "Everyone got raises but people are wondering how the government can afford it."

"Basic math, genius." Nora said. "All the private sector people making more money are paying more income tax. Plus everyone knows that the unemployment rate has plummeted and we're paying less for government health insurance. There will soon be no babies to vaccinate. Less and less government sponsored daycare. No more young mothers who can't work because they have babies. Everyone will have a job and money to spend. Do the math."

Mary nodded. "What's going to cause some distress we foresee is the reform regarding corporate perks. Any extra money spent on 'executive incentives' will be monetized and considered salary."

"You mean like it is for the rest of us?" Ted asked.

"Yes." Mary said. "They'll try to hide it but Task Force 200 has already anticipated the loopholers. A few CEOs might end up paying some hefty fines, which incidentally, will come out of their own salary."

Mary shook her head sadly. "I'm embarrassed that it took so long for anyone to take on corporate greed."

"It really is kind of crazy how some of these huge corporations have hired the masses for pennies while crying poverty about the cost of manpower as they bask in the most ridiculous luxuries paid for by the corporation!" Nora was working on her outrage. "How has it ever been fair to charge vacations and expensive meals and boxes at sporting events? Why is that a justifiable expense? What does it have to do with the business?"

"I guess they figure they have to wine and dine the customers in order to win the business in order to pay the employees. You can't argue with that." Lou reasoned. He was an excellent devil's advocate for his wife's diatribes.

Nora almost exploded. "Why can't they get the business by presenting a good product at a good price?! During business hours! In a conference room. With donuts and coffee?"

Mary put her arm around her daughter. "It will now come to that, honey. The whole committee agreed that companies don't have to impress each other in order to win contracts because none of them will have it in their budgets to wine and dine customers anymore. It's not like they lose customers. The customers will still need products. The executives who make the big decisions will just have to base their decisions on quality products instead of who gives them the most swag. I think they call it 'swag,' don't they?"

"Same with the feds. No need to wine and dine other countries in fancy embassies and outrageous White House state dinners. Work is work but you're on your own for luxury parties and fancy catered affairs. Seems right to me." Nora said.

"It's so simple, I'm surprised this is a new idea. I'm surprised anybody would argue about it." Audrey said.

"Oh, there will be some arguments. Plenty of outrage. There are executives out there who will not take kindly to this turn of events. I bet you some of the execs at the drug companies will break out in cold sweats at the thought of not having a gigantic budget for wooing doctors." Ted rolled his eyes.

Raf countered. "That's the beauty of this plan, though. They won't need a gigantic budget anymore because the competition won't have a gigantic budget either. It's strictly business. Here's our new drug, do you want it or not? There's no back and forth negotiating. Producers put forth a product. Consumers take it or leave it. No lunches. No theatre tickets. No Hawaiian vacations. You had something to do with this proviso, didn't you, Mom?"

Mary smiled. "We all reached this decision early on in our meetings. We knew there was plenty of money out there but the bulk of it is being spent unnecessarily and grossly disproportionately. Corporate entities are paying huge amounts in executive salaries which at first seems logical. But why are corporate entities paying for executives' clothes and cars and nannies? Shouldn't the executives being paying for their own personal items?"

"They sure as hell can't argue it when they watch the news and see what's happening in other countries." Nora grumbled. "I think it goes down easier too, when you tell them this is a temporary five-year-plan."

"True." Mary answered. "But in five years, I can't see anyone wanting to change it back."

"The next administration will have to decide." Ted said. "But, man, that'll be a tough sell."

Soon it became clear that only a small portion of the population was actually affected negatively. Most workers benefitted with a pay raise and nobody could argue that. Many executives' salaries were cut but the reduction still kept them in an enviable pay bracket. The initial threats of companies closing never happened. Some companies raised their consumer prices to combat the higher payroll but capitalism kept prices in check and it soon became clear that a population who earned good money, would spend that money. They would spend it on the consumer goods that were being sold by the weeping executives from companies who complained that they would have to go out of business if they had to adjust salaries. But it didn't happen. In a matter of months, people became more vested in their high paying jobs and more invested in their communities.

Watchdog groups kept an eye on the cheaters. The IRS focused on the loopholers. The playing field leveled with absolutely no fall out. The stock market tanked then shot up beyond hopeful expectations. The economy in the United States stabilized.

Chapter 11 - Joey is Seven Months Old

The last baby conceived through IVF at the Johnson Fertility Center was due in a week. Both Ted and Khan were on call for the delivery of Baby Milliner, each secretly hoping to do the honor since it would be a career finale. There was nothing else left to do at the Johnson Fertility Center after that. Dr. Lakey and Dr. Delgado had left the practice almost immediately after the Aqar outbreak, both now working as pediatricians in the area hoping to transition into another medical specialty when the time came. The rest of the staff had been let go with generous severance packages. It was emotionally difficult to break up the team that had worked so well together and Ted missed his crew, but there was simply no more work to be done. Sybil stayed on to wrap up the paperwork, see to the closing details and help with the packing. She knew there would be no more patients coming through the doors. Ted decided to keep the building as his private lab and man cave. It was close to home and Audrey would never know about the secret stash of Coca-Cola he kept in the break room fridge.

Ted held Joey and easily maneuvered him from arm to arm as he made his way through the maze of boxes. Joey was "helping" him while he checked on some samples. "Helping" as in chewing on his pacifier and grabbing everything that came within his chubby little arm's length. Allie was with her mother at the movies giving the boys a day out. Ted loved his kids so much that it hurt and he often wondered what the world would be like for them when they reached an advanced age, possibly the last inhabitants of the planet with no children on earth. His children would have no children or grandchildren. Would Allie and Joey have to tough it out alone? That thought kept him working on a solution. He couldn't bear the thought of his babies reaching old age and having no one to care for them.

The knock at the door startled him. Backtracking through the lobby he saw his old friend, Lily, tapping on the door, peeking through the glass. Surprised, he let her in noticing the suitcase and her disheveled appearance.

"What on earth are you doing here?" He hugged her but she was too busy fussing over Joey to notice. After a good deal of adoration and amazement as he clutched her finger, Joey gave in and let Lily hold him, his eyes never leaving her chunky necklace.

"I could use some coffee. I came straight from the airport." Lily plopped herself down on a waiting room chair and continued her devotion to Joey, who loved the attention and the necklace, while Ted found the coffee pot still plugged in and usable.

Ted brought her a mug from the Keurig machine and traded the coffee for his son. They caught up on the niceties and updated each other with family talk. Ted was delighted for the diversion. He missed his old school friend and was grateful for the chance to exchange Aqar virus news.

"Okay. How are things going at Carrel? Did you guys get my last report?"

"I read the report and you are on a completely different course. My esteemed colleagues haven't touched your data because they have dismissed your theories."

"Oooh." Ted said making a face. "Ouchy."

"Please do not take this as an insult. They are each one more arrogant than the next. So many cooks yet the broth is the least of their concerns and no one is managing the data. Pierre is too busy chasing young lovelies. I have resigned."

"What? Why, Lily? Why?"

"I was at first honored to be chosen for the team but I have now come to realize that this multi-country

68

initiative has very little concern for the human race. What I have recently learned has made my skin crawl."

"Your skin is crawling? Yikes." Ted bounced Joey on his knee, bracing for the news.

"When the WMA first pulled us all together and raised all that money to find a cure, what did you think they wanted to achieve?"

"Babies." Ted answered confidently like it was a no-brainer.

"No. Well, yes, but not for the reasons you think. Most of the people funding the WMA want only one thing: labor. Cheap labor. That is why they raised billions of euro and gave the scientists every imaginable resource. The world needs a steady stream of children and young adults so their factories will not slow down."

Ted shook his head. "That doesn't seem right. I find it hard to believe that even hardcore business people could be so cold."

"Oh, Ted. You have always been so sheltered, even naïve."

"I do like my rose colored glasses."

"Surely you have seen the human rights abuses year after year after year documented by advocacy groups. Your own mother is... *Ted*, you can't deny that this world has many human rights issues."

"I mean, I know. The Johnson Foundation supports a bunch of NGOs. I know that a few countries need to step up…"

"A few countries? Please take off those glasses. Every year, even now, millions of children are sold into slavery, forced into prostitution, consigned to military forces or killed when they refuse or are too sick to be marketable. You know this, right?"

Ted knew it but hated it. "Now with Aqar, maybe the bad guys will see children for the treasures they are. Maybe this was a wake-up call to the world and if we get back to having babies again, maybe things will be different. As soon as we find a cure.…" He paused long enough for Lily to finish.

"…the world will repopulate the factories, armies, rice paddies and whore houses."

Ted paced while shushing Joey to sleep on his shoulder. "You know, just because it's funded by these groups doesn't mean we should give up. We can work harder to support human rights initiatives. Maybe the world knows that we need to end the atrocities after this scare."

Lily shook her head. "We both know that won't happen. If we ever find the cure, if that is even possible, everything goes back to the old way of life. Throw-away children."

"So what are we supposed to do? Try *not* to find a cure? Keep deserving parents from having children because some bastards *might* abuse the system?"

"Don't you see how things are changing? Here in the States, your people are fine thanks to the Task Force and progressive leadership. This will never happen in most developing nations. The businessmen now, they are hurting because mothers and fathers are holding on to the children they have left. They cherish them. The factories lose workers giving existing workers some leverage. There's competition for good workers. Employers are forced to improve benefits. There's no line of people to fill the positions. There's a line of business owners begging for workers. Life for all of the working class has changed for the better. Maybe the bug is best left alone. Maybe this was meant to be."

"You think I should stop my research?"

"I would not presume to tell you what to do."

Ted sighed deeply. "I understand what you're saying, Lily. I really do. But there are good people out there and I owe it to my country to continue..."

"*Your* country? Ted, do you think the American business people are any different from the ones in developing nations?"

Ted shrugged defensively, like it was a given.

"It is your people, the American businessmen with factories overseas who most want their factories back in business. Back in the third world where the governments don't care how workers are treated. Don't look at me so shocked! These businessmen come to you in your clean, fresh world and say my pretty little wife wants a baby so we can post thousands of pictures on Instagram and buy so many little outfits. Don't you see how they pay for this, Ted? They pay for this by putting little foreign babies to work."

Ted sat down with the sleeping Joey, dreaming peacefully. Lily let Ted take in the reality.

"If you wish to work with the WMA, you will need to resend your last two reports. Nobody has read them but me. I will tell you that I think you are headed in the right direction. I do not wish to continue with the research."

They sat in silence for a moment. Ted absently rubbed Joey's back.

"Why don't you move here, Lily. You've always said you'd love to live in the States and now you can get a visa like in seconds. I heard they'll be handing 'em out at the border these days with coupons for a free t-shirt."

"That is the good news. I have come to Chicago for a final interview with Amnesty. I hope to relocate immediately if I am offered a position."

"Amnesty? My mom could probably give you a reference that'll open some doors. Wow, Lily, it will be great to have you so close. Will you be based in Chicago?"

"If it all works out."

Ted studied her face and had to ask. "Is there more to this, Lily?"

She squirmed before answering. "There was an ugly situation with Charbot. We were alone one night in the lab and he went too far. I cannot work with him anymore."

"Oh, my God, Lill, I'm so sorry. Are you alright? I ought to punch that guy's lights out!"

"Now, now, all is well. He is just such a.... shithead." Which made them both laugh.

"Hey, if we're going to be neighbors, maybe you can help me with some research I'm doing here... I've found some interesting..."

"I will not work with you if you intend to aid the WMA. I cannot justify curing this virus simply as a means to bring children into this world so they can live a miserable existence."

"I don't want that either, Lily. Come on. Let's go to my house and see what's for dinner."

"I would love to. Are you sure Audrey won't mind?"

"Mind? Are you kidding? She'll love it."

"I'm going to the Marriott, I will come after I get settled."

"Hey, have you ever met my brother, Raf?"

"I have not had the pleasure."

"Total dork. But, dreamy. *Very* dreamy according to North Shore News. He's like *the* most eligible bachelor in town. I keep razzing him about it."

"Oh, Ted. Stop."

Chapter 12

<u>Meet The Nation – NBS News</u>

Walter Safer: *The term "unemployment" will not exist. Everyone who wants a job will have a job because there will be ten times more jobs than there are people to fill them. Thank you, Task Force 200!*

Ira Wainstein: *Suddenly, young people have their choice of jobs. In so many fields!*

Walter Safer: *I saw it coming but the elegant distribution of wealth happened so quietly, so quickly. I think some CEOs are still huffing and puffing about having to pay for their own country club fees and security detail.*

Andy O'Hern: *Isn't it funny that suddenly most of them don't need a security detail when they have to pay for it out of their own pocket?*

Ira Wainstein: *Amazing how quickly they didn't need those private jet vacations with their extended families for* business *purposes.*

Andy O'Hern: *And somehow, their office décor didn't need modern art and antique furniture for them to do their jobs. Oh, how the system has changed, gentlemen.*

Ira Wainstein: *People have been complaining for years about the corporate executive perks that have become outrageous. Sure, we all brought it up but the response was that you need to give these big shots every possible luxury or how on earth could they be lured to work so hard up there in their two thousand square foot office with a view?*

Andy O'Hern: *Turns out, there are plenty of qualified applicants to run these corporations and they don't all need unlimited expense accounts and personal trainers to do it.*

Walter Safer: *Who knew?!*

Andy O'Hern: *The new pay policy means everyone in a company is valued and part of the team. That's what I like about it. Everyone's in on it. Everyone takes ownership and pride.*

Ira Wainstein: *The CEO can look down his or her nose at the janitor pushing a broom but the janitor knows he'll get his 100K salary annually, and live a very comfortable life with his family. Why, his wife might be the 100K barista across the street. It's all good! No more minimum wage jobs except for maybe the* teenagers who aren't part of the deal yet, but every man and woman can expect a living wage because the CEO of each company will want his two million dollar salary.

Ira Wainstein: *Still a pretty nice paycheck in this day and age.*

Andy O'Hern: *He'll need every dime of that money if he has to pay for his own dinner parties.*

Walter Safer: *Won't that take away incentive to work hard and move up?*

Ira Wainstein: *No! You'll still have the go-getters who want to climb the ladder. You'll still have the slackers who don't cut it, but guess what? The slackers get fired! That's still okay. But why would you want to get fired? That would be crazy! Even on your worst day on the job, knowing you got that nice paycheck coming at the end of the week, you'll tough it out.*

Walter Safer: *And if you do get fired, Ha! You're not getting a government check every week! No, sir! There are too many job openings to claim you can't find work and you can't argue that a fast food job doesn't cut it. You can offer fries with that burger all day long and still bring home a decent paycheck. You might not like the job, but it will pay the bills.*

77

Andy O'Hern: *The difference now is that everyone is held accountable, everyone has a fair shake and everyone truly can have a great life. If they choose to.*

Walter Safer: *Never thought I'd see the day.*

Ira Wainstein: *All because of a tragic plague.*

Chapter 13 - Joey is One Year Old

Mary Johnson hosted her annual summer gala, kind of like a block party but with caterers and a stunning back yard. Mary enjoyed spending time with most of her neighbors but really she seized the opportunity for fundraising and just plain awareness raising. She knew there was still work to do and money to be redirected toward the non-profits. The event gave Ted, Nora and Rafael a chance to catch up with childhood friends and say hello to the older crowd from town who had watched them grow up. Former neighbors who moved away usually travelled back for the chance to reconnect and enjoy a Johnson soiree. Big donors welcomed the chance to show their generosity but Mary also included old friends from town who might not write a big check but she expected to enjoy their company. One-year-old Joey toddled around on unsteady feet near his father while Allie circulated through the crowd. Mary took a stand on a raised dais and shushed everyone. Burke hovered nearby scanning the crowd.

Ted whispered to Lou. "...you're staying after this, right? We need to talk. It's important."

Lou gave him an annoyed look. "Would you listen to your ma talk, please?"

"...with great delight I have been given permission to inform you that there is now a long list of eligible, really eligible, foster parents looking for children instead of a long list of children looking for foster care. Adoptions are almost immediate and children in limbo don't stay that way for long."

She stopped to allow a huge round of applause. "Sadly, the shelters are still in use but not as heavily as they once were. Most families can get into a shelter immediately instead of waiting for beds to open up..."

Ted tried to listen to his mother but was on duty to chase little Joey through the yard. He passed by Rafael who stood uncomfortably next to Poppy, a 24-year-old heiress whose grandmother lived next door. Rafael was polite, even charming to the young lady but his gaze kept track of Lily across the pool where she was earnestly listening to Mary's speech. He couldn't help but notice that she looked beautiful.

Mary kept the message short and sweet. "I'd like to see a stronger focus on mental illness and addiction. Our progress is good but we can do better. State agencies finally have the time and resources to devote to true social services and we need to make sure they do it. With all that good news what could be the problem you might ask? With the new salary schedule, the government has slashed at its workforce but the beauty of the plan is that those social workers have found jobs working with charitable organizations that now supplement the government programs. Better yet, the government saves money by leaving the social work to the experts who will keep out the bureaucracy and get the job done. As citizens of this great nation, we need to give these new social workers more power to do what has to be done. Please! These wonderful people can be so effective and make such a difference. We can't let them be hobbled now when the progress has been so strong. We must demand that our politicians keep these angels in place. The Johnson foundation can provide back up to the government agencies and keep kids from falling through the cracks."

Nora yelled from the buffet table. "And give them all another raise while they're at it!"

Mary beamed at her daughter. "That's the spirit, dear! Please help me in my quest. Thank you."

The applause died down and the checkbooks emerged and conversation resumed. Lily turned to notice Rafael talking to a pretty young thing, which was nothing new. He was, after all, the ultimate bachelor. The few times she'd met him, he'd been very kind and attentive but standoffish. Shy. He was ridiculously handsome, eligible and sweet. He was also a few years younger and so hard to read. It was silly to even consider... As she walked toward the dais to shake hands with Mary, she had no idea that he was searching the grounds for her, while patiently listening to Poppy.

"...so people are wondering when I'll get the official promotion. But this guy's been there for, like, twenty-five years. I mean, he's got to be pushing fifty and he looks at me, the whiz kid, and he's petrified that I'll fire his sorry ass one day. He needs to learn where the talent lies and get out of the way. What does he know about fashion trends, anyway? You know what I'm saying?"

"Um, sure. How has the new payroll policy affected your company?" Rafael asked politely.

Poppy rolled her eyes. "Unbelievable, isn't it? Those idiots in the White House, what a joke. No offense to your mother, of course. But, yes, we were deeply affected. Wasn't every one of us that went to school, got our graduate degrees, and worked crazy hours to finally earn a respectable salary? Then, boom, the government gets to take it all away?"

"Your pay was cut?"

"Well, no, thank God. Some of the big shots upstairs got a pay cut which was better than paying the minions the kind of money they would never hope to see in their lifetime. God. They all got raises, every one of them. Like my assistant, who went to community college, mind you, got bumped up over six figures. Yeah. Crazy. And I'm lucky I even get to keep my assistant because some people," she whispered the heresy, "Have to go without an assistant." She shuddered.

"Well, I'm glad you were able to get through it without losing your pay and your assistant." Rafael offered uncomfortably.

"I lost a ton of perks. We used to have a clothing allowance. Gone. We travelled first or business class. Not anymore. We have to use our own upgrades or fly coach. Coach! Rumor has it that the company jet can now only be used for legitimate business travel and they are really getting picky about 'legitimate' business travel. Our expense accounts are being examined with a magnifying glass. You know how it is when you expense a nice lunch or dinner that wasn't technically with a client but your boss knew you needed it and you got reimbursed anyway? No can do. We are being nickeled and dimed because the company is suddenly cost conscious because the government sticks their nose into it. We have to make sure every dollar we spend is justified and necessary so we can pay these ridiculous salaries to the lower echelon. Uh, please. It's demoralizing. I just hope the economy gets back to normal soon. I have to use my trust money just to live on."

Allie jumped in between the couple and took Rafael's hand. "I can count to a hundred, Uncle Raf!"

Rafael was delighted with the distraction. "I would like to hear that."

Poppy could barely contain her irritation at the rude interruption by a child.

"One, two, skip a few, ninety-nine, one hundred!" Allie clapped, delighted with herself.

Poppy forced a smile and turned away, hoping they were done with the brat but Rafael seemed to find the whole thing, not just amusing, but acceptable behavior!

"That was cheating. Do it the right way." Rafael said, chuckling.

Allie obliged. Poppy hoped it was a diversionary tactic so that she and Rafael could get back to their conversation but Rafael seemed to be listening to the kid count. He was listening to the kid *count*. Poppy took control and talked over the noise, trying to divert attention back to herself.

"I have a niece about this age." Poppy lobbed the comment desperately.

"I didn't know that. How nice." He truly had never heard that Poppy's brother had children. He seemed to remember a wedding a few years back but his mother never mentioned offspring which she usually did during family get-togethers. Her way of pushing the baby envelope. Well, back when there was a choice in the matter.

"We don't see her since my brother's less than amicable divorce. His ex lives in town but she's so incredibly difficult so we figure, fine, until she can learn who she's dealing with, we'll stay away from Bella. Her loss..."

Rafael was genuinely taken aback. "How sad for the child."

"I know, right? All her mother's fault. She's got all these rules about car seats and language. She told my dad he couldn't smoke cigars around her. You know how he loves his stogies. So, fine. We told her that she doesn't make the rules and maybe we'll see Bella when she's eighteen and can make up her own mind."

"But you'll miss out on her childhood." Rafael couldn't fathom a world without his niece and nephew.

"What else can we do?" Poppy shrugged hopelessly.

Rafael searched for an escape route through the tortured conversation and was just about to excuse himself when Lily appeared out of nowhere like a ray of sunshine. He felt a rush of happiness along with a sheen of sweat.

"Hello, Rafael." She said it casually, with a very friendly tone as Poppy got visibly defensive.

Allie stopped counting somewhere in the fifties and jumped up and down to see Lily, the *nice* lady who was friends with mommy and daddy.

Even though his heart raced, Rafael smiled pleasantly and made the proper introductions.

"Bon Jour, Lily. I am delighted you could make it to the party. May I present Poppy Hanning."

Lily extended her hand which Poppy hesitantly acknowledged like a good debutante.

"How do you do?" Lily smiled.

"Oh, you must be the doctor friend of Ted's. I heard you were from another country but I just assumed you would be an old man."

"No?" Lily had no other way to respond.

Allie resumed her counting and got louder as she pushed her way in front of Rafael who patted her lovingly on the head. "....fifty-five, fifty-six, fifty-seven, fifty-eight..."

Poppy needed to put the pretty French doctor in her place. "Did I hear that you work for Amnesty International? Is that even still necessary? You're a fertility doctor like Ted, right? You left Paris where you could be on the news every night if you wanted and you wanted to come here? I see that Pierre guy and can't imagine the pressure he is under. I'm glad they're all working on it, I suppose but I gotta say, Aqar is working for me. Birth control pills were making me so bloated, but now, of course, who needs birth control, right? So everyone keeps asking me, have you gone down to a size two? Which, I have. Everyone has noticed. My assistant keeps saying..." Then she turned and lost it on Allie, "Will you *stop*!?"

Poppy couldn't help herself. This Lily person had rudely walked in on her meaningful conversation with the most eligible bachelor on the North Shore and, if that weren't enough, the kid wouldn't shut up!

Rafael defensively picked up Allie who was shocked to be yelled at. Lily patted her back and glared at Poppy. Audrey happened to be walking by with a state senator and her husband and caught the tail end of the conversation, enough to know that little ones should be seen and not heard. She excused herself and rushed to Allie, ready to take her aside for a talk. Allie was truly jarred by the scolding from Poppy. "Mama, I wanted to count for Uncle Raf but Poppy keeps talking and being mean. I don't like her!" She turned her head into Rafael's neck.

"Allie! That's enough!" Audrey was embarrassed and turned to Poppy. "I'm so sorry, Poppy, I don't know what's gotten into her."

Poppy stood in disbelief. Unbelievable in this day and age that kids would be allowed to talk like that to adults especially in this area. Shameful.

Audrey took Allie into her arms. "I don't want you to be a mean person, honey. Please don't say unkind things to people. You're a good girl who knows better. Please apologize."

"I don't want to!" Allie stood firm and pouted.

Audrey kept the same patient tone. "Well, then. You get to choose. You can go back in the house and miss the party. Or, you can apologize for being rude. Your decision."

Allie was pretty much over it but got her mom's point. She wiggled her way down and before running off said, "Sorry, Poppy!"

Audrey didn't at first catch the pointed look from Rafael as she reassured Poppy that Allie was acting out lately. Poppy basked in the victim role and tried to be magnanimous. "Children are naturally intrusive. I get that. As long as you know how to correct the situation."

"Yeah, I'm doing the best I can." Audrey could see the pleading look in Raf's eyes as she reluctantly gave Poppy even more attention. "I'm not just a mom, I'm a judge and a peacekeeper. It's a full time job."

Poppy gave Audrey a tight smile indicating she was done with the intrusion and turned to Rafael so she could get back on track with her story. Lily caught on and jumped in quickly. "The view of the lake here is lovely. Your mother has a magnificent home, Rafael."

"May I... Would you like me to show you around the grounds?" He choked out quickly.

"I would be delighted." Lily took his arm and they made their graceful escape while Audrey physically stepped in front of Poppy who had every intention of touring the grounds with Rafael and buttinsky, but Audrey took one for the team by asking Poppy about her job.

"Oh, great, great. I am so incredibly busy... meetings, business trips, in *coach*, it's just crazy. My assistant is like, when do you sleep?" Poppy gave in to the social requirements but vowed to catch up later with Rafael. In the meantime, it didn't hurt to schmooze with Ted's wife. He was, after all, Mary Johnson's son. "I'd give anything to stay at home like you, for just a week, to slow down and relax."

"I haven't relaxed in seven years." Audrey said amiably. Poppy laughed. "Oh, yeah. Ha, playing with kids. Yeah, Audrey, funny." She sipped her vodka cran and searched for her next social conquest.

Audrey saw that Rafael and Lily were a safe distance off so she prepared to move on but Poppy had more to say. "Audrey, you're educated, right? You could still do something with your life. You're relatively young and I'm sure there are companies that would hire you. It seems like everyone's hiring nowadays, which is ridic, but my point is, you shouldn't think it's too late to find a meaningful, fulfilling career."

"I know being a mom is not like being a marketing executive for high end purses like you, but I still have the will to get up in the morning."

Poppy expounded philosophically. "You just have to keep working your way to the top. It took me a few months but I can honestly say that my input at work sells handbags. My vision sells handbags. It's so important for a woman to know she carries the perfect purse, the one just right for her, so she can feel good about herself. We all know the right accessories will make or break you, right? My point is, you'll find your calling, too. You can get out of this funk you're in."

Audrey smiled patiently and felt no need to respond. She saw that Rafael and Lily had made it to the shoreline so she excused herself to find Ted and take over Joey patrol. *Funk*. Ha.

They watched the driftwood bounce on the gentle waves and took in the sunshine of a beautiful day. There were a few other guests taking in the water views but Rafael and Lily had the luxury of privacy with a beautiful backdrop.

"Your mother is a remarkable woman." Lily said. "She is tireless in her efforts."

"Mom is wonderful. Truly selfless. She won't rest until all children are properly loved and cared for. It's her life's work." Rafael responded fondly.

"And all of you have taken up her cause?"

"I never knew there was a choice in the matter." Rafael said with a laugh. "We were brought up to do this."

Lily cocked her head and considered. "N*oblesse oblige*?"

"None of us, including mom, are bluebloods. And we don't feel obligated to give back, we all *want* to. It's our passion. I can't imagine my life any other way."

"I've followed her trajectory, even before I met Ted. She's always been a role model for me. I don't know if Ted told you, but I was in the system. In France. My parents died when I was very young and there was only a derelict uncle to take me in. It was a frightening childhood. I was very lucky to come out of it unscathed."

"I had no idea. I'm so sorry." Rafael felt instantly bonded to her.

"Oh, I don't like to talk about it. You understand?" She looked down at the ground.

"I completely understand, Lily." He wanted to wrap his arms around her but he just couldn't make himself. He was paralyzed with fear and he hated himself for it.

Lily continued. "So, I learned about her when the state sent me on to my secondary education as a young teenage girl. I was very smart and I say that I was lucky because being smart gave me a better education and an escape. I read everything in the bibliothèque I could get my hands on. I saw that a woman like her could change the world and I wanted to be like her in every way."

Rafael had no immediate response, the panic was overwhelming but she didn't seem to notice. Or she was too polite to bring attention to his muteness. Either way, he was falling in love and having a panic attack simultaneously.

"Your mum, she was rather left in the lurch by her husband, no? A young widow who inherited a fortune and everyone expected her to go off quietly into the sunset and lunch with her lady friends."

Somehow, maybe a divine intervention or some such miracle, but Rafael found the strength and the courage to interact with this beautiful woman. Maybe it was all those years of making small talk at parties but he came off sounding normal. Conversational. He felt a release of endorphins and easily responded. "My father was quite a bit older than my mother. I know it sounds odd to call him my father but that's how we have always referred to him. Anyway, my mother wasn't nearly ready to take on the foundation at her young age with so little experience."

"But she had her Brown education, a doctorate from University of Chicago and a burning desire to help the world." Lily filled in.

"So, you really have read the biography?" Rafael asked, enjoying the discourse.

"How could I not? What a story. She took charge of the foundation while the advisors all tried to talk her out of it. Not only did she exceed expectations, she increased the fortune, adopted her children, raised a family and went on to help so many in need. She is my hero."

"Mine too." Rafael confided. "And Ted, of course. He's my other hero but please don't tell him. I'd never hear the end of it."

"You are so much like Ted in your devotion to others."

"We get it from our mom."

"He was like my big brother during our fellowship at Weill-Cornell. He is naturally a paternal figure, I think. I always knew he would be a good father and I can see the way he loves and cares for those two little darlings that I was right."

"He was our father figure growing up. He took it upon himself as a child to be the man of the family. Which is why he acts like a child now, I suppose." They both laughed.

"What a wonderful family. How lucky you all are." Lily concluded.

"I know." Rafael was handling the pressure but getting uncomfortable with the familiarity. He silently cursed his lack of endurance in the game of social skills but Lily seemed to sense the need for an easier topic and that helped. She gestured toward the sanguine man who seemed always in the vicinity of Mary Johnson. "Who is that big, giant brute that is with your mother?"

Rafael was happy for the diversion to safer waters. "Oh, that's Burke. He's her driver, really more of an assistant.

Well, he's like her companion, I suppose. He's a godsend, really. He travels with her and takes great care of her. They've been together for years. More friends than employee/employer at this point."

"How reassuring to know someone is watching out for her. I have a feeling she's a handful once she makes up her mind to do something."

"You have no idea! She was always with us when we were young but as we got older she trotted the globe and built orphanages and hospitals and distributed mosquito netting and brought food packs and water bottles to every country under the sun. We're hoping her generosity will keep her stateside for a while. We are all concerned about her schedule with the foundation and the Task Force and all."

"That's what brings her to sainthood status! It's not just that she gives so much of her time and money, it's that she's so efficient at it! She runs the foundation so responsibly. I've read that she gets more work done with the fewest number of people because the people she hires are great at what they do. No nonsense. There are no layers of middlemen, just smart, pragmatic employees who cut through the details and get the job done. She's the opposite of corporate America. She's the opposite of the WMA. I wish she would run for president because I would vote for her in a second. Well, when I become a citizen, that is."

Rafael laughed. "She ran our household the same way. We all had our chores to do growing up and we did them without question. There were never any excuses for mom. She has a household staff but the bare minimum. I remember when Ted got his driver's license, he was expected to drive us younger kids to and from school. Then Nora had to do it."

"Of course you were all given nice new cars when you were able to drive?" Lily queried.

"Not a chance. Ted got a ten-year-old Honda Accord and it got passed down to Nora then to me when I turned sixteen."

"That's what I love about her. She is so down to earth. I have heard she owns a jet but it was not meant for passengers. Is this true?"

"That may be a bit of an urban legend. Mom does own a jet but it's used more for cargo then people. She finds it easier than trying to get supplies through in commercial or leased aircrafts. She actually has a very nice passenger section right behind the pilot with room for twenty people. It's quite comfortable, almost luxurious but whenever I've flown with her, the passenger section is stuffed with boxes of MREs or supplies. She doesn't like to waste space."

"How wonderful. She's such a sweetheart. You'd never guess when meeting her that she is the driving force behind so much goodness. She comes off so gentle and unassuming."

"She means the world to me but I share her with the world. And I'm perfectly fine with the arrangement."

"You were brought together for a reason, Rafael. She is just as lucky to have you in her life." She genuinely meant it as she looked into his beautiful brown eyes. But he turned away uncomfortably.

"It was destined, I suppose. Ah, as if on cue.... Mama. Wonderful speech."

Mary approached, smiling happily, kissed Rafael then embraced Lily.

"Thank you, darling." She turned her attention to Lily. "Lily, I'm so glad you could make it today."

Lily was nearly breathless with adoration. "Thank you so much for your kind invitation. It is my honor to attend this lovely party."

"How are things at Amnesty, dear?"

"Oh, my we are so busy! I have been traveling quite a bit but we are making such great progress."

"Do you see much improvement in human rights worldwide?" Mary asked, hopefully.

"Attitudes are changing, for sure. It is fascinating what Aqar has done for the remaining children on earth. So many orphans are being adopted by good, caring parents. There is still much work to be done, of course, but it feels good to know things are getting better."

"I'm so happy to hear it. I do hope you'll come around to visit more, Lily." Mary smiled graciously, ready to move on and leave Rafael to his wooing.

"It would be my pleasure, Mrs. Johnson." Lily glowed.

"Please call me, Mary. I insist."

Chapter 14

The kids were in bed. The last of the caterer's staff were gone and the family, finally alone, relaxed in the library and spoke of the day, even chuckling at Poppy's aggressive attempt at romance. Nora couldn't resist a few jabs at Rafael's expense. She did a dead on imitation of Poppy eliciting a great deal of laughter from everyone but Rafael. Eventually, Mary set down her cup of tea and gave Ted a nod.

"We have a wonderful announcement," Mary started.

"You're adopting a new brother or sister for us?" Nora asked with a straight face.

Mary laughed. Her kids were so witty! "No, dear. No more siblings for you. This is even better news."

Lou wanted answers. "Just tell us, ma, we're dying to know!" He'd had a few beers and was feeling fine.

Mary looked radiant as she broke the news. "Ted has discovered an IVF procedure that will allow women to become pregnant again." She grinned from ear to ear as the information enveloped her family.

"Holy Crap!" Nora exclaimed. That was the only sound for a full thirty seconds until Nora continued. "I knew you could do it, kid." She hugged Ted while Lou shook his hand, sporting a huge smile.

"Thank God." Rafael was relieved and elated.

Lou threw up his hands. "If anyone was going to save mankind, it'd be Ted." He bear hugged his brother-in-law while Ted struggled to breathe.

"When are you going to make this... public?" Rafael asked while hugging first his mother, then Audrey.

"Soon, soon, soon," Ted responded, shaking Lou off. "We want to talk to all of you first."

"I bet that French guy went nuts when you told him." Lou said. "Bet he was all, 'mon dieu merde.'"

Ted cocked his head. "Well... I haven't exactly told Dr. Charbot."

Nora, Lou and Rafael stood silent, confused, waiting for more.

Mary had her arm around Audrey. "We have an idea...."

Ted stepped up. "A while ago, Mom bought the old Victory Hospital in Waukegan."

"Wait. *What?* You bought a hospital?" Nora asked.

Ted smirked. "I know, right? It's all ours and since it's a fixer-upper, we got it for a great price. Turns out there's not a lot of people looking to buy old hospitals so we made a competitive offer and…"

"Okay!" Nora had to stop the inevitable meandering topic drift.

"Ted technically hasn't cured the bug but he has made it possible to work around the virus." Audrey helped. She was beaming as much as the rest of the family.

"Yes." Ted continued. "Through a simple IVF procedure. One that I invented, I might add; women can now get pregnant if they come to the new Johnson Fertility Center! Two visits, maybe three. Nine months later… Baby!"

The family was shocked at first but as the news sank in, they started to grasp the possibilities. The world wasn't doomed. Life would go on.

"So what's the hospital for?" Lou wanted details.

"The procedure will have to be done in a controlled environment. Same old IVF but I'll be using a new procedure that blocks out the Aqar virus long enough for fertilization to happen in the dish and stay strong enough to hang on in the uterus."

"Ted, I'm serious, right now. Do you need human test subjects?" Nora grabbed her brother's arm as she said it.

Ted grimaced. "Yeah, but ewwwww, if you think I can perform a girlie procedure on my own sister!"

Nora stared him down. "Like I would ever let you? Seriously. I'd get a real doctor..."

Lou covered his ears. "I can't listen to this. It's weird. Please stop."

"We're all uncomfortable," Rafael added with obvious discomfort and impatience as he looked askance at his brother and sister. "Please move on."

"I wasn't talking about me, moron." Nora responded to Ted. "I know of some great people out there who were turned down for adoption because there are no more kids left to adopt. I'm just saying, let me know if you need test subjects and I'll give you some deserving couples."

"Funny you should phrase it that way, Nora. I will need to vet some potential mommies for the Beta but more important I will need some help from you and Raf and Lou."

"Just tell us what you need." Rafael said, meaning it. "We're here for you."

"Eventually, we'll need to bring all patients here to my new hospital... That sounds weird, 'my new hospital.'" Ted in a silly voice.

"Slow down, Ted, how will this work?" Lou said. "Why do they have to come to you and your new hospital?"

Ted shrugged. "That's what we're about to talk about right now. What has been the mission of the Johnson Foundation all of our lives? What has mom worked for? What's our common goal in this family?"

Silence. They were all rhetorical questions.

Ted took a deep breath. "Lily's not here tonight even though I thought about asking her to come. Seems Prince Raf over here has cast some sort of spell. Dude, I really think she's into you. Can you not see it? Why don't you..."

"Oh my God, Ted, SHUTUP, and tell us what's going on!" Nora had her arms crossed. Rafael looked down into his lap.

"Okay, sorry." Ted continued. "She's always supported the same NGOs as us. Hell, she worked for UNICEF during her breaks from med school. Maybe that's why we bonded when she came to New York. She's completely and totally about human rights, specifically children's rights, like us. We all got the drive from Mom but Lily's passion came naturally. I want her to be part of this."

Lou looked puzzled. "What exactly is 'this'?"

Ted got sort of serious. "The thing is, I think I put on some blinders here in luxurious Lake Forest. I write the checks to charities, I spend a couple weeks in a Costa Rican clinic once a year but there's a really crappy world out there...." Ted didn't know how to continue so Mary did.

"Ted is conflicted. He has come up with a formula to strengthen the embryo through IVF and the first crucial weeks of gestation with a natural additive but he cannot mass produce this, this, this... additive which means there are a limited number of women who will be able to take advantage of this breakthrough. We don't have enough additive for everyone who will want to get pregnant."

Nora raised an eyebrow and waited for it. There was complete silence until Ted responded.

"I'm going to need you all to come and work with me." Ted said. "I'm calling it the Johnson Project. You see, someone has to decide who gets to procreate and it looks like we're going to be the ones to do it."

Chapter 15 - Joey Is Eighteen Months Old

Nora and Lou sat in war-torn seats in the waiting area. Nora couldn't stop her leg from tapping, Lou alternately paced and sat. Paced and sat. During one of the pacing moments, Nora stopped him by putting both of her hands on his shoulder and looking him straight in the eye. "We can do this. We're ready."

"I know. I know. I know. But so many things could go wrong. I just...." Lou had sweat on his upper lip. He hugged his wife and it calmed them both temporarily.

Lou pulled back and cupped her cheek. "You're going to be a great mom, Nora."

Her eyes filled with tears. "You're going to be a great dad, Lou."

A door opened behind them. They both turned to see a smiling woman holding an old winter coat. The woman held the door open and beckoned someone behind her. Lou and Nora held their breath. Billy came shyly through the door, smiling but obviously nervous. His glaring scar was evident but fading. Nora opened her arms and he ran to her and hugged her fiercely. Lou got a hug in and picked up the boy while Nora hugged them both. "Are you ready to go home, Billy? Your forever home?" He nodded and hugged Lou's neck as he cried.

Nora had been watching Billy's situation since the last custody hearing. She had even made it a point to regularly visit him at his foster home because there was something special about this boy. She was drawn to him and for the first time felt maternal love. Eventually she brought Lou to one of her visits and soon all three looked forward to the weekly events. On one occasion, Mary joined the trio for an outing at a McDonald's playland. She, too, immediately fell in love with the little guy and made a vow to use her resources to make a better life for him. Somehow. But the situation was in a bureaucratic stalemate. Lou personally checked on Billy's mother and her husband who were still together. He noted they spent a great deal of time fighting but still cohabitating. He found a few domestic violence calls at their address but no follow up with the police or court. It seemed Billy would not have to move back in with his mother since she had no intention of breaking up with her abuser but she refused to give up her rights to Billy, thinking one day the court would rule in her favor and she could have her family back together again and if Billy could just behave and she could watch her mouth, maybe Ron would be nicer and things could work out.

In the meantime, Billy moved from one foster home to another and his life stood in limbo while the adults tried to figure out what to do.

It was Ron, ironically, who brought the checkmate. Only days earlier, in a rage over a ruined dinner as evidenced by the burned steak in the kitchen, he beat his wife with a tree branch and then slammed her head into a tree when she escaped into the yard. After setting fire to their home, he took his own life with one shot to his temple. He must have realized he finally went too far and he couldn't get bailed out of this one. Billy was told three days later at his foster home. Nora and Lou acted quickly. With Mary's help and by calling in every favor with the court, they were given temporary custody until an adoption could be finalized.

The family Christmas party was in full swing at Mary's house. "Where are Nora and Lou?" Raf asked after swinging Allie around like a helicopter.

"They texted to say they were running late. They'll be here soon." Mary was sitting near the tree doing a puzzle with Joey. There were only six puzzle pieces but Joey couldn't fit them together without gnawing on them first; the chewed lumps of cardboard were never going to be the same and they sure weren't going to fit into the puzzle. Mary tried anyway as she smiled benevolently at her drooling grandson. Audrey entered with an armful of wrapped gifts to add to the pile already under the tree. "Does anyone know what the big secret is?" Ted asked.

"Nora has been keeping something secret but I can't guess what." Audrey sat by the huge fireplace and cradled her cup of tea. Rafael smiled at her. "Maybe they're finally moving out of the city," he suggested.

"That's a given," Mary said. "I happen to know that I will soon be getting new neighbors." She smiled happily but couldn't be persuaded to reveal more. Rafael had recently moved to town, working with the family on the Johnson Project. They were using Ted's deserted medical building as an office while the new hospital was under construction. Nora and Lou were transitioning out of their city jobs to work on the project and Mary knew the whole family would be living in the same zip code very soon. She was thrilled they would all be working together and living nearby. She loved seeing her kids every day. It was as if her dreams were all coming true.

Soon, Lou and Nora showed up in the entryway full of Merry Christmas cheer, exchanging greetings and announced that they had some news for everyone. Even Allie gave her full attention.

"We thought you'd all like to meet the newest member of our family," Nora said with tears in her eyes. She was too choked up to continue. Lou went around the corner and came back holding hands with a nervous Billy who was still trying to grasp the notion that he was now part of a family. Even though they tried to contain themselves for Billy's sake, it was impossible not to hug their new nephew/cousin and everyone got a little weepy at the monumental life event. Billy took it all in and even relaxed a little. He stayed close to Nora and Lou and gaped at the gigantic Christmas tree and the plate of cookies that anyone could just take from. He couldn't imagine that any of the million presents would be for him but he was happy to be with nice people who smiled and made him feel welcome. Allie was thrilled to finally have a cousin and she eventually lured him away from his new parents to show him her toys and books. He even had a baby cousin named Joey who staggered all over the place and banged his hands on the chairs. Lou and Nora beamed with happiness as they hovered over their new son. The evening was full and happy. Billy fell asleep that evening in Mary's arms with a smile on his cookie crumbed face. She kissed his forehead and held him close and silently welcomed him to the family. She was beyond grateful for her new little grandson.

Chapter 16

The Christmas season was a joyous one for many Americans and Canadians. The payroll statute stabilized the economy then boosted it to where even Task Force 200 never imagined. Anyone who wanted a job, had a job. Not necessarily their dream job, but a job with a salary that paid the bills until further education or experience could land the dream job. But even that didn't matter because every job was tolerable as long as the pay was good and all the co-workers were happy. Some undesirable jobs were hard to fill. Custodial work, housekeeping, jobs that were previously considered menial, almost subservient, were not drawing many candidates. It didn't take long for the demand to boost the salaries to where enterprising individuals eagerly took on the tasks to get the premium pay and ended up only having to work part time. It was perfect for those who wanted to use their spare time for other interests while cashing in their paychecks that rivaled some of their bosses. Most of the "bosses" didn't care as long as they didn't have to do the dirty work so everybody was happy. It also made hiring a cleaning lady something of a tradeoff. The true middle class had to consider how badly they wanted someone to clean their house because they would pay dearly for it. Same with landscaping and other luxuries but people were happy to trade off for wants and needs.

Immigrants arrived daily. Once they were cleared by Homeland, private organizations gave temporary housing and filtered individuals and families to whatever cities had housing and resources to give them a start. It was handled efficiently and happily with local volunteers who knew where to fill in the gaps. The new residents didn't have to stay put but they did need to find work, establish some savings and support themselves before moving on to another part of the country if they so desired. Most opted to stay where they landed. Many started out with the undesirable jobs, but with the high pay, they were quickly able to save up, experience life in the United States, learn the language and settle in. They also paid taxes and spent their paychecks. Top executives from big corporations still grumbled and occasionally made public statements about getting back to normal but there seemed no reason to go back to the old normal when the new normal was near perfect. There was still something of a poverty level but where the government had long ago given up, private organizations were stepping in to help. Government agencies were given more resources to deal with mental health issues which helped to get many homeless off the street and also helped those with drug addictions. The only thing missing in everyone's life was the pitter patter of tiny feet and the knowledge that the world would be passed on to a new generation.

Chapter 17 - Joey Is Two Years Old

It took a lot of overtime and two construction crews but the hospital was retrofitted into Johnson Tower and operational less than two years after the Aqar virus first gripped the world. It was a beautiful seventy-acre campus to begin with but now looked like a resort on the outside and a state-of-the-art medical facility on the inside. Ted and Lou chased Joey around the front lawn while discussing security with Burke who wanted a full rundown of the property and the security detail now that the public would be granted access.

"The perimeter fence is air tight. There's motion sensored cameras every ten feet and a highly paid security team that will take a bullet for you and any of the docs on staff." Lou boasted.

"Good to know," Ted responded. "But kinda weird. Hopefully there won't be any bullets to take."

"Mary and you kids can go through the underground garage?" Burke asked, all business as usual.

Lou liked Burke and trusted him like he would another cop. "Yeah. The family can get in and out without going through the parking lot or front gate. You saw the private elevator from the garage to the eleventh floor. The family is safe."

Burke relaxed a little and looked around the grounds. He was always on alert.

Ted watched Lou. "You worried?"

"You've read the papers, Ted. There's too many people involved now for there not to be leaks. There's nutty people out there. I have no idea what to expect."

"It's gonna be cray. Are your guys prepared for announcement day?"

Lou held up his hand in a pledge. "We are prepared to open our doors to the press. All internal security is fully trained. But until tomorrow, nobody's getting into this compound without authorization."

Ted nodded toward the bus roundabouts. "Except, apparently, Mickey Bruce." Burke was already on the run. Sure enough, strolling across the grounds came intrepid reporter, Mickey Bruce, holding up his arms in an "I Surrender" gesture. Ted picked up Joey as Lou raced to meet the other three guards who were just catching up with Mickey, ready to tackle. Burke had Mickey in a chokehold within seconds. Lou was furious and embarrassed. "What the hell happened?" he yelled to the security officers who had no answers for him. Mickey accepted the blame.

"I'm good at scaling fences. Can't we let this one slide, Ted? Lou? Big Guy? Come on. You know I come in peace. Why not show a little love for the local journalist?"

Lou shot daggers at the guards. "Get him outta here."

Mickey persisted. "Ted! Ted! I hear this hospital is not for wayward orphans! Rumor has it, you beat the team in Paris and you're gonna start making babies. Can you confirm?"

Ted considered a straightforward answer but instead said, "Come to the press conference tomorrow like everyone else, Mickey. Well, if you can make bail."

Mickey managed to squirm away and turn to Ted. "Why can't you give me the scoop?"

He was gone with his captors. Lou came back to Ted to say, "I'm gonna go fire some guards over there. Burke followed him, disgusted with the breech. "This won't happen again." Lou assured while he and Burke jogged off toward the rear of the building. Ted made his way into the air conditioning with Joey happily clapping as he went.

The lobby was massive but homey and inviting with live plants and trees arranged with cozy waiting areas. Behind the welcoming reception desk he was thoroughly scanned by live guards before passing through to the elevator bank where he provided a retinal scan to get on the elevator. He let Joey down in the elevator and used his key card to swipe an infrared reader which allowed him access to the eleventh floor where the executive offices were housed. They called it the executive floor but really it was just a nice grouping of office suites including a play area for Allie, Billy and Joey, a kitchen, dining room and every amenity the family might need while in the building. There was also a kennel for Billy's dog, Tuffy, although Tuffy was rarely in it. He tended to run around the floor peeing on things and hoping Joey would drop his Cheerios. Everything on the eleventh floor was considered personal property of the Johnson family and not funded in any part by the Johnson Project or the Johnson Foundation. The family paid rent to the Johnson Project for use of the eleventh floor and even paid the utilities and cleaning costs from their personal funds. The Johnsons zealously upheld the Payroll Statutes almost to a fault.

Ted found Audrey in her office with Mary and Nora. Ted set Joey down who immediately toddled toward his mother as Tuffy eagerly approached his little friend.

"What's going on around here?" Ted asked.

Mary smiled. "Just gearing up for the big day."

Audrey turned to her husband. "Sybil's looking for you."

Ted looked over his shoulder. "Oh, no. Did anyone foresee her transition to megalomaniac?" Before anyone could answer, Sybil popped into the office carrying a clipboard and walkie while talking into the microphone of her headset. She signed off with her caller before turning on Ted.

"Ted, can we revisit the dress code situation? One of the new physicians is wearing shorts. Shorts!"

"I think we've all decided that there will be no dress code, sooooo...." Ted grimaced.

"It's just that we all appear more professional when..."

Ted held up a hand for her to stop. "Still no dress code. I don't care how it appears. Everyone should be comfy." He tried to sidestep her and escape but she stood in the doorway.

"And another thing, Ted. I heard a couple of the nurses refer to the sperm donation rooms as 'wanker' rooms." She said indignantly.

Ted didn't crack a smile but it took some effort.

Sybil continued. "I told them they would get written up if I heard it again and they told me that *you* called them 'wanker' rooms!"

"Okay, to be fair, I may have once made a joke..."

"How will the teams come to respect us if we allow this kind of malarkey?"

"The teams will respect us if we earn their respect. Also, you really don't have the authority to write anyone up, Sybil, although I'm sure you'll try. And, you're way too young to use the word malarkey and be taken seriously."

"Fine." Sybil spun on her heel and flounced out of the room.

Nora grinned. "It's like having a teenager."

Mary agreed. "She means well and, my goodness, she is efficient."

"She keeps me on my toes," Ted admitted. "But she makes me crazy."

Audrey beckoned. "Hon, can you take a look at this page of the website? Did I get the medical jargon right?"

Ted leaned over his wife and read through quickly. "Yeah. You got it. When does this go live?"

"During the press conference. Sybil will hit the publish button just as soon as your mom reads the reveal. I'm just adding some finishing touches now before Nora rips into it again with her fine tooth comb."

"Good." He turned to Nora. "We all covered on the legal front?"

"Hell if I know. It's not like this has ever happened before in the history of the world. Ever." Nora shrugged. "I mean, as the law stands today, we're perfectly within our rights. Everyone's license is up to date. I think they'll go that route first but we're safe. Then they'll get some temporary injunctions but nothing that could possibly stick."

Ted snapped his fingers as he suddenly remembered. "Oh, Mom. Burke's head is gonna fly off his body 'cuz Mickey Bruce got through the gate. Sorry in advance."

Mary smiled her most benevolent smile. "He's such a dear. Always worried. He'll be fine. What did Mickey want?"

"A story. He climbed the fence or some damn thing. Lou body checked him and we're all safe now."

"You have to admire Mickey's determination." Audrey said.

"No, we don't. He's a pain in the ass." Nora answered. "And he hates our guts."

Ted nodded. "Well let's enjoy this last day of normalcy, shall we?"

The day ended with taco night at Mary's house.

Chapter 18

The press conference was scheduled to start at ten a.m. sharp. The local and Chicago media had been invited for "a significant announcement." Some had heard rumors about an orphanage, others were mildly curious but not expecting much. Most expected it was a publicity stunt to draw attention to the Johnson Foundation, maybe a new headquarters in the suburbs. But it was only a forty minute drive north of the city so what the hell? Representatives from the networks arrived, the papers sent the usuals including Mickey Bruce, newly sprung from his twenty minutes in jail. He was prepared to spend the night in a cell and make the most of the ugly experience but the Johnsons did not wish to pursue charges so he was released, much to his dismay. The jail thing would have made a great opener.

The local news stations sent 'About Town' reporters who would stand in front of the building and announce whatever was happening at the midday news if they could fit it in. The majority were expecting another philanthropic endeavor from the Johnson family, most likely a new children's hospital which seemed a little crazy since the world was running out of children, but the Johnsons always put out a nice spread for the press. After passing through security, each reporter was given a badge and led through the impressive lobby to the auditorium where they were treated to a breakfast buffet before being seated. The stage contained an oblong table with five chairs and a podium with a microphone. The family came out at ten o'clock sharp without fanfare or introduction and sat at the table while Mary took the podium. Lily waited in the wings giving the family a thumbs up and a nervous smile as they got seated.

"Welcome everyone and thank you for coming today." The audience murmured polite responses.

"The Johnson family is proud to show you our newest facility here in Waukegan, Illinois. It was built with love and hope. It has been a year and a half since the last child was born on this planet. The nurseries have been too quiet." A dull murmur and some shuffling followed by shushes meant the press was actively listening. "So I am delighted to announce that my son, Theodore Johnson, has discovered a safe and surprisingly simple procedure to once again allow women to become pregnant through In Vitro Fertilization."

A roar of applause startled Mary but she smiled and waited for the revelry to end. In the wings, Sybil hit the publish button that made the Johnson website visible to the world. Her job at the press conference was done sufficiently so she headed upstairs to resume her reign as office manager.

Mary continued. "Our test subject is now sixteen weeks pregnant and doing just fine. The baby is absolutely thriving..."

More roars from the crowd. "Someone's already pregnant?" "What's her name?"

"Thank you, yes, we're so excited. The parents have asked not to be identified just yet."

Someone from the back yelled, "Can everyone get pregnant again?"

Mary frowned. "No. The procedure will only be made available to those couples who can prove they will be good parents."

Every hand shot up and the murmur evolved into a dull roar.

Mary pressed on over the noise. "A press release has just been sent out to all major U.S. and Canadian newspapers and news outlets. A website is now available to the general public for couples interested in applying for consideration."

The screen behind the table posted the website address: www.JohnsonProject.org in bold text. The address would be hit ninety-seven million times by the end of the day.

Mary continued. "Applicants must meet the following criteria before being considered...."

Uproar from the crowd. *Criteria?*

"It's really very simple so I'll relate the overall requirements and you can check the website for details. You can find everything you need to know on the website and we would appreciate if potential patients would direct all correspondence through email. For now, I'll give you the basics and we'll be happy to answer your questions." Mary took a deep breath and made her case. "Interested parents must meet the following criteria before being considered for our program. To start, all couples must provide five notarized affidavits from references willing to testify that applicants have the characteristics of good parents. Applicant couples must provide notarized copies of their last five tax returns to prove they have the means to raise a child. We'll need bank statements to back this up and social security numbers so that we can run a credit report. Applicant couples must provide proof of health insurance. Both parents must be over the age of twenty-seven. If either partner is a convicted pedophile or sex offender, neither will be accepted. Ever. If either partner has had more than one DUI or DWI, they will not be considered without a minimum of five years participation in AA or NA plus a notarized statement from their sponsor. Couples are not required to be married; however, both potential parents are required to sign legal documents ensuring financial support for the child through college age. Applicants must pay the fee of twelve thousand dollars."

Mary looked up to the disbelieving expressions before her. Nobody in the audience was seated. There was some murmuring and a stir but they were hungry for more details as they struggled to believe what they were hearing. Rafael gently escorted Mary to a seat at the table where Nora hugged her. Lou took the podium with a rapt audience waiting for more.

"You can get the application on the website and apply on-line. All the instructions are there. We just need copies of all the documents scanned and attached to your app. If you have falsified any part of the application or send any forged documents, you will be turned down and placed on our black list which means you will never be allowed to apply again. If all of your info checks out and you pass the background check, you will be accepted and scheduled for a personal interview where you will be given a lie detector test and a drug test. If you fail any of that, both partners will go on the black list so choose your co-parent carefully. If you break the rules, for instance, if you try to buy someone else's time slot, you will be put on the black list. Basically, if you try to circumvent the process, you will not prevail and you will never again be considered as a candidate. For now, this offer goes out to Americans and Canadians. Any questions?"

The sheer strength of the roar surprised him and made those at the table look at each other with unease. Lou was afraid they would storm the stage as he saw the desperation for new information.

"Please calm down. We won't get anywhere if everyone talks at once. How about we start with you... there." Lou pointed to a female reporter in the front row.

"I... I... can you describe the procedure?" She was shocked to have been called on first and then given the chance it was her first instinct to get the 'how' question answered.

Ted leaned forward into his microphone at the table. "It's the same IVF that was done worldwide prior to the Aqar virus. The difference today is that we've added a natural component, literally in the Petri dish, that strengthens the embryo and makes it viable. The embryo is implanted in the uterus and Mother Nature takes it from there."

Lou pointed to another reporter who was shocked but ready. "Can you tell us about the component?"

Lou looked to Ted for the answer. Ted considered the question then leaned into his microphone and said, "No."

The reporters were getting used to the news and were anxious to meet deadlines. They behaved and waited their turn. Lou pointed to the next reporter.

"What gives you the right to determine who gets pregnant and who doesn't?"

Nora put her hand on Ted's arm, afraid of what he might say so she answered. "Since the procedures will be limited, we see it as a responsibility to ensure that only the best parents are given this opportunity."

Lou pointed to the next reporter, a television personality.

"Why don't you share this procedure with the world so every doctor will have access to this breakthrough?" The pack nodded and anxiously awaited an answer to the million dollar question.

Ted leaned in. "The breakthrough isn't the procedure. The breakthrough is the natural component which is limited in supply. We are the only facility with access to the component."

Lou pointed to the next reporter.

"Where do you grow this secret component?"

Ted nodded, "Right here."

"Can we see it?"

Ted shook his head. "Ummmm. No. You can't."

Lou pointed to the next reporter.

"Why do you say just Americans and Canadians? Can women from other countries come to your facility for the procedure?"

Lou took the question. "At this time, no. We do not have the means to adequately check the backgrounds and financial circumstances of foreign citizens. Except Canadians. We will add other countries to the line-up as soon as we can."

A female on-line reporter stepped up. "My husband and I have been praying for this moment. Can we start now? Can I be the first?" She was choked up with emotion.

Lou smiled. "By all means get your paperwork in and you'll be considered. We are now officially accepting applications so..."

The reporter slapped her laptop shut and ran up the aisle. Her story would have to wait. The crowd smiled and took pictures of her departure. It was a nice moment. Lou continued. "We'll be taking applications immediately but we expect some legal pressure and possibly a cease and desist. But get the apps in and we'll schedule the interviews in the order received."

More reporters, male and female, left the auditorium.

Nora came to the podium next to her husband. "What we are doing is, well, unprecedented in case law and medical history. It may not seem fair to some people but, believe me, we've gone to every extreme to make sure our selection process is fair and impartial. I'm sure our decision will stir some debate."

More chuckles as keyboards were pounded and the story of the century took hold. A black, female reporter pushed to the front of the crowd. "Shame on you, Miss Johnson-Berger, for allowing this kind of discrimination on your watch."

Nora honed in on the reporter. "Was that... a question...or... ?"

The reporter continued. "Obviously, African Americans will be most affected by this... ethnic cleansing."

Nora stared daggers at the reporter. "Ethnic cleansing, Ms. Parker? Yes, I know who you are. Our search for good parents does not preclude color, race, religion or lifestyle. It's meant to weed out people who are not ready for the responsibility of..."

"You think our sisters on welfare will be able to afford a twelve thousand dollar fee?"

"Maybe you hadn't noticed but there're not many sisters left on welfare. The new economy has got just about everyone working."

"Not so fast, Miss Johnson-Berger. This temporary economy has given some new jobs but we still have plenty of single mothers struggling to make it."

"Why would they want to have more children if they are struggling and single?"

"How dare you shame women who are trying their best to make do."

"How am I shaming them?"

"By taking away their choice to have a baby. By setting the fee so high, they could never hope to pay like the children of privilege. Our people still need help just to survive!"

Nora barked. "If they were able to afford the fee, they shouldn't be on welfare. If they're on welfare they should wait to have children until they are *not* on welfare."

A hushed gasp was heard among the reporters. This was getting juicy.

"Some of them can't afford a computer to get to the website to get to the application."

"Then they shouldn't have children! Welfare gives people the chance to get back on their feet. Once they are financially stable, that's when they should consider having a child. Not while they are struggling."

The reporter was outraged. "And you want to put our people through the indignity of a drug test?"

Nora nodded. "Yes, I do. I want all people to take a drug test. Every last applicant."

"And you don't consider that discrimination?"

Nora considered. "I consider it discrimination against drug users, so, yeah, I'm discriminating against drug users. News flash: They shouldn't be parents."

Lou had enough and called on the next reporter, a curmudgeon who'd been covering news since the first Daley administration. Until now, the old cuss thought he'd seen it all. "I see what you're doing. Okay. But there are plenty of good people who are not using drugs and not dependent on welfare but still can't afford your fee. Black, white, Hispanic, whatever. I'm thinking of the young adults who are just starting a career. What about them?"

Nora was ready to blow so Rafael nudged her back to her seat and answered the question. "Yes. Good question, sir. I do sympathize with those young people who are anxious for a child. But, I'll say it again, our resources are limited. We have to reduce the applicant pool and we thought long and hard about the age limit and we eventually agreed on the minimum age of twenty-seven. If you think back to your early twenties, would you really recommend parenthood to people in that age range? They have a lot of living to do, my mom calls it 'sowing your oats,' which makes it seems like a dating game but really it's about taking the time to find your true life partner. It's also about finding a career that you love and ideally, saving enough money to build a solid foundation for a secure life and *then* adding a child to it."

Lou silenced the reporter with one look and moved to the next.

"Maybe the government should subsidize the payment...?"

Rafael responded. "If the government wants to pay for the procedure, we have no objection as long as the applicants meet the requirements."

The reporter continued. "What if the government wants to step in and regulate your operation?"

Nora got up from her seat and stood next to Rafael. "If the government tries to interfere with our operation, we will shut our doors and go home. Then nobody gets pregnant. Our family and our organization do not believe it is a civil right to bear children."

The audience reacted audibly. Lou pointed to the next reporter.

"How many doctors are here and how many procedures will you be able to perform at peak capacity?"

Ted leaned into his microphone. "We currently have thirty-five doctors on staff and we're looking to hire more. Incidentally, if you're from an IVF practice and would like to relocate to northern Illinois, please send resumes to my attention. It's a great job. We offer really good benefits, steady work, there's a 401K thing, we have a weight room, an awesome cafeteria with great coffee and I'm trying to get a softball league started..."

Rafael shot him an intense glare which Ted caught and reluctantly changed the topic. "Anyway, factor in vacations, part-time docs and all the staff working round the clock, we aim to have an average of thirty-twoish doctors each performing ten procedures a day, which works out to about three hundred and twenty per day so one hundred and seventeen thousandish pregnancies a year. But you gotta factor in a miscarriage rate and, sadly, an infant mortality rate, sorry, but that comes to about one hundred and nine thousand, eight hundred happy bouncing babies per year." Ted smiled. The audience gasped.

The reporter continued. "That's it? That's all you can do?"

Ted was taken aback. "That's where we'll start but we hope to double our efforts the following year, maybe stay at that rate for a few years..."

"Three years ago, we had almost four million births in the United States alone. How can we build the population back up with two hundred twenty thousand births a year being your top capacity?"

Ted rolled his eyes. "Who said anything about trying to rebuild the world's population?"

"I think we all assumed when you made your announcement that that you would bring the population back to where it was. We already have an eighteen month loss..."

Nora jumped in at her table microphone. "We don't want to make the numbers. We want to make sure that every child is brought into a loving home."

"I get that, but how is the economy to survive with only a couple hundred thousand babies born every year?"

Rafael answered. "I think the better question here is how will the economy thrive with fewer drains on our dwindling resources?"

The same reporter had to ask, "What is this secret component?"

Ted leaned into his microphone petulantly, "I'm not telling."

The reporter was indignant. "The public has a right to know."

Ted leaned into his microphone. "How do you figure?"

The same reporter hesitated and then said, "Are you hoarding this secret additive to keep the reproductive business in your control and make all the profit?"

Rafael gave Ted the evil eye and answered. "Hold on, hold on. The twelve thousand dollar fee will cover operating expenses and overhead. The majority of expense for this project will come from family money and the Johnson Foundation. While we are not obligated to report *any* of our numbers to you, we plan on making public every dime that is spent including our expansion plans. We will keep you, the press, updated on every development and hold regular press conferences to keep you apprised of the budget and statistics."

Lou pointed at the next reporter.

"Once a couple passes all your tests, do they have to reapply for the next one?"

Ted leaned into his microphone. "There won't be a next one. Every couple gets one chance."

"You mean people will only be allowed to have one baby?"

"Yes. That's exactly what I said."

"What about people who already have children?"

Ted frowned. "They are ineligible."

A roar from the crowd.

The next reporter got her turn. "What if a woman doesn't want a man involved in her life? What if she wants to raise a child alone?"

Rafael glared at Ted and Nora and answered the question. "She and her sperm donor would need to apply like everyone else and pass the test like everyone else. After she gives birth, she and the father can go through the proper channels to legally terminate his parental rights."

The now angry reporter felt like she scored a point. "The father may not want to terminate rights after going through all that."

Raf nodded. "That would be his right. He is the father of the child."

"Where does that leave the mother?" The reporter dunked her shot.

Rafael was honestly confused. "It leaves her with a devoted father for her child."

"Are you seriously saying that a woman needs a man to have a child?" The reporter snapped.

Ted raised his hand and answered. "I'm the doctor here and I can confirm that, yes, a woman does need a man to have a child. It's been scientifically proven. In a lab. In a clinic. Five out of five doctors agree."

The audience laughed.

The reporter was angry. "This is outrageous!"

"To who?" Rafael asked.

"To women!" The reporter answered.

Rafael was shaken. "I've worked with a number of young, single mothers, ma'am, and I can assure you it is very difficult to …"

"You've worked with them, huh?" Snapped the reporter. "Women should not be denied their right to raise their children the way they see fit."

"Neither should men." Rafael answered.

There was no easy answer for that so the flustered reporter asked, "What if you get more 'qualified' applicants than you have petri dish stuff? Are you going to turn people away?"

Rafael was prepared. "We believe we have enough additive to accommodate the couples who are eligible for the procedure. We firmly believe we won't have to turn away any applicants who qualify."

Lou took control. "Okay, who's next?"

A local reporter stood. "What about gay couples?"

Rafael nodded. "Homosexuals will not be denied because of their lifestyle but obviously they would need a third party, a surrogate mother, or in the case of lesbian couples, a sperm donor. Again, all parties must apply, qualify and be accepted."

Mickey Bruce finally got his turn. "I wonder if everyone here knows this is a family operation."

The panel did not respond.

"Yeah, I've been checking this whole deal out and learned that you, Ted and Nora Berger are the children of Mary Johnson, heiress to the Johnson fortune."

Rafael answered. "We've never tried to hide that, Mickey."

Mickey continued. "Your mom's got billions in holdings, you all have trust funds that I could only dream about but you've poured a good chunk into this place. We all know about the Johnson do-gooders philanthropy..."

"Your point...?" Rafael asked.

Mickey played his ace. "And all of you are adopted."

The three racially diverse siblings look at each other. Ted couldn't resist. "Good sleuthing, Mickey. What made you suspect?"

The reporters laughed. Ted would provide some nice bites.

Mickey continued without humor. "You don't need to do this. You've probably given yourselves some nice salaries but if this doesn't work, your money is gone. One bad lawsuit, you could run out of your secret component. Charbot could come up with his own procedure. There's no guarantee of a win. Why risk it?"

Rafael jumped in. "We're obligated to do what we think is right. None of us want to see the end of mankind, yet we are forced to make a choice and we think our decision not only keeps our species from extinction, but it also might improve upon our treatment of children. Yes, it will cost us a lot of money but what good is money if you sell out your conscience?"

Mickey nodded. "Nice. Hey, how come your sister, Penny, isn't involved?"

Silence.

Mary leaned into her table microphone, shaken and defensive. "Who's next?"

A new reporter stepped up leaving Mickey in the dust. "When do you expect to get more of this... secret sauce?"

The whole room burst into laughter. Ted took the opportunity to change the subject. "You waited all this time to ask a question and you ask about the *secret sauce*? For the last time, we only have a little of the secret sauce. We can't rush production of the secret sauce, and sharing the knowledge of the secret sauce will not make it grow any faster. Now, enough about the secret sauce!"

The next reporter took his turn. "Why the Johnson family? I mean, you're holding a huge amount of power. Why is it all in your hands?"

The family all looked at each other. Ted took the question. "Because we're the only ones in the whole world making babies right now and if you want one, you're gonna have to play by our rules. That's why."

There was nothing left to say and the family didn't feel obligated to continue despite the pleas from the crowd. They all knew it would take time to sink in and they also regretfully knew that a backlash was imminent so they left the stage and braced for the fallout.

Chapter 19

Back on the eleventh floor, the family planned to meet for a private lunch but Sybil was waiting just outside the elevator with a wide-eyed temp by her side. Sybil was beside herself with importance and anxiety as she held up a handful of pink message notes while trying to explain her predicament to the family. "The calls have not stopped! The temps can't keep up..." She started.

Audrey, holding Joey, stepped over to calm Sybil. "Just keep referring them to the website. None of us will respond in person just yet...."

Sybil shrieked. "But you don't understand. They have the private numbers! How, how, how..."

Mary tried to help. "All of the information they need is on the website."

Sybil flipped through the pink messages. "Peter Jennings, BBC, Anderson Cooper, some guy from Fox News, Diane Sawyer, Oprah!!!"

Nora wasn't hearing it. "We are not doing interviews. Period. Just tell the temps to be firm."

Ted was genuinely impressed and stopped to look at some of the notable names on the call-back slips but the others kept walking toward the dining room.

"I get that you're not doing interviews but there's a lot of international calls coming in from, like, governments." Sybil exclaimed. "Some guy named Kim, and that Pierre Charbot guy, oh, and a king!"

The family seemed to consider her anxiety which gave Sybil the attention she wanted.

"All the information they need to know is on the website." Mary repeated. "Royalty or not, everyone has access to the website."

Another temp came running up to Sybil and anxiously whispered in her ear. Sybil turned to the family. "This temp has Hillary Clinton on hold. Yeah. Are we supposed to refer her to the website? The president of the United freaking States is on freaking hold!"

Before Mary could respond yet another temp ran up to the group. "I seriously have Pope Francis on line two. I'm not even joking. The *pope*! Line two."

The temp next to Sybil let out her frustration. "I have the Sultan of Brunei demanding to speak with someone. He's on hold and he is *mad*."

Ted raised his hand. "Mom, let me just talk to the president. I'll give her the spiel. It would be so cool to talk to the freaking *president*."

Sybil read from another pink note. "The Prime Minister of Canada says he will wait all day if he has to. Should we really make him wait all day?"

"Oh, dear," Mary looked around. "Let me talk to Mrs. Clinton and you can talk to the Pope. Wait. Perhaps I ought to speak with the Pope but, really Ted, please use your best manners."

Ted cheered and ran to his office while instructing Sybil. "Send the president to my desk phone, Sybil. Woot!"

Audrey ran after him. "Ted! Please don't talk about wanker rooms or cafeteria coffee. Oh, dear Lord."

Mary addressed the temps. "Please send Pope Francis to my office. Thank you." She turned to Rafael. "Honey, can you talk to Prime Minister Trudeau? I met him once and he's lovely. I suppose we should have mentioned this earlier to President Clinton and PM Trudeau but I wasn't thinking."

"Sure, mom." Rafael hustled to his office.

Lily asked Sybil for the message from Pierre Charbot, figuring it was time for some smack talk. She didn't want to brag but this was going to be sweet revenge.

"I'll take the Sultan of Brunei." Audrey said happily. "Yes, let me talk to the Sultan of Brunei. How many wives and kids does that guy have? He better be calling to say good luck with the new venture because I am in no mood."

"Wait!" The frazzled temp answered. "He will only speak to a man. He said no *wimmins*."

Audrey smiled. "Even better. Put him through to me."

"Nora, can you talk to the attorney general?" Sybil pleaded.

"Yeah, I can. Put him through."

Sybil turned to Lou. "I got a National Guard guy, an FBI guy, a Homeland guy and the Waukegan chief of police. Pick your poison."

Lou shrugged. "Give me the Waukegan chief. It's good to stay nice with the locals."

When they finally all met for lunch in the dining room of their eleventh floor second home, they were ready for some peace and quiet. Mary set Joey in his high chair while the caterers set out the food and the family looked out the window to the chaos down below outside the closely guarded gates. Ted held Allie up so she could see the mass of people. Lou had Billy up on his shoulders. They watched the protestors, law enforcement, eager applicants but mostly the press. The security team kept everyone outside the gates. They were instructed to make no exceptions.

Audrey closed the door with instructions that the family should not be disturbed during lunch regardless of the caller's importance. And, yes, that included Bono.

Mary had a hand over her heart. "I had the loveliest conversation with Pope Francis. What a kind man, he is. He has given his blessing on our project so that will relieve many. I told him we weren't Catholic or even particularly religious but he asked me to pray with him so I did. Very sweet."

"I got hung up on." Audrey reported. "The Sultan wanted all of his wives impregnated immediately. Here's the funny part. He couldn't be bothered to come here so he asked that we send a team to Brunei. Today!"

"Nervy bastard." Nora mumbled.

"He offered ten million bucks." Audrey added. "So he tells me all this thinking I'll run to the nearest man in charge but I told him no and he hung up on me."

"Does anyone care what my new best friend, Hils, had to say?" Ted was tickled. "She's so cool with all this but wants me to keep her in the loop. You know. 'Cuz we're besties."

Nora nodded. "Good endorsement. I got the same from the AG. But he warned we're about to have every government agency examining every square inch of the place. I told him we're ready to allow all necessary and legal inspections. Let the games begin."

"I wish Pierre Charbot would be happy for us but he is skeptical and vows to take us down. I do not see how but he is quite angry and claims we are liars." Lily shook her head.

"Spoil sport." Ted sniffed.

Lily shrugged. "He wanted every detail about the 'secret sauce' but I told him he was on his own. He should have listened to Ted when he had the chance."

"What about the Canadian PM, Raf?" Audrey asked.

"Excellent conversation. He just wanted a heads up since Canada is part of the applicant pool. This will affect their economy, of course. Certainly their future."

"I feel another meeting with the Task Force coming on..." Ted said to his mother.

"Yes. I anticipate a quick meeting. I hope my colleagues aren't angry that I wasn't more forthcoming with this announcement. Nothing changes, really. But we may want to tweak the statutes."

Lou carried Billy back to the table and got him started on his mac and cheese. "I had a nice talk with the sheriff.

He's pissed. County guys are pissed. State guys are pissed." He went back to the window, worried.

Allie and Billy found the word 'pissed' to be hilarious which made Lou clamp a hand over his mouth when he heard the giggling. "Hey, I warned everyone in advance that there would be traffic issues after the press conference. Not my fault they didn't care. Oh... crap..."

Lou stopped midsentence. Rafael and Ted stood to see what silenced Lou. "Should there be a convoy of black SUVs approaching the building or am I missing something?"

Lou headed for the door. "Guess I forgot to tell the Feds what was going on. Well, it looks like we got some company. I'll let you all know. Finish your lunch." He was gone.

The lunch continued but the conversation exceeded the eating. Everyone was feeling hopeful until Lou walked in holding a sheaf of documents. He held up a pile of blue tri-folded packets. "We've been served." He set them down next to his wife and grabbed a sandwich but didn't bother sitting down. Nora quickly looked through the papers. "As expected."

Lou choked down another bite. "Get this, we already got applications. On-line, but also, some people are throwing their apps over the fence tied to rocks!" He held up more paper. "I'm gonna take these down to admissions but there's no way they coulda got all the paperwork requirements so quick. Man oh man, you get one shot and you blow it like that? Morons. Anyway, only a few genuine crazies out there. We're good. We may need to send over a little donation to the Waukegan force, Ma." Mary nodded. Lou continued. "They're gonna be busy for a while. And, hon," he turned to Nora. "No way I'll be home tonight. See ya." He gave Billy a tickle, kissed Nora and Lou was gone.

Allie piped in, "Uncle Raf, are you ever gonna get married and have a baby?"

Rafael nearly choked but started down at his plate to hide his sudden blush. Lily concentrated on her salad until Nora broke the awkward silence. "We have to answer to all of this through the courts but it won't take long."

Mary was delighted. "Oh, I can't wait! More babies in nine months."

Audrey picked up one of the documents that Nora was sifting through. "This has become about discrimination?"

Nora sneered. "Yeah. Some ACLU sharks have already determined that we are discriminating against low income families, Christian Scientists... Jeeeez, crap, one

147

of these C&Ds claims we are discriminating against handicapped women because we are not allowing drug users to have the procedure. We should let heroin addicts get pregnant? Not on my watch."

Lily looked concerned. "Will this stand up in your courts?"

Nora shook her head. "No, it just hoses us up for a few days. Not a biggie but I'm gonna be in front of a lotta judges this week."

Mary brought her cheek next to Nora's affectionately. "It's best we hold our temper and let the process work its course."

"I know, Mom!" Nora rolled her eyes at the gentle scolding knowing full well her mother was correct.

Ted leaned back in his chair. "We'll win. Hils and I talked about this at length."

Nora couldn't resist. "I'm sure she was diplomatic in her endorsement until all of the polls have spoken."

Lou burst through the door. "Back again. Guess what? You're each getting a bodyguard for at least the next week."

"Nooooo." Nora exclaimed as everyone voiced their own dismay.

"Sorry," Lou continued. "There's too many nut jobs calling in threats. I had some of my guys on call just in case so get ready, they're on their way. I'm gonna be hiring some more permanent staff but for today, none of you leaves without your muscle."

"What's happening, Lou?" Audrey asked, concerned.

"I'm just erring on the side of caution. Please, you gave me this job because I know what I'm doing. I have to insist on this precaution and I don't have time to hear your protests."

They all knew it was the prudent course but nobody was happy about it.

"On another note, we've started to run security checks on our first applicants and we've officially rejected five couples already. Huh. That was quick." Lou shook his head. "And... some guy tracked Sybil through her Facebook page and offered her a million bucks to get on the 'to do' list. Sybil has since made her Facebook page private. You all might want to do the same."

Ted smiled ruefully. "Is Sybil okay?"

"Yeah, she's good and starting to realize her life is about to change. Then she made sure the doofus was number one on the blacklist."

"I cannot believe we already have a blacklist." Lily said.

Lou grabbed a lemon bar and headed for the door. "Took less than an hour."

Ted, curious, turned on the television and went right to CNN. Everyone turned to watch footage of the press conference. "Hey, we're on TV!" He said, studying the picture. "Audrey, you're *wrong*. I do *not* need a haircut." Nora shushed him as they listened to the commentator: *The decision to limit access to the procedure has caused friction worldwide. So far, no comment from any of the Johnsons.*

Ted flipped to the local ABC station where Mickey Bruce was live outside the gate.

News Nine Investigates with Mickey Bruce – Waukegan

The Lake Forest Johnson family has long been known for their philanthropic community service, especially the voice for children in need. Matriarch Mary Johnson has been the leader in this worldwide effort to help children for the last forty years. Adopted son, Theodore, has been a big name in obstetrics since medical school at University of Chicago. Adopted daughter Nora Johnson Berger was an attorney with Social Services Family division and youngest adopted son, Rafael Johnson joined Doctors Without Borders after a Stanford education and went on to work in the Chicago Public School system as an advocate for at-

risk youth. All of the Johnsons now work exclusively for the Johnson Project here at Johnson Tower. There is no doubt that this family is qualified to speak on behalf of voiceless children in need but making this step to hand choosing all future parents, well, more on the legal fallout as more information comes in. And what is the secret sauce? That's what has international scientists scratching their heads. Researchers in Paris are skeptical and angry that Dr. Ted Johnson was not more forthcoming with his data. Head of the WMA, Pierre Chabot, claims this highly experimental procedure may not be the panacea we've all been waiting for. This is Mickey Bruce, News Nine. Back to you, Brad.

The feed went back to Brad in the studio in front of a chart listing the criteria. Ted hit the mute button. "If this isn't a panacea, I don't know what is!"

"Why do they always say we're *adopted*? Like we're not exactly the legitimate progeny, we're *adopted*."

Mary hugged her daughter. "You are legitimate progeny to me."

Nora rolled her eyes. "Thanks, mom. I get all warm inside when you tell me I have a pretty face and that I'm legitimate progeny." They had a good laugh.

Lou entered again followed by six men dressed unobtrusively in casual clothes but all wearing ear pieces and packing. Introductions were made and instructions were given. The family reluctantly agreed.

Chapter 20

Nora took her bodyguard to the court house where she spent the rest of her day. Audrey took her kids and Billy home after lunch with her new bodyguard in tow. Audrey hoped the poor guy wouldn't mind a quick stop at the library followed by a ballet lesson at three. The rest of the Johnsons and Lily left shortly after six down the private elevator and into the underground garage. The bodyguards followed. After making sure their mother was safe in her car with a slightly miffed Burke scowling at the intrusion of another man appointed to protect Mary, they waved her off. Ted slapped a palm to his forehead. "Ah, Lily, I forgot to tell you. I can't drive you home. Audrey told me to stop and get some throwy-uppy meds for Joey and she wanted it like two hours ago. Raf, would you mind taking Lily home?" He smiled at the ploy Audrey had come up with earlier.

Ted left them and told his bodyguard he was going to love the Lake Forest Walgreens. The bodyguard nodded in agreement, ready to take on the Lake Forest Walgreens, as needed. Rafael opened the car door for

Lily and couldn't believe his brother's transparency. He wanted to punch Ted but he was also reluctantly grateful for the opportunity. As he settled into the driver's seat, he realized his first date with this dream woman would be chaperoned by the two hulks who awkwardly climbed into the back seat. Lily fiddled with the radio buttons and found a news station covering the announcement. She shook her head. "I wish there was a way to get a public read on the issue instead of the talking heads repeating the same thing over and over."

The younger bodyguard leaned up. "Why don't you find a talk radio station? I'll bet the calls are coming in like crazy, people weighing in on the topic."

"Great idea! What's a good talk station?"

"Put it on WLN AM. That's Ron and Bill. They'll be talking about it for sure." The young guard said, happy to help the pretty doctor lady. Lily found the station and they all listened in:

The Ron and Bill Radio Broadcast – WLN AM

Bill Meyer: *I was offended. I'm all done having children but, still... who are these Johnsons and what the hell do they think they're doing?*

Ron Cone: *I always heard about Mary Johnson when I was growing up. I knew she was big in the social scene up on the North Shore...*

Bill Meyer: *What? Were you moonlighting as a caterer or something?*

Ron Cone: *Will you listen to me? Did you see our coverage of the Johnsons this afternoon, Bill?*

Bill Meyer: *I did not.*

Ron Cone: *Way to support the hand that feeds you. Anyway, they did the whole rundown of the family and, oh my God! I am not worthy. They can make whatever rules they want to as far as I'm concerned. If they have to dole out the secret sauce with a dropper, I'm glad they're the ones doing it. They are like the most selfless people on earth.*

Bill Meyer: *Good people.*

Ron Cone: *Yeah. And if you think about the rules, they make perfect sense. I mean, why would you let a nineteen year old have a baby? Why? Really. Why?*

Bill Meyer: *I wouldn't. The nineteen year old doesn't appreciate it now, but she will. When she's thirty. Thirty-five.*

Ron Cone: *You should be able to afford babies before you make babies, doesn't that just seem obvious?*

Bill Meyer: *To me.*

Ron Cone: *Why should I pay for your baby?*

Bill Meyer: *You've never so much as sent a gift.*

Ron Cone: *Because you have everything you need! That's my point. Let the Johnsons make the rules and if someone doesn't pass the test, boot 'em the hell out of there!*

Everyone in the car smiled.

Lily lived in a rented coach house on swanky Green Bay Road. When they pulled into her driveway, she casually asked Rafael in for a glass of wine. He accepted and nervously escorted her inside hoping he could finally get the nerve to tell her how much he admired her and hoped she would consider a possible relationship.

His hopes were dashed when he realized that bodyguards have a tendency to stick around. Lily couldn't stand the thought of them guarding outside so she invited them in. It made for an awkward first date, if that's even what she considered it. But the four settled in to watch television in the cozy front room and keep up with the newscasts that interrupted every network schedule for the evening. Lily and Rafael sipped red wine while the guards stuck with coffee. Rafael managed to respond appropriately as Lily commented on the newscasts and replayed the events of the day. Many of the newscasters were not as open to the project as the talk radio people. Lily vented. "I wish we could just start making appointments and get the ball rolling but it seems like the whole world is against us. I'm sure public opinion will shift as we bring more children into the world."

The older guard seemed to catch on that he and his colleague were a third and fourth wheel and eventually took his partner outside to "recon" the perimeter. Rafael took a deep breath and decided to go for it but Lily had work on her mind.

"I can't believe this is happening." She said with a sigh. "I mean, we all knew it was going to cause controversy but I thought eventually it would make sense to people."

"For a little while. It's hard to... understand. People are so angry with us and we're only doing what seems to me so perfectly right."

"Given your experience, it is no wonder you feel as you do."

"Doesn't everyone think a child should be born to capable parents?" Rafael asked

"So many of us weren't."

"Now everyone will be."

Lily was focused on his eyes. "You are a very good man."

"No."

"Why do you work so hard? Why do you want so badly to help the children?"

"Because they can't help themselves. Some can't even hope for a happy life because they've never seen a happy life."

"Are you unhappy?"

"Once, when I was a child. Not anymore."

"What would make you very happy?"

Rafael leaned over and kissed Lily gently. He pulled back awkwardly but she took his face in her hands and kissed him back. Lily enthusiastically brought her arms around him and got closer but he pulled away suddenly as the security guards made a grand and somewhat loud entrance into the front foyer.

"I better go." Rafael said, looking down at the ground. She couldn't resist hugging him and wished he would stay.

Chapter 21

Nora spent a week fighting injunctions with her legal team. In the meantime, the Intake Department advanced the first group of applicants who were passed on to the Background Check Department. The applications that passed muster were sent to Interview Scheduling and First Appointment Booking. Of the forty-eight thousand applications that came in since the announcement, fourteen thousand made it to the Interview Scheduling Department. Mary, Audrey, Rafael and Lily helped with the initial rush of screening and scheduling while the doctors on staff waited to be called in for duty. The local couples were given weekend appointments and eager non-local couples arranged transportation to arrive within hours of contact. As long as they didn't perform the disputed procedure, they were free to do prenatal checkups and arrange future appointments.

One hundred and eighteen couples were scheduled for Monday. All hands were on deck for the first day of intake, cycle evaluation and procedure scheduling. The staff worked together seamlessly, efficiently and enthusiastically to make the day special for the potential new parents. There were gatherings and celebrations in the lobby throughout the whole week. Mary made sure there was plenty of good, healthy food for the new potential mommies as they came through. The press numbers outside the gate were legion, causing the Waukegan police, fire and highway departments to be on hand to deal with the traffic and satellite trucks that lined the streets surrounding Johnson Tower.

Nora hung up her desk phone and shrugged at her brother. "The FDA doesn't know what to do with us."

Ted shrugged. "I told you. They spent more time in the cafeteria than the lab."

"Did they even ask for the secret sauce?"

Ted grimaced. "Of course they asked but I told them it was secreted in the gel in the petri dishes. The patients are not ingesting the stuff so…"

"Did they want a sample?"

"I'm sure they did but it's not required so I told them no."

Nora thought for a minute.

"Is that the last hurdle?"

"Yeah."

"Will this put all the lawsuits to bed?"

"No, but, you can legally do your thing while I'm in court for the rest of this nonsense. There's nothing they can do to stop us now. They'll try.... but for now we're in the clear."

"I've got at least one patient on the list who's ready to go now. Today. Can I bring her in for the actual procedure? You know, put a baby in her tummy?"

Nora nodded enthusiastically. Ted headed for the door but stopped again and turned. "Better tell Raf to stop the presses around the world!"

"Yeah, I'm about to call him." She reached for her phone.

Ted hesitated again. "You'd think he'd get more of a charge out of controlling the schedules of every major medium in the world but he's more like, Oh, yeah, whatever, I'm stopping the presses. *Again.*"

"Get to work, Ted."

He tore off. Nora hit a key on her phone. "Raf. Big news. We're open for business."

Dr. Cathy Radio Broadcast - Syndicated

Dr. Cathy: *It's been one week since the announcement of the century and I have been inundated with calls, faxes and e-mails asking for my opinion. I have*

161

remained silent until now. Before the bug, in order to get pregnant, women had sex with men. It didn't matter if she was drunk, stoned, lying about birth control, underage, stupid, manipulative or even consenting to the sex in question. What we ended up with was a lot of unplanned pregnancies, unprepared parents, angry men, DNA testing and court ordered child support. The Johnsons have made sure that both men and women are stepping into parenthood with eyes wide open. Monumental decisions should <u>not</u> be made in the heat of passion. To the Johnsons I say, Bravo. My only complaint... they may just put me out of business. Let's hope so.

Chapter 22

A sea of reporters surrounded the stone staircase leading to the Carrel lab. Word of a counter announcement was rumored and since Pierre Charbot always made good press, the street was packed. He loved to make the lead story on CNN World News and would prefer that all stories regarding Aqar go through him but Ted Johnson was now stealing the show; hell, he owned the show and it was starting to piss him off. Charbot stepped out of the double wide doors in a manner that was not unlike a papal entrance. Several minions in white lab coats whose only purpose was to look medical, stayed behind him as he waited for perfect silence. Questions were tossed out, mostly in French and English but many other nationalities were represented as well. Charbot slowly turned his head from one side of the crowd to the other so that all cameramen could get a still shot. His hours of practice in front of his mirror had perfected the look of intelligence coupled with a patient ennui reflecting his selfless duty to the world. Finally, he held up his hands in a practiced gesture for quiet and made his proclamation. "Please do not get your hopes up with this Johnson Project. We have no data yet as to viability and certainly no proof of its practicality. As to the ludicrous demands the Johnsons are making... they are showing themselves to be conceited and bigoted. That is all."

He knew the reporters were screaming inside their heads with rage. They wanted more of him but he wasn't their pawn nor would he let anyone call the shots. He pointed his index and middle finger at one of the minions to let the man know they would be 'pretend' talking on their way back into the building on a subject of no consequence or even coherence. It always looked good on the news, as if he suddenly had a breakthrough and needed to discuss it post haste with a minion.

He hoped he was able to mask his fury in front of the press. When he and some of his key researchers watched the press conference the night before, he may have let slip some of his anger issues. He may have fired a few people, he sure as hell pissed off most of the staff, but they were the stupidest bunch of smart people taking up space in what should have been his victory. It didn't help that Lily defected months ago against his wishes. He wasn't used to being turned down by any woman but to be turned down and then have her switch to Ted's team?

It would take a long time to recover. A long time. He needed to light a fire under some of these doctors who were riding his coat tails and get serious about this secret sauce over in the States. None of his subordinates suggested that the post-fertilization process could be manipulated and they were going to hear about that for the next couple of weeks. At least his research could focus on that aspect and they could rule out some of the dead ends. He'd recently bought a jet for research purposes, of course, but maybe he needed to get away from the losers at Carrel and concentrate on his new desire for a few days. He would pilot himself to the Seychelles, maybe check out some orangutans and get himself through the humiliation. Let the minions shiver in their boots and earn their keep.

Chapter 23

The editor had been on his case for weeks and it was driving Mickey crazy.

"They have the money, Andy, to cover up any skeleton that may be in their cedar lined closets."

"This is the story of the century, Mick. You have unlimited resources and a ridiculous expense account. What's the problem? Why aren't you coming up with... something?"

"They're not real, these Johnsons. I'm looking for an ulterior motive, a hidden agenda, hell, I'd be happy with a little adultery. It's just *NOT* there."

"They hold the future of the entire world in their hands. They could be making trillions! But they have a game room on site. A goddam game room for their employees! It's weird."

"Still no luck with any of the docs?"

"They're not talking. They were recruited and thoroughly vetted. That's been Ted's job these last few months. They're all IVF specialists, all people he knew from school or friends of friends' kinda thing. They all moved here and bought huge houses then settled in for a nice long ride. They probably had money before, but I'm sure they're taken care of even more so now. No one's gonna screw that up."

"There's gotta be someone willing to talk."

"Why would they? They've just landed a sweet job with a huge paycheck. I'm sure they signed airtight contracts. Nora Johnson-Berger has a team of lawyers working for her. Obviously, we know what she's been doing these last few months. You know they came up with ironclad agreements for all employees."

"What about the support staff?"

"They got secretaries and cleaning people and drivers and janitors. All recruited and vetted. Their houses are only slightly smaller than the docs'."

"So the Johnsons followed the payroll law?"

"To the letter. Probably more so. If you sling hash in the Johnson cafeteria, not only are you part of the team, but you're also set for life financially. No one is going to risk losing that by talking to me. I tried chatting with one of the guards at the gate. Like talking to one of those guards at Buckingham Palace. Nothing. Of course, I been on the shit list since I got through that first day. A couple of them got demoted, not fired, but demoted after that. The guards all hate me now. They're all ex-cops and they got no need to be on the take because they're getting paid crazy money with crazy benefits and living *la vida loca.*"

"Someone's bound to get fired eventually. Someone will screw up and want to talk about it."

"I got feelers out. Believe me, I'll expose and widen any crack in the foundation."

"What about Penny Johnson. The black sheep."

"I'm working on it."

"Work harder. And try to figure out Ted. What's his Achilles' heel?"

"That Ted is a piece of work. I've never seen him take anything seriously. Always the joker, always cracking wise. Real funny man."

Audrey heard Ted talking in the bedroom and popped her head in to see him sitting limply on the bed with the phone next to his ear. He was hunched over, resting his forehead in his palm. His voice sounded brusque like he was ready to bawl.

"...I...thank you, Dorothy. I really mean that. No."

Audrey quietly walked in and sat next to him. The 'Dorothy' calls were always rough on Ted.

"You take care, too. Bye."

He carefully hung up the phone and looked up at his wife. He hastily brushed away the tears. She put her arms around him.

"She's drunk every time. Still gets to me."

"Why did she call?" Audrey asked gently.

"Mickey Bruce offered her thirty thousand dollars for an interview. She's on a fixed income but she told him to take a hike. She wanted me to know that if any other reporter called she'd send them packing, too. Said she knew when she gave me up that I'd make good someday and she promised she wouldn't spoil it."

In the kindest tone she could muster, Audrey had to ask, "Did she want money from you?"

Ted shook his head but his face crumpled into a sob. "No, no. She just wanted to say she was proud of me."

Chapter 24

As Lou predicted, the Johnsons were forced to make lifestyle adjustments but they rolled with it. They were still able to spend family time together including house parties and holidays at Mary's. Billy was thriving in his new life as a Johnson-Berger, living in a manner he never even dreamed existed. It wasn't just the material windfall that made his little mind think every day was Christmas, but his new doting parents and the extended family that all cared about him and loved him. He stopped being afraid and the horrible days were quickly fading from his memory. He sometimes thought about his old mom and wondered if she went to heaven after Ron killed her. Grandma Mary said there was a heaven for everybody even the bad people and maybe his old mom wasn't so bad that God would make her go to hell like Ron was always saying she would. Ron was definitely in hell, Billy was sure about that. He knew it wasn't right but he was glad Ron didn't become his new dad and he was glad Ron did what he did. Billy knew he'd hit the jackpot in the new mom and dad department. He was safe from now on and there was no more yelling or closets. It didn't take long to make Nora his forever mom and Lou his forever dad. Life was good.

Chapter 25 - Joey Is Two and a Half Years Old

"I'm worried because the maternity ward has been getting dusty over at Lake Forest Women's Hospital," Ted told the family over brunch. "I told them to get moving because she could go early, you just never know." Ted was excited to be on call for the Beta delivery. There were now thousands of women pregnant in the U.S. and Canada but none as far along as Patricia Myerson, the brave test subject who happened to be a friend of Nora's and also happened to live in Lake Forest.

"The foundation is completely renovating the maternity unit." Mary informed everyone. "Obviously it will be much smaller, only two delivery rooms, and chances are that will be too many." She paused to sip coffee.

"Why don't they just incorporate the maternity unit in with the surgical suites?" Nora asked. "Why even make it a separate section of the hospital?"

"Security." Lou answered. Billy was seated on his lap eating Lou's scrambled eggs. "Most hospitals around the country are doing the same thing. Hacking out one small area for delivery but with high-tech surveillance and specially trained security teams when there's a baby born."

"I guess it stands to reason." Audrey said with a frown.

Ted piped in. "They say kidnappings will be on the rise again but it will be near impossible for someone to suddenly show up with a baby or a kid now that they are so rare. It won't change much even after we start pumping them out on a regular basis. They're so evenly spread around the country that each little tyke will be a novelty. They'll stand out in their communities."

"Did you see the crackdown in Thailand?" Lou asked. "After kidnapping became a cottage industry over there, they finally pulled their shit together and dealt with it. I don't think it's gonna become big in the States. I really don't."

"The press covers every movement Patricia makes now." Nora offered. "With the coverage after the birth, good god, there's no chance anyone could kidnap her baby."

Ted rolled his eyes. "She wants to let the press into the hospital when she goes into labor. Like I need more reporters in my life. I put a kibosh on having them in the delivery room. I got no time for that."

"I had a talk with Patricia." Mary said gently. "I know she's excited but she needs to consider what all this scrutiny will do to her baby."

"I've seen press from all over the world in town, getting ready for the perfect shot. I've seen them climb trees near the hospital. I have to admit, I'm kind of excited, too." Audrey confessed. "The first baby in over a year. I just want to hold her."

"Me too!" Mary admitted.

Carla! The Carla Martin Network (transcript)

Carla Martin: *Give us the timeline.*

Marilyn Cronin: *We had our paperwork together the same day as they made the announcement. We borrowed from our 401k.*

Walter Cronin: *..and took the penalty for early withdrawal!*

(audience laughter)

Marilyn Cronin: *We didn't care. We drove the whole package six hours that same day. We knew there would be a million applications.*

Carla Martin: *I remember reading this. You turned in the application to someone inside the gate and just kind of stood there. At the time, as I recall, the Johnsons were sorting out the legal fallout so they weren't even letting people on the premises. So, you went home and how soon before you heard from them?*

Marilyn Cronin: *They called us two days later. They told us we had passed the first phase and they wanted us to come in for the interview, the polygraph and drug test....*

Walter Cronin: *We thought, oh no, this is where the dream dies but they scheduled us for a Wednesday at noon so we got up at the crack of dawn, ah, who are we kidding, we didn't sleep that night. We made it there by eleven the next morning.*

Marilyn Cronin: *These people went out of their way to be nice. The waiting rooms were beautiful, they had tea and, like, juice and drinks and stuff. In the waiting room for the interview, we got to talking with some of the other couples, they were from all over the country. So, every few minutes an interviewer came out and called a name and we all said good luck to the couple going in. Then, you won't believe the interviewer who came out next and called our name! It was Mary Johnson doing the interviewing. Herself! We had seen her on the television but didn't think she would be talking to average Joes like us.*

Walter Cronin: *She was great. I mean, we were so nervous, expecting the third degree and, let me tell you, the interview was not about "why did you miss a payment on your Sears charge ten years ago?" Just simple talk about having kids and what not.*

Marilyn Cronin: *When Walter and I talked about it later, we figured the interview is all about them trying to see if you got a screw loose but also to see if you know what you're doing.*

Carla Martin: *And did you?*

Marilyn Cronin: *I guess so!*

Walter Cronin: *She told us there on the spot that we passed the test and she personally escorted us to the medical area and hugged us both when she said good-bye. She hugged us!*

Carla Martin: *What did you have to do after that?*

Walter Cronin: *Marilyn got all checked out with her cycle and all that. I had to give a sample if you know what I mean.*

Marilyn Cronin: *Walter, stop! We saw a nice lady doctor and she told us what to do at home. We got the medical green light and I got some pills and a calendar. Luckily I was rarin' to go within about six weeks. We came back for the procedure....*

Carla Martin: *And...?*

Marilyn Cronin: *I'm six months pregnant.*

(Audience applauds)

Chapter 26

Lou stormed out of the lobby elevator and approached a woman talking crisply into her cell. He didn't need a description to figure out she was the one. The woman ended her call when she saw Lou approach and extended her hand in greeting. Lou didn't return the courtesy.

"You're Ms. Daltry?" He asked.

"Yes. I was expecting to meet with Ted Johnson or Nora Berger..."

"I thought we made it clear the first twelve times you called that Ted and Nora have nothing to say to you. It wasn't necessary to harass the receptionists." Lou thought this would embarrass her but it didn't. In fact her tone turned condescending.

"I guess I didn't make my point clear with the girls. We can work this out, I just thought I should go right to the top so we can get this matter settled immediately for my clients. We're facing a time crunch here. I represent Mr. And Mrs. Dillon Headstrom. In case you haven't heard of them, both are incredibly important people on Wall

Street with substantial financial security. Well, I'm sure you must know who they are."

"I know who they are from their application. I don't know jack about any bigshots on Wall Street and I really don't give a good god damn."

This gave Ms. Daltry pause and a reason to set the record straight. "That's why I'm here. They were both stunned, I mean *stunned* that you would turn them down without considering their standing in the business world. These people have a daughter who is pampered and well taken care of..."

"Who takes care of her?"

"I'm sorry?"

"Who takes care of their little girl?"

"Mrs. Headstrom is a wonderful mother. She takes care of the child and wants to add another child by the end of next year, so you can imagine the sense of urgency...."

"The little girl is raised by a nanny, isn't she?"

For some reason, Ms. Daltry found the statement amusing because, *of course* there was a nanny. Three, in fact. People didn't always understand so she explained with a chuckle. "Mrs. Headstrom is a very busy woman who travels extensively. Yes, she has help but she is a very involved mother."

"No, she's not." Lou answered.

"I beg your pardon." She kept the smile but it was forced.

"She's not involved at all with her kid except for some photo ops. I did the background check on her. She's a tycoon in business but she sucks as a mother and the really amazing part of her application, which we all found horrific by the way, is that she couldn't even get five buddies to swear she was a good mom. There were some lukewarm letters but...eh, she would have failed on that alone."

Ms. Daltry was no longer chuckling. These people were honest-to-god serious. "I'd like to point out that Mrs. Headstrom has been a huge supporter of the new government financial policies and she even came out last week in support of the Johnson Project." The lawyer smirked, thinking she was making headway. "You might remember she was one of the first executives to support the president when the new payroll initiatives were announced. She immediately fired the corporate masseuse and held a press conference to announce her bold, pioneering decision. Don't think she didn't take flak about that debacle. We're talking about a very progressive woman whose name will continue to dominate the news. You might want to keep that in mind before you make a bad decision. You might want to let

Mary Johnson know that Mrs. Headstrom is not to be taken lightly."

Lou never changed expressions. This lady was simply not worth it. He sighed and answered. "On paper she didn't pass because she already has a child, so this whole conversation is a waste of my time. It's not a waste of your time, though, because you're getting paid by the hour..."

"I resent your implications."

"Which ones?"

"The Headstroms have the money to give a baby everything. I would think if someone higher up could take a look at her application and financial statements, they would give her the go ahead immediately. Now, they can be here next week but not before Tuesday..."

"Are you not hearing me? The Headstroms don't meet the criteria. Fail. Done. Not gonna happen. They already have a daughter and the affidavits from their friends were carefully worded, checked by a lawyer and don't say a damn thing."

"We'll get new affidavits if that's a sticking point with you."

Lou was disgusted and turned away before he lost his temper but turned back suddenly because he couldn't take it anymore.

"Why don't you write a letter swearing that the Headstroms will make good parents? You gonna sign it, have it notarized and swear under oath that Mrs. Headstrom would be a good mommy? Well?"

She paused thinking of the best answer to his question. She was losing but maybe with the right amount of legal persuasion.... "It would be inappropriate for me as counsel..."

"Is having another child very important to the Headstroms?" Lou asked quietly.

"That's why I'm here. I came all this way..."

"Yeah, *you're* here. Where are *they*?"

She kept quiet.

"If it's so all fired important for them to create a new life, why aren't they here themselves, pleading their case?"

"Please. They are very busy people and they hired me to take care of the details."

"Details. Don't you think kids deserve better than that? Have you thought about who you are fighting for?"

He left her in the lobby.

Chapter 27

WLN News Chicago

Pictures of one-day-old Mary Hope Meyerson have been released today; the first infant to be born in two years! She weighs in at a hefty nine pounds eleven ounces. Here she is with Dr. Ted Johnson in the new maternity ward at Lake Forest Hospital. Parents, Alex and Patricia Meyerson were the first couple to test the in vitro procedure offered by Dr. Ted Johnson at Johnson Tower center. In fact, Dr. Ted delivered the baby girl himself.

Mary Hope is the only baby on the planet right now and she will be receiving all sorts of goodies from local residents and businesses who want to welcome her into the world. Representatives at Proctor and Gamble have gone into their warehouses in search of newborn diapers and promise to keep her pampered with left over stock until they resume limited production. Her celebrity status will end in about five months when the rest of the pack now known as the Johnson Babies or

Generation "J" will arrive to anxious moms and dads in the U.S. and Canada.

"I almost forgot how to do it." Ted joked at Mary's dinner table. The whole family was together enjoying pie and coffee while the kids played nearby. "But, as it turns out, kinda like riding a bike."

"I'm glad we went with a local test subject so we could be part of the process." Mary said. "I went to visit the Myersons in the hospital today and I got to hold baby Mary. What a feeling! I do wish one of you would step up and give me a new grandchild. I'm not getting any younger."

"Oh, here we go." Nora said. "I told you, Mom, we might consider another adoption but I'm probably not cut out to be a pregnant person. My mood swings are crazy enough without hormones throwing me into a tizzy."

Mary looked disappointed but turned hopefully to Audrey.

"Nope. Nope. We're done." Audrey said while cocking her head in Rafael's direction. Mary turned in his direction as did the rest of the family. Rafael concentrated on his plate and waited for the onslaught. Nora innocently spoke to her younger brother. "You know, Raf, it's a small town. I drive by your house every night on my way home from work. Your car is never there."

Rafael shrugged it off. "I go to the library."

Lou raised an eyebrow. "Were you at the library last night at eleven o'clock?"

Ted joined the fun. "You must have been at the library's pre-dawn program this morning when I drove by..."

"Can I go to the library with you, Uncle Raf?" Allie asked earnestly as she ran through the great room and overheard the exchange.

Audrey eyed the adults and answered Allie. "I don't think so, dear."

Rafael blushed but he was smiling, too. "Will I ever stop being the *little* brother?"

Mary was next to him and patted his arm adoringly. "I think what we're trying to say, honey, is that we all know..."

Ted interrupted. "...so does everyone at work, by the way. Sybil's been spreading the word."

Mary shushed Ted and continued. "It would be nice if you would invite Lily to family dinners."

"And married her and had a baby." Ted added nonchalantly. "For mom."

Rafael looked around at the people he loved most in the world and sidestepped the issue. "Speaking of Sybil, she said that Muammar Qaddafi's son called three times today. He's very anxious..."

"Don't go changing the subject to Muammar Qaddafi's son." Nora said.

"Like you always do when the conversation is uncomfortable." Ted added.

"This is the first time I have ever brought up Muammar Qaddafi or his offspring if I'm not mistaken! Not that it's any of your business, but Lily and I are taking things slow. We have an excellent working relationship and a very nice private relationship but we don't want to jump into anything."

"Dude, you've been dating almost a year!" Ted reasoned.

"If you move any slower you'll go backwards." Nora added.

The doorbell saved Rafael from further deflection. Audrey excused herself, although she wondered why the security guard at the gate let someone through. Well, maybe it was Lily herself, speak of the devil. She hoped so as she left to answer the door.

Mary wondered too, and thought it was probably a delivery of some sort from the Tower. It was not uncommon but usually the guard accepted correspondence. She turned her attention to Billy. "Who would be out on a night like tonight? Probably a snowman, don't you think, Billy?"

Billy found this preposterous. "Snowmen don't come to houses, Grandma!"

Lou jumped in with authority. "I dunno, the abominable snowman usually makes his way to Lake Forest, oh, I'd say this time of year. He may just want to scare us and be on his way."

Allie and Billy exchanged a look and realized they were being toyed with. It was to be expected.

"Don't scare me, daddy." Billy said with a giggle.

Audrey appeared in the doorway looking stricken. The whole family stopped smiling as they noticed who was behind her. Penny stepped into the dining room, her coat was dusted with snow, her cheeks flushed. She waved a greeting to her family. "Hi, everyone. I'm home!"

Chapter 28

Mary was the first to greet her with a warm embrace which told the siblings what they already suspected: That Mary had been supporting Penny all along despite the "tough love" stance they all took after her last stint in rehab and prison. It was frustrating beyond belief. Intellectually they all knew that Penny had to hit rock bottom in order to heal. But, logistically, she needed a roof over her head and food to eat and Mary never could make that final cut to force Penny to help herself. Thus, Penny kept using, Mary continued to enable and her siblings shook their heads at the constant cycle of family love.

The conversation started out fine. The family was almost feeling encouraged about this new promise from Penny to reform. She asked about their lives and smiled at the children, all good signs. She seemed pleased to meet Billy who couldn't believe all the relatives he had. After the kids were in bed, they gathered in the family room by the fire. Penny asked for a glass of wine. Ted and Rafael were surprised but obliged. Nora knew they were in for another disappointing crash but kept quiet listening to Penny's latest update on her new and improved life.

"His name is Frank Bauer and he's gorgeous. You guys would not even believe how good looking he is."

Audrey saw this as a good, although shallow, sign and encouraged Penny to continue. "What does Frank do, Penny?"

"Well, he's still deciding. He's gotten a bunch of job offers but he'd consider working with the family. You know, if you've got something good. And he'd insist on getting paid under the table." She downed the last of her wine. No one offered her more so she found the bottle herself and filled up her glass anxious for her family to know about her triumph.

"Why would we do that, dear?" Mary asked.

"Well, his bitch of an ex-wife is money hungry and is always on his back about more child support, more child support. So he likes to keep his business private, ya know, so she can't garnish his wages."

Nora kept her anger in check. "How many kids does he have?"

"Three." Penny sipped her wine, annoyed that her boyfriend had three children.

"Is he against taking care of his kids?" Ted asked in a friendly light manner.

"Only because the bitch can't get off her ass and get a job. Why should he pay for everything? She gets food stamps and I know, if Frank gives her any more money, she'll just blow it on clothes or crap for the kids."

Nora was losing it. "That's what she's supposed to spend money on! Her kids!"

Everyone was startled by the outburst from Nora including Penny.

"Like he should give *half* his money to *her*? He hates her! God, Nora."

"He didn't hate her when he was lying down and making three children with her!"

Penny glared hard at her sister, ready to pounce. Lou put his arm around Nora while Mary looked pleadingly at her daughters. Nora seemed to gain control of her temper.

Penny was petulant. "Okay. I get that you guys are all into families and kids, whatever. You don't realize that there are some real bitches out there trying to make it difficult for me to start a family. I mean, come on."

Ted smiled. "We have a pretty good grasp on things, Penny. We only want what's best for the children."

Penny chugged her wine. "That's what I'm saying about Frank. When him and me have kids, he'll take care of *our* kids. Really. It's different with me. I can promise that he'll do everything for the kids he and I make."

"As long as he has his priorities straight." Ted said, sarcastically.

Nora leaned forward. "What makes you think you and Frank will qualify to have a child?"

Penny laughed like Nora was telling a good one. "Um, I better be moved to the head of the line coming from this family. I'm pretty sure I'll pass that test you guys all make people do." She quietly burped and chuckled.

No one wanted to start a fight but Penny was clearly back to her own selfish ways and someone needed to set her straight.

Penny looked around at the faces of her family and let them in on her excitement. "You guys have no idea how good looking Frank is. Wait until you see him. When we walk into a room, people stop and stare because of how we look. We'll have the most beautiful kids. Well, you'll see. And," she added coyly, "a baby may just get him to pop the question." She was giddy at the thought of a marriage proposal. "I know he'd marry me if I got pregnant." She was quite confident.

Lou was holding Nora back. Ted took charge. "You know about the criteria to qualify, don't you? I think it's been on the news. A little."

191

Penny shrugged, bothered by the question because it didn't really matter in her case.

Lou was uncomfortable but said, "I can tell you right now, you won't pass the test, Penny, and I doubt prince charming even comes close no matter what he looks like, but fill out the forms, give me your bank statements and... I'll let you know." He really hoped Mary would back him up on this decision.

Penny barely knew Lou which made his statement that much more ridiculous. "Who do you think you're talking to, Lou? I'm not filling out a goddam thing. I can't believe you would embarrass me like that. God. What am I supposed to tell Frank?"

"Tell him to take one of those job offers." Ted answered helpfully. "It will seriously boost his credibility."

"You're not getting the procedure, Penny. You're not going to have a baby! No way in hell." Nora burst out. "You can't take care of yourself! How can you take care of a child?"

Penny turned to Mary for help. "Mom! You know I'm trying."

Mary looked down, she couldn't look Penny in the eye. "You haven't been sober for five years, honey. That's a mandatory requirement for you to be considered."

Penny glared at her mother. "Wow. You really know how to rub salt in the wound, don't you, Mom? Nobody cares that Nora drinks. It's not fair!" Mary looked away.

Nora lost it. "Maybe I do but at least I can function! Hold a job! Raise a son! I came out of a shitty situation, too, Penny, but somehow, I can drink without getting twenty DUIs. I've never used Crack. I've never hocked mom's jewelry. I've never been to prison or rehab. So shut the fuck up! We keep waiting for you to get better but you never do and it's always somebody else's fault. Now you've hooked up with the biggest deadbeat on the planet and want us to believe that having a baby will make everything right. Well, I got some news for you, sister. Even if you somehow pull yourself together, get sober and qualify to become a parent, it won't matter! Your loser boyfriend doesn't take care of the kids he has, no way is he getting more!"

Penny needed to explain because her stupid family was just not getting it. "He doesn't want that family. He wants a new one! If you could see him, you'd understand and be happy for me. God! Why do you always do this to me? I do something right and you shit all over my happiness!"

"We can't change the rules for you, Penny, even if you are our sister." Rafael said.

Penny stormed out of the room and found her coat in the front hall. "Fuck you all. None of you are my real family and you never will be." Mary ran after her and begged her to calm down but everyone knew that wasn't how it worked. Penny was in full tantrum mode and there was no stopping her. Mary would try to placate and Penny would win the battle.

"You're all so perfect and wonderful. I hope you know the whole world hates your guts and that eventually people are gonna figure out your secret sauce. Reporters call me, ya know. Maybe I should start telling family secrets, how about that?"

Mary was desperately trying to palm some cash into Penny's hand but the threat pulled her back.

"Why would you hurt us like that, Penny?" Mary was crying now.

"You don't care about me! You never have!" She grabbed the money out of Mary's hand and headed out the door. Audrey quickly arranged for the guard to stop her at the gate and drive her home or wherever she was headed. Probably to gorgeous Frank. They retreated back to the great room and worried about Penny.

Chapter 29

As the United States and Canada welcomed anyone looking to start a new life, Mexico and South America provided a lot of takers. Instead of being stopped at the border or worse, shot at the border, immigrants now risked their lives on the *south* side of the border as desperate drug lords struggled to hold on to their workers and soldiers. Private agencies on both sides of the Rio Grande assisted millions up North. The drug trade still existed but production in Mexico dried up as the enforcement in the U.S. and Canada became more strict. The drug lords were getting desperate but there was not much they could do with a dwindling work force and a smaller consumer base.

Cities and towns up North were filling up but the job market increased as the population increased. Construction crews were at a premium as new homes and businesses were built to accommodate everyone. There were no such thing as abandoned buildings anymore. The worst were torn down and rebuilt but most were renovated as fast as possible. It was a great time to be a civil engineer and carpenters and tradesmen could name their price for any given job. Citizens never felt so much a part of the solution as groups formed to discuss expansion while still others met to ensure the forest preserves and national parks were protected. Everyone worked together toward the same goal and communities grew stronger while the federal government got smaller.

Australia and New Zealand were in a similar situation and handled the transition just as beautifully. Some wondered why there had ever been an issue with allowing foreigners into their country. It made for a colorful collection of neighbors and a delightfully vast choice in restaurants.

It did leave an open wasteland on some continents. NGOs were gaining power and money from grateful donors. Not only did the influx of money provide jobs, great jobs, to good people, it provided an underground railroad for many who would not otherwise have the chance to start again.

Chapter 30

Mickey Bruce wasn't sure if the trip to Cleveland would be worth the expense of the flight and the rental car but his boss said okay and it was Cleveland for crying out loud. Less than an hour flight from O'Hare and he could turn around and get back to civilization before he needed a hotel room. He was chasing a slim lead but, if nothing else, he was curious to see how the Johnson's handled this sweet old lady when they stole her only grandchild from her bony, arthritic hands.

Paulette Timmons lived near the airport in a tiny little house, most likely two bedrooms, one bath, Mickey appraised when he pulled into her short driveway. The lace curtains swayed in the front window as he got out of the rental. She had probably been waiting for him. No doubt she would offer tea. He brought his notebook to the door but didn't expect to be writing too much. He mostly wanted to hear her thoughts on the Johnsons. Find a chink in the armor that he could pick at and there might be a nice Sunday exposé with his byline.

She answered the door with a sweet smile and ushered him into the front room where he sat in a delicate wing chair and accepted her offer of tea. He called that one. There was only one framed photograph in the room and it looked like Paulette when she was a bride a million years ago. No kids. No grandkids. Hmmmm.

Paulette brought in two delicate cups of tea in bone china. Mickey was trying to assess how to open the conversation but the old lady jumped right in. "I guess you're wondering why I didn't adopt Billy after my daughter was murdered."

Mickey nodded. "It's none of my business, Mrs. Timmons, and I'm not trying to upset you. I just want to make sure you had every opportunity to keep your family together without the Johnson's threats and intimidation. I want to make sure you were treated fairly during the whole ugly situation."

Paulette Timmons set her tea down and started to speak. She hesitated like she didn't know where to start and then she gave Mickey her side of the story. "I don't know what you heard, Mr. Bruce, but I was never threatened, intimidated or even pressured into giving up Billy. I had every opportunity to take custody and I considered it. Briefly. I love him though I barely know the child. My daughter and I were distant anyway, ever since she was a teenager, but marrying Ron didn't bring us any closer, he saw to that. He had control over everything she did and that included Billy. I tried to stay in her life. I tried to have a relationship with Billy but I hadn't seen him since he was a baby. Everything changed when Ron took over. She used to tell me on the phone how happy she was but always so busy. Yes, always too busy to visit or even talk long on the phone. I sent Billy gifts on his birthday and Christmas. I could tell things weren't perfect in their home but I had no idea how bad it really was. I certainly didn't know he was in the foster care system when it came to that." Paulette stared off into space for a minute, maybe thinking she could have tried harder. "Part of me was a little miffed at being put off by my daughter. I assumed once Billy was older, she would have more time for me but I also realized that Ron wanted her all to himself. I would never be welcome in that family. The sad part is, I was actually happy that Billy had a man to raise him. My God." She choked up as she said it but didn't give herself the luxury of crying. "I should have seen what was happening. I should have known. I should have protected my daughter and my grandson. Somehow." She wiped hastily under her eyes.

Mickey was mildly interested but he really wanted to get to the meat of this story. Unfortunately, he had to let the lady tell it her way or he might miss something. "It's not your fault, ma'am. That Ron was a sick fu... ah, criminal. He was an animal. But he kept up appearances on the outside. Nobody knew what a monster he was."

Paulette shook her head. "That's not quite true, is it? My daughter knew. She knew right from the start yet she let it happen. The abuse toward her was bad enough. Maybe her mental state made her think she deserved it, that's what they always say. But I'll never understand why she let anyone touch her baby. I can't forgive her that. She's just as much to blame as Ron. Maybe more so."

Mickey was surprised by the old lady's take on the situation. "I don't want to pass judgement on anyone here. I was just concerned for you dealing with the loss of your daughter then losing the chance to raise your grandchild because of the Johnsons. I always thought it was so unfair..."

"What makes you think the Johnsons took away my right to raise Billy? What have you been told?"

"I just assumed you were strong-armed into giving up your rights." Mickey blustered.

"Mary Johnson called me right after I heard from the police that my daughter was dead. I was in shock and she helped me deal with the grief. Not just that. The next day, she came here, to my house and sat right there where you're sitting. Nora and Lou Berger came too. They didn't strong arm me. They offered their condolences and offered to help me raise Billy right here if I chose to. They offered to help me financially. They said they would cut through all the paperwork to get him here quick and set him up with a psychiatrist to help his little mind make sense of his life. They told me they had been visiting him and encouraging him and giving him hope. They were the only bright spots in that boy's life. I never knew such kindness from anybody." Paulette paused as she remembered the day. "I knew right then and there that this was the family for my little grandson. Nora and Lou were the parents he deserved, not an old lady like me. The kindest thing I could do was step back and let Mary be his grandma. I made the decision to back out of his life so that he could have one consistent family. You think the Johnson's did me a disservice? I'm telling you, they gave me the greatest gift I could ever ask for and I took it and I gave that gift to Billy."

Mickey gulped. Not much he could say to that. "I didn't know it went down like that. Um, wow. That must have been real hard for you Mrs. Timmons, but I can see it was a great act of love. He's a lucky boy. I guess I keep wondering if it's in the kid's best interest for you to miss out on all the stuff coming up for him. His baseball games, his graduation, his wedding..."

"Nora sends me notes and pictures all the time. It warms my heart to see how happy he is with his cousins and extended family. He loves that dog, Tuffy, I can tell from the photos. Those pictures brighten my whole day. Nora is such a dear. No, I couldn't have asked for a better outcome. I get the feeling you were looking for some gossip for your newspaper but the only story here is a happy ending. You see, shortly before my daughter's murder, I was diagnosed with stage four ovarian cancer. I won't be around to see any of Billy's milestones anyway and it would be selfish of me to put myself in Billy's life only to have him suffer another lose. I would love more than anything to see him again, even one last time, but it's not what's best for Billy. It doesn't matter what I want. It only matters what's best for Billy. Do you understand?"

"I'm glad it all worked out." Mickey chugged his tea and mentally calculated the next flight home. What a waste of time.

"If you want to shed some light on a tragic situation, why don't you focus on abusers like Ron? Or the psychological state that keeps women in abusive relationships? Why do abuse victims keep going back? It's a puzzle I'll never understand."

"That's a wonderful idea, Mrs. Timmons." Mickey answered politely thinking it was a terrible idea.

"That's the enigma, isn't it? There are those that get away and get help and see the light, yet some go back to the abuser. Why? Let me give you some reading material to get you started." Mrs. Timmons left the room leaving Mickey to wonder what kind of pamphlets he would have to dispose of at the Cleveland airport. She came back with a shoe box and thrust it at him as she showed him the door. He could see there were tears running down her cheeks. "These are my daughter's journals. The police advocate sent me some of her things but I could barely stand to open the box. Most of her things burned in the fire but they found all this in the freezer of all places. She must have thought it was the one place he wouldn't find her personal things. I never finished reading the journals. I know she suffered from a mental illness but her words don't paint a very nice picture of the woman she had become. I don't want to remember her like that. I'd rather her frightful journey be used as a resource for women who may be drawn into the same situation. Maybe you could write an article about emotional abuse and its victims especially the poor souls who go *back*." She made a move to close the door so there was no way for Mickey to politely decline. He nodded and carried the box to his rental car. He had no intention of opening it. But he didn't want the old lady to feel worse.

Chapter 31 - Joey is Three Years Old

The press release was scheduled for Wednesday, June 10th, 2020 at 10:00am. Rafael took the podium. "Thank you all for coming, today, especially such a large representation from the foreign media. You've come so far... I know you were all hoping for a positive announcement." He let the words hang. The press rustled suspiciously. "Uh... regarding our expansion. But... we... have decided that we cannot, in good conscience, share our operation with... well, most of the world."

There was a moment of silence followed by a burst of reaction.

Rafael soldiered on. "Please remember, we want what is best for the children. Therefore we have established a plan to provide reproductive service centers only to those countries that have stable governments with no imminent threat of war, no habitual human rights violations, countries that provide equal rights to women, that do not knowingly allow slavery, child labor, torture or blatant drug trade. I'm sure you can all assess which countries will be approved and which countries will not."

The buzz got louder. The cameras didn't move but the hand held devices were in full swing.

"Our center in Brussels will be open soon for all approved countries in Europe. A center in Adelaide is part of our expansion plan for Australia and will be ready next year."

The reporters seemed to hold a collective breath devouring every word.

"Dr. Khan Patel, who was instrumental in opening this center will be running the Belgian site. Press releases with the application have been sent to major European newspapers in approved countries. The American website will take you to the specifics for your country." He took a needed breath. "I believe it will be more efficient to announce the European countries that have NOT been approved due to human rights violations or instability: Albania, Belarus, Bosnia and Herzegovina, Croatia, the Czech Republic, Latvia, Lithuania, Moldova, Northern Ireland, Poland, Romania, Russia, Slovakia, Slovenia, Turkey, the Ukraine and Yugoslavia. Citizens of all other European countries may apply and make their own travel arrangements to Belgium. Any questions?"

The room roared. Rafael calmly pointed to the first reporter in his line of sight.

"You haven't mentioned Mexico? Can Mexican citizens apply for the Waukegan location like you hinted at before?"

Rafael leaned closer to the mike to make sure he was clear. "Mexico has not been approved due to human rights violations and a prevalent drug trade."

The reaction lifted the din then hushed. Another reporter got the nod. "What about Latin America?"

Rafael held his head high. "None of the Central or South American countries have been approved."

The reporter was flabbergasted. "So these countries...just *end*?"

"If they do nothing about their civil wars, human rights violations or drug trade, then, yes, their population will dwindle to... nothing."

Another reporter stepped up. "What about the Middle East...?"

"We would like to open a center in the Middle East, however none of the countries meet our criteria. Should that change in the next few years, we will reassess."

"What about Israel?"

"Israel will not be approved. It's not a safe place to raise a child."

A huge reaction.

Rafael continued. "Nor will most Asian nations. For obvious reasons."

"What about Africa?"

"None of the African nations will be admitted to the program."

"Can you explain what you mean by equal rights for women?"

"Exactly that. Any country that does not treat women as equals will not be considered."

A roar from the crowd.

Mary, Audrey and Ted watched the live coverage from the conference room on the eleventh floor. Ted murmured, "...and then the death threats poured in."

Sybil burst in. "President Clinton on line one!"

Mary picked up the phone. "Hello, Madame President." After a lengthy pause. "No ma'am, it was not our concern."

As much as she wanted to hear the outcome from the president, Audrey could see Raf's distress and needed to jump in. "I can't stand the whining down there. I'm going to help Raf." She bolted out of the room.

Ted turned back to Mary who couldn't seem to get a word in edgewise. Finally, his mother said proudly, "We made our decisions based on how governments treat their people, including women and children. With all due respect, Madame President, why would we want to do business with a government that allows children to die in the streets?"

Ted made a "Yikes" face toward his mother and then turned back to the screen where another reporter was tearing into Rafael.

"...which can only ensure the eradication of the black race. Hasn't Africa been through enough?" Ted watched proudly on the screen as Audrey crossed the stage and gently took her brother-in-law's arm to indicate she was taking over. Rafael was happy to turn over the podium. Audrey addressed the reporter. "Mr. Parker, would you like to raise a child in Benin? Libya? Congo? Sudan? Ivory Coast? Even South Africa?"

He blustered at the question. "You're white washing!"

"All we are asking is that governments stop hurting children and come down harder on the drug trade. We will not endorse any country that allows, even passively, child labor, trafficking or child abuse. As soon as they get a handle on human rights, we will be happy to jump in and build a center. Why do you object to that?"

"You are punishing the people for a few bad apples in government! That is not fair to the good people of Africa!"

"Nor is it fair to bring a child into a world where the probability is that they will either die at birth, be born with AIDS, suffer starvation and dehydration, be sold into slavery or tortured for no reason other than it is the whim of the current government. Next." Audrey dismissed the blustering reporter and turned to the next.

A new reporter stepped in. "You are interfering with age-old religious traditions. In some cultures women are not equal but they are happy. How can you deny them the one gift they can give to their husband?"

Audrey answered. "Some fundamental religious groups allow women to be beaten, raped, tortured, and killed for the slightest infraction. For instance a woman who dishonors her family by being raped is actually punished for it! Some allow, I should say encourage, female genital mutilation."

The same reporter shook his head at her lack of knowledge. "That's a tiny percentage of women in remote areas..."

"One hundred and fifty million women." Audrey interrupted.

The reporter persisted. "You can't speak for those women! How do you know they're not happy with their lives?"

Audrey stared quizzically, genuinely puzzled, at the reporter who asked the question. "Oh, I've got a pretty good idea. I wouldn't want to live in those conditions but more important, I wouldn't want my daughter to live in those conditions and that's what this is all about. What kind of world do we want to leave for our children? Would you want to raise a child, let's just say a female child in any of the countries that allow this sort of disparity?"

"I don't have any daughters but I concede that some women are oppressed. It's true. But some men take care of their women. They practice fundamental beliefs but hold their women in very high regard. It is important for these men to continue the family tradition by producing an heir."

Audrey responded easily. "Their fundamental beliefs do not allow women be seen by a doctor. If their fundamental beliefs are so important that they'll let their women suffer through a yeast infection, then they will not be interested in our modern day method of procreation. Right? You can't have it both ways."

The reporter had no comeback which didn't matter because Mickey Bruce had pushed his way to the front. "So what the Johnson family wants to create is a world that lives on three continents?"

"We want equality in every continent but the choice will not be ours." Audrey answered. "From the way it looks now, it seems that the population will be concentrated in North America, Europe and Australia. If the other continents choose to let their citizens fade away by not improving human rights conditions, well, that is their option."

"That's a nice white world for you. Say, didn't Hitler try that?" Mickey loved to provoke a fight but Audrey was nonplussed and answered him. "All races will prevail. Because of our own declining population, more and more foreigners are coming to America, Canada and, presumably now, Europe and Australia. Hopefully, we will welcome immigrants to a new way of life, a democracy with equal rights for all and a haven to raise their children."

"How about Asia? You gonna ban all the Asians, too?"

"We're not banning anyone, Mr. Bruce. We're offering our services to the countries that can provide a decent standard of living to all families. Asia is no different. As it stands now, some Asian nations will be accepted into the Johnson Project, some will not. All of the Asian nations have a few years to solidify a human rights policy before the final decision is made."

Mickey Bruce silenced the room. "Why don't you share with us the names of the Asian nations that are approved by the Johnsons?"

Audrey wasn't playing. "If you read your own newspaper, Mickey, you'll see which countries meet our criteria."

Mickey shook his head like he couldn't believe it. "You're seriously going to tell the People's Republic of China that they will not be given a Johnson reproductive center? Seriously?"

"If China wishes to end child labor, slave labor, religious persecution and make women equal, we will build a site in downtown Beijing. It is their choice, not mine."

"You claim you don't have enough secret sauce for the world. What happens if China corrects its human rights violations? How can you make good on your promise to build a center in Beijing if you claim you don't have enough secret sauce to give them?"

"We anticipate a boost in production in the next few years. If China can make a better life for its people, I will personally deliver the additive myself. If they don't, the surplus goes to approved countries and we allow deserving couples to have more than one child. Next..."

Mickey backed down.

A BBC reporter got the nod. "You must know that you can't force other countries to behave like they are children that need to mind you."

"The Johnson Project is not trying to force anyone to do anything. We've offered a deal. Take it or leave it."

The reporter scoffed. "I come from a country that you've approved but I'm still stymied as to how you think your family should control the code of conduct in other nations. It's horrific. I'm not even sure I understand what you mean with this criteria of yours."

Audrey smiled. "It's very simple. Everyone should be equal regardless of race, gender, religion or orientation."

The reporter was baffled by the simplicity. "Well, that's not going to happen, is it?" He said with a sneer.

Audrey considered his question. "It's already happening, sir."

Contrite silence. Finally, a young reporter got his chance: "So what are the innocent people of these warring, unequal, child-abusing, drug-dealing nations supposed to do?"

"Move." Audrey said.

"What?"

"Move, move, move away! Move to a country where people live in peace. Move to a country where children don't live in fear, where they have a fighting chance."

"Many people can't afford to move..."

"Please." Audrey interrupted. "There are any number of organizations that bring families to the United States and Canada. Europe and Australia will follow suit, I'm sure. There are representatives literally standing at the borders of oppressed nations, ready to assist those in need."

"I don't think you're going to change the minds of these leaders." The reporter answered.

"I don't have to. If the people leave, the leaders will have no one left to lead. Are you following? They have no more power. No one to fight battles for them. They can wander around their palaces twiddling their collective thumbs."

"Yeah, but the people have to give up the land they love. That's not right."

"I guess they have to ask themselves what they love more. Their land or their children."

An Al Jazeera reporter stepped forward. "Your husband will need to justify his reasons and prove these ridiculous allegations against our culture. We will wait to hear back from him and in the meantime, we expect equal treatment with the procedure or I can promise you a higher court will intervene..."

Audrey smiled sweetly. "I am speaking on behalf of the Johnson Project and I can assure you that this decision is final and not negotiable." Audrey interrupted.

The Al Jazeera reporter shook his head angrily. "This is far from over." The men around him agreed.

Audrey smiled. "Your leaders have been given the criteria necessary to bring reproduction back into your culture. If they choose not to participate, your country will not get a fertility center. There are no exceptions to the rule. There are no shortcuts and there will be no further dialogue. The ball is in your court. The choice is yours."

Audrey and Rafael left the press with many unanswered questions.

Media around the world covered the story. The reactions from approved countries were joyful and celebratory. World leaders made announcements to their people promising a plan to accommodate the Johnson Project and restructure their school systems to accommodate the new babies. There was also hope that because of their approved status, they would attract more desperately needed immigrants. Many had taken on economic plans similar to the U.S. and a surge of new citizens would secure their financial future. There was much love for the Johnsons from all of those that were promised a second chance.

The reaction from every other country ranged from sadness to outrage. Leaders in non-approved countries promised retaliation and economic sanctions against the U.S. but Homeland couldn't even take the threats seriously anymore. The hostile nations were going broke and their people were being guided out, usually in the dark of night, by the willing and able humanitarian groups. Heads of state were losing control rapidly although some had loyal militaries willing to fight to the end, they would have to go up against the strong countries who had superior intelligence and a vigilant population eager to defend their way of life. There was really no way to negotiate or appeal the Johnson's decision even though some foolish dictators tried. They all heard Audrey's ultimatum ringing in their ears. They had the option of complying with the outrageous terms that the Johnson's had established. Once upon a time those dictates would have been laughable but now, well, now they weren't going to rule out the possibility of equality for all people. As crazy as it sounded, there would be long and hard debates within the leaders' gated walls, palaces, compounds and bunkers in the weeks following the unimaginable announcement.

Chapter 32

Meet The Nation – NBS News

Walter Safer: *We can expect even* <u>*more*</u> *of an immigration movement to this country. Now that we know which countries didn't make the cut, we can expect the young people to move here for certain.*

Andy O'Hern: *People will come for the jobs. I would. Banned countries will have no industry left. Everything will shift to North America and Europe.*

Ira Wainstein: *Don't forget Australia.*

Andy O'Hern: Ah, yes, the Aussies have been approved by the Johnsons. So all the jobs and the people move into North America, Europe and eventually Australia and at what point do we say, no more immigrants?

Ira Wainstein: *We don't. We have plenty of room and we need them. It's working very well right now. The immigrants move here and get a great job with great pay. They settle down into a nice cozy house and they start paying taxes. They start buying groceries. They go to Home Depot and Best Buy and Target. They* contribute to their new communities. *Why would anyone put a stop to that?*

Andy O'Hern: *Mark my words, gentlemen! The United States will start paying immigrants to move here!*

Ira Wainstein: *The Charitable organizations already have! Our government doesn't have to! The NGOs pay them, in a way, with a house and head start but they end up giving us more then we give them.*

Walter Safer: *They get all the benefits of being an American and if they play their cards right, they eventually qualify to have a baby. Every kid who is born will be born into privilege which means a full education and a decent high-paying job.*

Ira Wainstein: *The playing field just keeps on leveling.*

Andy O'Hern: *The salaries of the CEO and the factory worker are already getting closer and closer.*

Walter Safer: *And the developing nations of this world will simply...end. No more poverty, fighting....the continents of Africa, South America, and most of Asia turn to seed....*

Andy O'Hern: *A geographical do over!*

Ira Wainstein: *You know what's beautiful about this flawless plan? I'll tell you. In the very near future, I'm talking within our lifetime, gentlemen, the United States will easily take control of abandoned nations.*

We can take control of the oil nations without a war, without so much as a paper cut. We simply march in and help ourselves to the resources that we need. Maybe even resettle. Start a new nation without all the prior baggage.

Andy O'Hern: *I don't see a downside, do you?*

Ira Wainstein: *All I see is a win, win, win, win.*

Andy O'Hern: *The only people who lose are the ones who should have lost a long time ago.*

Walter Safer: *Cui Bono, gentlemen, cui bono?*

Ira Wainstein: *It's not the Johnsons, they lose money on this deal. They gain no political clout with anyone. They're not currying favor from anyone and they're not getting rich from all this.*

Andy O'Hern: *They're not looking for that, never have. None of them belong to a political party. None of them belong to a church, temple or mosque. Strange breed, the Johnsons. They gain nothing personally by doing this.*

Walter Safer: *Then I'll ask again: who benefits?*

An unusual silence among the men. Finally...

Ira Wainstein: *We all do.*

Allie, Billy and Joey loved the noisy arcade room. They were each given a roll of quarters, a slice of pizza and a high fructose soft drink before being set free into the chaos. Ted, Lou and Rafael watched from a safe distance behind a glass partition which helped block out the noise but allowed for loose supervision and a chance for the men to have some guy talk. Most Saturdays involved daddy time with the kids and on this occasion, Rafael was invited because Mary felt he needed some brotherly advice since his relationship with Lily didn't seem to be progressing as fast as she would have liked. Lou got right to the point. "We all know you two are tight. Why is it such a big secret?"

Rafael rolled his eyes good naturedly. He was used to his family knowing no boundaries. "Nothing is secret. We date. We're taking it slow."

"Too slow if you ask me." Ted chided. "You guys act like co-workers."

"We are co-workers!" Rafael responded.

"We just want to know when you're gonna do right by that young lady." Lou reasoned.

Rafael hesitated. He hated to open up to anybody, it made him feel exposed. But these two goofs meant well, and he was certain their wives put them up to this little talk, but he could use some advice and maybe it was time he reached out. "Okay. We're both kind of at an impasse. We both know it's time to decide about a future, but we're both soooo..." Rafael struggled for the right word.

"Geeky?" Ted helped him with what he thought was the right word.

"No, Ted. We both have, you know, issues, obviously. We haven't been able to follow through on... certain parts of our relationship."

"What's that mean?" Lou needed clarification.

Rafael literally blushed and looked away. "I don't... We can't..."

Ted got it. "You two haven't... gone the distance?"

Rafael nodded but couldn't look either his brother or brother-in-law in the eye."

Ted and Lou wanted nothing more to do with the conversation but they had opened Pandora's Box and now they were stuck with the fallout. Lou swallowed hard and did his best. "Uhh, I thought you were practically living there in her coach house. I just assumed you were... you know."

"We sleep together but without any intimacy. She backs away from anything more than a kiss. She's never seen me, you know, naked..."

"Do you need a prescription?" Ted asked.

"No!" Rafael responded. "That's not the problem. We just need more time. To adjust. To get used to being a couple, I guess."

Lou wanted, more than anything, to end the whole line of conversation so he studied the glazing of the glass partition and hoped they could go back to talking about sports. Ted looked a little more concerned. He knew more about the childhood traumas endured by both Rafael and Lily and it hurt him deeply that they were both still suffering the consequences. He put his arm around his brother and meant it when he said, "You'll get there. You both might need to open up a little more. You both might want to have a painful discussion about all the crap you've been through. You gotta make yourself do it, maybe talk to a therapist."

Rafael nodded but they both knew there was more to the story.

Ted continued. "You know about the situation with her uncle, right?"

Rafael nodded again. He did, indeed, although Lily never spoke of the details. He knew the damage was deep seated. Eventually, both he and Lily would have to face the demons from their childhood and he was willing to wait as long as it took.

Chapter 33

Ted led Penny into his office. He was leery when she called and asked to come see him but hoped maybe she was finally on the road to recovery. She had to recover eventually, right? Penny went right to the picture window to enjoy the view of the budding trees.

"You really got it made, don't you, Ted?" She said without thinking. Sometimes the unfairness physically hurt her and she couldn't repress the anger or filter her exclamations. Ted was clearly the favored child and it pissed her off. He was so fucking perfect.

Ted got defensive. "I worked hard for it, Penny."

"Yeah, and mom's money sure helped."

"You had it, too." Ted felt compelled to add, "Until you blew it."

"Whatever."

"We just want to trust you again, Penny."

She shrugged and then froze when her gaze happened upon two Petri dishes sitting on a bookcase near the window. Just sitting there. She made herself look away as if disinterested but couldn't help but smile at her good luck. Ted sat at his desk and rummaged in some drawers.

"Hey, I'm not here to whine about the past." Penny said.

"I'm sorry. I just need to get better."

"Good. We love you and want to move forward. We really do, Penny."

"I'm ready to go all the way this time. I know I can. I've been sober for thirteen days now. With the right kind of support and a steady income, I know I can beat this. Just you watch."

Ted tried to read her. "If you want the job in transportation it's yours." He offered, hoping.

"That job to schedule the van from the airport to here? For the customers?" She edged closer to the bookcase.

"We call them patients, but yeah. You'd be like the dispatch, coordinating the drivers. We can't let you drive, obviously, but I think you'd be good at scheduling. It gets a little crazy when flights are delayed. Weather and stuff. We really need someone who can work with the airlines and deal with the shuttles..." He had his back turned to her as he rummaged through a file cabinet. Penny reacted quickly while snapping at her brother. "That's pretty insulting, Ted. It's degrading. I'm still a Johnson, you know."

"It's a great job! We'd get to see you every day. You could be part of the family…"

"I'm better than that. Give me something that people will respect. Give me something with some dignity."

"You can start out with this and we'll see how you do. If everything works out, you can work your way into a different position. You need to prove yourself, Penny. We need to see you're all better."

"I'm gonna tell mom you're forcing me into this. She knows I'm getting cut off from unemployment with these new stupid government restrictions. She knows I'm desperate for money. She won't make me take a simpleton job."

"It's kind of a hard job and it was Mom's idea."

"You're the worst, Ted. You really know how to kick me when I'm down."

"What job would make you happy? If you think we're going to give you a placeholder position where you get a paycheck but don't have to work, think again."

It was exactly what Penny was thinking but obviously her family wanted to punish her some more. "Shut the hell up, Ted. Soon as Frank gets a job, I'm outta this state. I don't need you or this fucked up place." She moved toward the door, away from the bookcase.

"Then why are you here?" He was done with the conversation.

"We're waiting for Frank's disability check, that's all. I thought maybe my family could lend a hand. But I see now it's all about humiliating Penny. Forget your stupid lowlife job offer!"

She stormed out the door a little too quickly. Ted glanced at the bookcase and saw only one Petri dish of secret sauce.

Chapter 34

Only the top doctors were shored up in the lab waiting for Pierre Charbot who had insisted they stay past midnight claiming, once again, he had made a breakthrough. There were few researchers left who felt they were anywhere near a breakthrough and they all secretly agreed that they were decades away from a cure. The money was good, the perks were plentiful but most realized they wouldn't live to see any long term fame as a result of their work with Charbot. There would never be a sense of accomplishment when they got the job done. They might go down as a footnote in history but Ted Johnson would be the hero and rightfully so. Things weren't looking so bad for the world right now. France would survive and really, some of the problems around the globe would be solved. Hell, some of the researchers would get to be parents soon because of the Belgian Johnson Center that would open next year. Life in Paris was great for everyone especially children and Charbot had nothing to do with it. They were being paid openly by the WMA and privately by some individuals who didn't know about a Hippocratic Oath and wouldn't abide by it if they did. Charbot was definitely getting the best deal out of the situation. The most money, the most notoriety and he would capitalize on his position if they ever did make a breakthrough but for now, they weren't coming up with any answers. They were sleepy and unimpressed when Charbot made an entrance into the lab from his office. They waited patiently but still unimpressed for his **communiqué**. He didn't immediately say anything, just stood there with that smug expression. Finally, he pulled a Petri dish from his lab coat pocket and held it up for them all to see. With a wicked smile and a new reason for living he calmly said, "Nous avons le secret sauce."

Chapter 35

Lou and Nora had their heads cocked, trying to understand what Ted was telling them.

"What exactly was in the Petri dish?" Nora asked.

Agar, of course. Some of Tuffy's pee, a little bleach, part of a fruit roll-up, a shiitake mushroom, a drop of Frappacino, a teaspoon of the Des Plaines River and some extract from the fern in Mom's office. I blended all the stuff like a smoothie, don't tell Audrey 'cuz I used our blender at home. Anyway, it'll take them a while to analyze all this stuff and when they do, they'll know we were messing with them."

"That was pretty stupid of them to hire Penny. Don't they know she's a fuckup?" Nora said, disgusted with her sister.

"She's just one of many." Lou responded.

"You think if they used her there's more spies out there?" Nora asked.

"You mean better spies?" Ted clarified.

Lou nodded. "Yeah. Not like they didn't have a plan B when they hired her. I think there's more people trying to get their hands on the secret. There has to be. We might want to take a closer look at the new hires. We been bringing in people so fast lately. It's great that we expanded so quickly but it does cause some security concerns. I know we vetted everyone to the nth degree but it doesn't hurt to double check. Makes sense they would plant someone on the inside."

"You think one of the docs?" Ted asked.

"I dunno. We just gotta keep an eye on things."

"It's just me and Khan who have access to the sauce. We're the only ones performing intracytoplasmic *sperm* injection when necessary and I'm the only one with the code for the incubators in the IVF lab. We cook the embryos in the sauce for a few days then personally distribute the goods just before uterine implant." Ted assured Lou.

"I hear ya. And I know we keep the IVF lab locked tight as a drum. Even the most trusted docs who have been here since day one haven't been in there." Lou knew it to be true but he had to keep watch. "I know Khan is clean as a whistle but is there any chance...?"

"Don't even go there, Lou." Ted broke in. "No way in hell. I'd trust him with my life. I'd trust him with Allie and Joey's life. No. We never have to worry about Khan. Swear."

Lou conceded. "Chill, man. I'm just doing my job. I like Khan a lot. He's a good guy and a helluva soccer coach for Billy. But I also know that breeches come from the most unlikely places. They come out of nowhere and you're left wondering how you trusted anybody. Still, those morons at Carrel have to know a mole isn't going to get in very easy."

"We made it pretty easy for Penny. You'd think they would be suspicious." Nora said.

"They'll realize their mistake when they get the lab results from the Petri dish. I wonder how much they paid her to transport Tuffy urine to Paris." Ted pondered.

"Still can't believe she would sink so low. Betray her own family." Lou said.

"She probably needed the money." Nora added. "I bet Frank planned the whole stupid thing. I bet he forced her into this."

"She still had a choice. She always has." Lou said, kindly.

Mary stared out the window. "I got her too late. Her own mother kept convincing judges she was fit. It was back and forth until she was twelve. If only I could have gotten her earlier. She'd be a different person." Mary looked miserable. She'd been somber lately partly due to her realization that Penny wasn't going to change. Nora walked over to her mother and gave her a hug.

"Are we going to confront Penny?" Rafael asked, hoping the answer was no.

"No. Please, no." Mary begged. "No harm was done so let's just pretend it never happened. Please."

Her family looked at the distraught matriarch and understood her pain. There was no point in accusing Penny, she would deny it and blame someone else, anyway. It was better to let the matter go and keep a close eye on her. Now they knew for sure, for the hundredth time, that Penny was not to be trusted.

Chapter 36

Rafael was given the unenviable task of addressing reporters once a month. Mary felt it was only right to keep the world updated and she wanted the press to have ample opportunity to ask questions. Not that the family was obligated to answer every one, but it was nice to address issues that they might not even know existed. Rafael, with his calm demeanor, was the perfect choice to host the standing-room-only crowd that showed up every month. Mary had witnessed Ted and Nora in action with the press, meaning, Rafael got the job. Lou was zealous in allowing press passes but didn't discriminate against the reporters who asked difficult questions, however he was quick to ban those reporters who were rude or disruptive. That was his only criteria and it was working for him. There was nothing new nearly two years into the project but Rafael stood at the podium with a short update on numbers and procedures.

"...in closing we hope more countries work toward compliance instead of fighting against basic human rights. We'll have another forum next month as usual. Are there any questions now?"

An Indian reporter from Delhi stood up. "We have made our peace with Pakistan yet you still refuse to allow India in the program. What more are we supposed to do?"

"You are a role model for the world. We are very much aware of your government's concessions to keep the peace and we applaud your efforts and beg you to continue. Now you need to concentrate on your poor."

"But we also have a very wealthy, cultured upper class who have nice homes and healthcare and much love to give a child. Please explain why these people cannot have babies."

Rafael took a deep breath and considered before responding. "Those wealthy, cultured, loving people need to look at the starving children in the street and take care of them. They need to pressure the government to make a better country for all children, not just the wealthy children. You have come so far in education for your people, why do you insist on this "class" system?"

The reporter balked. "You do not understand how it is in India!"

"I lived in Calcutta for six months and I understand your country very well. Your wealthy citizens have every amenity and comfort imaginable yet thousands of children are left to die in the streets because their mothers are too sick to take care of them or are... dead or insane. I took care of an untouchable woman who was dying of HIV. Her sole job in life was cleaning human waste from a public rest room. She spoke of her six children with little emotion. You see all were born with AIDs and all died of AIDs. She was never allowed in a hospital. She made babies and watched them suffer and die. Her fate was sealed before she was even born. Likewise, her children."

A respectful silence ensued as the reporter backed down with his arms crossed. There was no reason to argue. In fact, he already knew that there was a huge movement in his country to help the poor and it was really only a matter of time before there was no caste system left at all.

Mickey Bruce jumped at the chance to shoehorn in. "I guess I'm okay with holding back on some of these third world countries. Seems fair that they clean up their act. What I got a problem with is the criteria in a good country, why do you guys get to decide who is a fit mother?"

Rafael sighed. He wished Lou would take Mickey off the press list but so far his behavior had been close to courteous. In fact, his last few articles were almost congratulatory to the Johnson Project, although grudgingly, as the city of Chicago became less of a war zone and more of a haven.

"What is it you want us to do Mr. Bruce? How do you think we should be handling the selection process?" Rafael asked patiently.

"I think you should draw straws. Let the government or this WMA run it. After people have a baby and it doesn't work out, well then, take the kid away. That's fair."

"By then it could be too late." Rafael reasoned.

"You don't know that. Plenty of kids have come through abusive situations and became better people because of it. Plenty of kids had to struggle and they appreciate things more because of it. Sometimes having a baby can really straighten a girl out."

Rafael paused. "I knew of a teenage girl who had four children, three boys and a baby girl. She started burning the children with her cigarettes and then moved on to the iron, eventually holding their hands over the burner on the stove. When teachers started asking questions, she pulled them out of school. The baby girl cried a lot because the mother sometimes forgot to feed her and

238

rarely changed her diapers. One day the crying got on her nerves so she filled a pot with water and patiently waited for it to come to a boil. She dipped the baby's feet into the water and held them there while the baby screamed. The baby kicked some boiling water onto the woman so she dropped the infant into the pot of water. She was angry that the baby had burned her. Mercifully, the infant girl died soon after."

"So the system failed. We all know you have a million horror stories, Rafael. We've read your resume. You've seen the worst cases and you think it's the norm. They're not. Like in this case. I bet they got the other kids out of there and everything was fine."

"No, the boys stayed. You see the judge said she used poor judgement but was still fit to raise children. One day, the day after her boyfriend dumped her, she tied the boys down to their beds and poured boiling water on their torsos and legs. This time, she was careful to wear protective clothing and oven mitts so she, herself, would not get burned. She left the boys there for days with their skin peeling away in strips while she sat on the floor and smoked and drank beer and cried over the mess her life had become. The boys were in agony, the wounds festered and nobody responded to their screams for help. Finally they were too weak to scream anymore and

239

just whimpered. The oldest and the youngest boy finally died. The middle child lingered on the brink, praying to die. He cried for his brothers, his baby sister and wondered what he had done wrong. The pain was excruciating. Eventually, the mother got hungry and went to a diner down the road where a waitress noticed her unkempt appearance and started asking questions that led to concern. Only then did the police intervene and remove the one surviving boy from the home. My question to you Mr. Bruce: Where were the neighbors, her employers, her boyfriend, social services? Why did it take a *waitress* to stop the abuse? When does someone help the children? After three are dead? When the fourth is maimed?"

"Yeah, it's sad but you can't take away the right to have children because the mom *might* screw it up."

Rafael considered and asked. "Let's say I live in a one room apartment, no savings but I have a pretty steady job. I want a horse. I can't afford to keep a horse but I want one. Somebody is willing to give me a horse. Should I take it?"

"What's all this? All right I'll play along. No, you do not take the horse because you don't have a place to keep it and you can't afford to feed it. And the horse needs to be out riding every day. I get your point. But a kid is different."

Rafael couldn't believe that Mickey wasn't getting the point. "Yes. A kid is more important than a horse! Yet the ASPCA has more power to remove that horse than our social workers have power to remove a child."

"It's hard to take you seriously, Rafael when you have no idea what it's like to live in a one room apartment. You don't know what it's like to struggle with the bills, you've had it easy, everything you ever wanted. You grew up in a mansion and you have no clue about us little guys down here in the real world. You are not qualified to tell me these sob stories about tortured kids because you have no clue... "

He stopped talking because Rafael stepped next to the podium and took off his jacket. His tie came off next. As he unbuttoned his shirt, he stared down at Mickey.

"What the hell are you doing, Rafael?" Mickey was uncharacteristically confused.

Rafael removed his shirt to reveal a hideously deformed chest with skin dripping down like candle wax. Deep lacerations and small cigarette burn scars glared at the flashes as the photographers snapped pictures. For a moment, the only sound was the clack and whir of a hundred cameras.

Rafael answered. "I'm qualified. And I'm alive today because of a kindhearted waitress who gave a damn about a little Puerto Rican kid who didn't have a chance in hell."

Most of the reporters wrote up and transmitted the story while Rafael put his shirt back on. He got back to the podium, back to business, and addressed Mickey who hadn't moved or taken any pictures during the revelation. The story and pictures would lead every news station that night.

"Why are you so angry, Mr. Bruce?" Rafael asked.

Mickey's face caved. He was outdone and it showed. "My mom was sixteen when she had me. She never would have passed your test. If it were up to you, I never would have been born."

Rafael sympathized. "Neither would I. Neither would my brothers or my sisters, and when I say brothers and sisters, I mean both biological and adopted. Believe me, the irony has not gone unnoticed. And, you and I, Mickey, we're okay now but that doesn't mean we should let future children suffer our fate and hope they come out okay, too."

"I am not a mistake! I just don't want people to say that I'm a mistake!" Mickey cried out in a choked voice.

"Children are never a mistake, Mickey. Never. But getting pregnant and keeping a baby when you cannot provide for one is not fair to anyone. All we ever wanted was for people to think before getting pregnant instead of struggling to catch up after the baby is born."

Mickey turned and walked away without comment. He was shaken by the revelation and humbled. He needed to think outside. His departure opened up a frenzy of activity but Rafael watched the defeated Mickey walk slowly up the aisle. His reverie was interrupted by another reporter who seized the opportunity. "How did Mary Johnson find you?" he asked gently.

Rafael turned back to the front row of inquisitors. "Um. She was visiting the hospital where I ended up. She was passing out toys and she came into my room and fed me ice cream ...and... she took me home. Now she's my mom and I love her very much."

Lily was between procedures and happened to catch the news conference in the medical lounge. Her eyes were flooded. The other employees who were resting in the lounge were respectful as she sobbed. After swiping away her tears and shedding her lab coat and stethoscope, Lily made her way to the holding room next to the auditorium where Rafael was waiting. She ran into his arms and sobbed into his chest. He cried, too, but he was relieved to have his private shame revealed. They hugged and cried until Ted and Nora stepped into the room. Then everyone hugged and cried.

Poppy's mother texted her as soon as she saw the footage on the afternoon news. Poppy got caught up with the story on her Yahoo news feed. She watched dispassionately on her laptop from her high rise office suite. She knew her crush on Rafael Johnson was ridiculous and this proved it. Her father told her over and over again it was a mistake. He couldn't get past the Puerto Rican heritage but her mother liked the idea of being related to the Johnsons. It could have worked but now, she wasn't sure. Despite his muscular physique, those scars were pretty darn hideous. She was already a little turned off even though she'd been dreaming about fucking him for years. Maybe this was the kick in the pants to let go of the crush and move on to a man with whiter skin who wasn't deformed and didn't carry all that cheap, ugly, thrift-store baggage. Damn, it was hard to let go of her girlish obsession with the boy next door but, really, this might just be the impetus to move on. Yeah, the thought of touching that.... Not to mention the embarrassment of having everyone know. Why the hell would he announce it like that? The Johnsons were so weird.

She was staring out the window at Lake Michigan realizing that maturity brought better life choices and it made her feel kind of grown up. Her daddy would be so happy with the news. Her assistant burst in with the ancient news that Rafael Johnson was on every news station in the world. God, she was lame. What an idiot. She wanted to tell her to print out the close up shots of Rafael's torso so she could remind herself what she almost jumped into until she remembered that assistants cannot be asked to run personal errands and that included Googling information that was not work related. What a pain. It really was all the Johnsons' fault, too. Why, just the other day, the unthinkable happened. Poppy went for a blowout at her salon on Michigan Avenue where she'd been a client for years. Very upscale, where they would never dare call you by your first name. They always had a flurry of girls asking what you needed and then going to fetch you a glass of champagne or they'd sit down and massage your feet. Anyway, Poppy went after work since the stupid new work policy made you wait until after business hours for personal appointments. Unbelievable. Anyway, she got there for her 5:30 appointment, a little late because she had other things to do. So she got there at 5:45ish and the foreign bitches told her they couldn't fit her in because she was late. They honest-to-god told her she would have to make an appointment for another day. As she was telling them off, she happened to see her community college assistant having her hair done like she belonged there. Like she honest-to-god thought because of her salary increase, she could start going to upscale salons. Christ. The world was changing in the worst way, just like her father predicted. Too many people with just enough money to squander and suddenly, customer service goes out the window. Service people talk to you like they're your friends. Her mom just told her the other day that the cleaning lady from home bought a new car. A Lexus. The same make, model, and color as Poppy's. God. This whole nightmare better be over soon. In the meantime, she needed a new crush. Too bad Rafael Johnson blew his shot.

Chapter 36

WLN News On The Street

Older Man: *I don't give a hoot about national security or trade relations. Seems to me before all this Aqar plague happened that the government would 'a kept human rights in mind when they was agreeing to do business with some of these countries.*

Teen Girl: *I'm like so psyched about it all. It means everyone is going to be nicer and kids won't have to suffer so much.*

Middle-Aged Mom: *At first I thought they were dreamin' but now I'm thinkin' this just might work. Maybe it'll help some kids and, who knows, maybe it'll stop all these drugs on the street and the crime and that.*

Mary told Burke he was free for the day because she was exhausted and just wanted to read her book and go to bed. Burke dropped her off at the front of the house and made sure she got inside and closed the door before he pulled away. The staff was off duty so Mary looked forward to a quiet evening in front of the fireplace in her sitting room without the worry of anyone noticing her episodes. It was getting more and more difficult to function these days. The memory lapses were getting longer and sometimes she would be speaking with someone and realize she had no idea who they were or what they were talking about. She was able to cover by excusing herself but it was frightening and so difficult to keep covering up the fact that she was not fully herself. She found it peaceful to be alone because she didn't have to worry about blanking out or losing track of time. It still happened when she was alone but she didn't have to excuse herself of suffer the pitiful looks of the younger generation who only saw a demented old lady. The kids were worried, she could tell. They seemed to think she was having a few senior moments, a natural part of aging. They took good care of her and loved her. Burke was the only one who knew the full extent of her dementia. He helped her through the worst episodes and guided her out of awkward situations. Thank God for Burke.

While pouring herself a cup of tea in the dark kitchen, she realized she was not alone. She heard a door squeak and knew the sound was coming from her own bedroom upstairs. This was not one of her episodes, she knew it.

Although her heartbeat escalated she calmly punched in nine one one on her cell phone and was poised to hit the call button when a familiar voice called out. "Mom, is that you?" It was Penny. Oh, Thank God! Mary went into the front hall and found her daughter coming down the staircase with a man in tow.

"Penny! You scared me to death! What on earth?" Mary gripped the railing for support.

"Sorry, mom. I was just showing Frank around. Frank this is my mom. Mom, this is Frank."

Mary was gracious enough to shake the man's hand but her heart was still racing and the intrusion was very upsetting. She wanted to be understanding with her daughter but found this invasion unacceptable. "It's very nice to meet you, Frank, but I'm afraid these circumstances are not appropriate. Penny, how did you get in here and may I ask what you were doing upstairs?"

Penny rolled her eyes. "Oh my God! I can't believe you're making a federal case out of this! The guard recognizes me, mom. He let me in. The alarm code is always one of our birthdays. Duh. I *am* Penny Johnson. I grew up here and I have every right to come to my own home. I told you I was showing Frank my room. Now I feel stupid because you're making this deal in front of Frank and embarrassing me."

Frank took it all in stride. "I guess we should have expected this reception, Penny. Fine, we'll leave. Nice meeting you, *Mary*. We'll go away now. Is this the way you always treat family?" He shook his head. "Great way to get to know my future mother-in-law."

Mary was brought to tears as Frank and Penny made a show of heading for the front door. She might have tried to stop them, maybe invite them in for a visit but Frank's attitude and the glassiness of Penny's eyes stopped her from trying. These two were responsible for stealing a Petri dish from Ted's office and selling it. Far different from the time Penny took Mary's diamond necklace and pawned it, actually worse. Penny would betray the family and then think nothing of lying her way into the house. The other kids were right. She needed to truly exert tough love in order to help Penny. She wept anyway as she double locked the front door and set the alarm.

Chapter 37

Mickey Bruce waited patiently in a dark corner booth nursing his diet coke. He'd never really been a drinker because a long time ago he realized he liked alcohol so much that he knew he could never let it into his life. It would consume him. So he stayed sober even when he was meeting a lead in a bar.

She was over an hour late but from researching her lifestyle, he wasn't surprised or even worried. He knew she would show up because she came right out and told him she needed the money. He could smell the desperation.

He saw her come in the door followed by her handler, Frank. It was obviously the dude who was whispering to her while she talked on the phone, telling her what to say. He was the guy calling the shots, running the show and Mickey would play into that dysfunction as needed no matter how manipulative. This was going to be a great story.

"Hello, Penny. This must be Frank. Nice to meet you, Frank. Here, sit down. Can I get you a drink?" Mickey played friendly suck-up guy. Penny looked to Frank who nodded. Wow, she needed permission?

"We'll just have a couple beers, thanks." Frank got comfortable in the booth with his arm protectively, maybe restrictively, around Penny. Mickey flagged a server and ordered while his two interviewees sized him up, barely able to contain their information.

"I recognize you from the news." Frank offered. He was mildly impressed.

"Thanks. Yeah, I get that a lot."

"You really know how to stick it to the rich guys, huh?" Frank asked. "I've seen you with those asshole alderman and their bullshit. I like your style."

"I appreciate that. I hope I'm helping the little guy, ya know?"

Frank nodded. "That's why we're here. We think we can bring down an empire that's been ruling too long now. Penny's been shafted enough by the Johnsons and it's time we told the world the whole story."

Mickey tried to hide his excitement. "Sure. I've been doing my homework on the family and it looks like they kicked out poor Penny for no good reason. That really sucks. I'm sorry to hear about what you've been through."

Penny smiled regretfully. "It's been horrible and I'm ready to tell my story."

"I'm ready to put it out there." Mickey assured her.

Frank audibly sucked in his breath. "The thing is, we know damn well this story would be of interest to a lot of people. So..."

Mickey nodded. "You want compensation?"

Frank shrugged. "Well, yeah. You're gonna benefit from this so why shouldn't we?"

"I don't have a whole lot of money."

"But the newspapers do. The news stations do. I would think they would be willing to pay for a story like this."

"That's the thing... what are we looking at here? Is this story going to scar the Johnsons or just embarrass them a little?"

Frank leaned forward and whispered, "It's going to take them down."

Chapter 38

Mickey could barely drive his car. He had a lot of fact checking to do but if that jamoke, Frank, was telling the truth, even a little bit. Mickey was about to win a Pulitzer. He was tooling down Sheridan Road listening to some talk radio while he tried to get his head on straight. Something about the subject matter gave him pause.

The Ron and Bill Radio Broadcast – WLN AM

Bill Meyer: *So, as most of you know, I live in the suburbs while fancy pants over here lives in the big city.*

Ron Cone: *Why do you say it like that?*

Bill Meyer: *What? So, this past weekend was our annual block party.*

Ron Cone: *Are you still hungover? I know how your block parties go. Usually it ends up with your next door neighbor passed out in the peonies.*

Bill Meyer: *Not this time, though I didn't look this morning. We've gotten new residents over the last couple years and I'm going to say the face of the neighborhood has changed since I grew up there. Let's just say we don't have hotdogs and hamburgers at our block party anymore. The kids look forward to it because we block off the street and they can ride their bikes. The adults look forward to it because of the food.*

Ron Cone: *What'd you eat?*

Bill Meyer: *My God! I told my wife, don't bother with your potato salad, you'll just look like you're not trying. We can just graze over by the Ptasenskis because Lina always makes a bunch of different kinds of pierogis.*

Ron Cone: *Mmmmm. Was there any souvlaki this year?*

Bill Meyer: *Oh, yeah. Stavros and Anna bring that every year. But the new lady down the street, Lan is her name, from Viet Nam, brought these little meat things, <u>Bánh bèo</u>, she called them. I wanted to eat the whole plate, I just stood there and ate like, forty of 'em and now she thinks I'm a pig. Not a good first impression.*

Ron Cone: *Well...*

Bill Meyer: *Shut up. And Gemma made these egg rolls that were so unbelievably delicious. We didn't need a main course! I filled up on the appetizers. But the best part of the night was the music! We had our own* mariachi band, then Stash got out the polka music so Ian goes and gets his bagpipes. It was GREAT!

Ron Cone: *Sounds... uh, noisy.*

Bill Meyer: *It was, but all good. We were throwing back the Cachaça like nobody's business then Balthazar and Ling get to arguing about the Cubs and the Sox and I'm like, hey, five years ago, you never even heard of the Cubs and Sox, now you're acting like a native Southsider versus a native Northsider and I'm worried Muhammed is gonna cry like a baby 'cuz he was trying so hard to slam Vlad in the dunk tank and he couldn't concentrate with all the racket so Shmuel comes over and shows him how to nail it like an all-star. Then we all went and played corn hole. It was surreal.*

Ron Cone: *That's every day in my neighborhood. I mean this immigrant thing, it all happened so fast but it's been great, you know what I mean? It's like, we're all the new kids on the block, and I don't mean the heart throb boy band. We're all involved with our communities like we never had to before and there's all these cool, new people who want to be a part of this great country and it's working! Somehow, it's all working.*

Bill Meyer: *Who would a thought?*

Ron Cone: *The times they are a changing.*

Bill Meyer: *Yeah. It's nice, isn't it?*

Mickey liked the story. The imagery. Kind a cool to live in a neighborhood like that. Grow up in a neighborhood like that. So many kids were living in safe communities with a colorful cast of neighbors and experiences. Nice. It was happening in the cities, suburbs and farm communities. He just finished a story about the new Detroit, Michigan. Rebuilt, refitted, reborn. A few years ago, they were about ready to close down the place and the crime was ridiculous. Now it was this beautiful haven full of gardens and parks and pleasant city streets. Jobs were plentiful. The automobile industry was thriving and the people all seemed happy. Crazy.

Chapter 39

CNN News

Pierre Charbot: *Since law enforcement in the States has failed to force the Johnsons to cooperate with us, we are slightly behind schedule but I can assure you we are close to a breakthrough.*

Reporter: *When you finally get your own secret sauce and start to perform IVFs what sort of criteria will you place on the mothers who wish to get pregnant in your facilities?*

Pierre Charbot: *The list will be much shorter than my colleagues in Waukegan, Illinois, USA. I will make my procedure available to all who wish to have children. I will not discriminate or ask for money.*

Reporter: *How will you pay for your facility and your staff?*

Pierre Charbot: *What a ridiculous question but if you must ask, well, I will get paid, of course, by the governments of all nations. They will gladly pay my fee. No one would expect me to work for free.*

Reporter: *What if a teenager comes into your facility and wants to get pregnant?*

Pierre Charbot: *She is capable of making up her own mind. I do not presume to tell her she cannot make a baby.*

Reporter: *What if she's being dragged in by a middle-aged man who claims to be her husband but you know darn well she's being forced.*

Pierre Charbot: *I am not a social worker. These are not my concerns.*

Reporter: *What if a crystal meth addict comes in and wants a baby?*

Pierre Charbot: *Well, then, I would let her have the procedure but let the proper authorities deal with her if she is found to be unsuitable.*

Reporter: *You would let her get pregnant knowing she intended to use meth during the pregnancy?*

Pierre Charbot: *It is not my place to question her. I simply get paid to perform the procedure. I cannot play nursemaid to the masses. I am not a Johnson.*

Reporter: *What's your reaction to the CDC announcement this morning?*

Pierre Charbot: *I am told they have ruled out my theory that Aqar was transmitted through mosquitos. As you say in America, Whatever. It means nothing that they have found no infected insects with the virus. It means nothing.*

Reporter: *Well, doesn't it mean that Aqar was not spread through mosquito bites?*

Pierre Charbot: *No. It means that this interview is over and I do not want to hear any more of your stupid questions!*

Mickey was holding a time bomb and it was making him crazy. He had the nut of the story but some of Frank and Penny's revelations were not playing out. No way was he going to put out the story without the facts; the full complete story or there was no point. The next fourteen hours would be spent at his home computer which had full access to most of the world's newspapers. He had a paper calendar and enough coffee to get him through the research. He didn't get anywhere until he homed in on the Mosul refugee crisis back in 2017 when those idiots in Iraq nearly killed their own people rather than ask for international help. Morons. There was some kind of drought... Mickey pulled up the images, there were a ton, because Iraq finally let the NGOs in but they also let the press in. The pictures were depressing, what a fucked up world we used to have, he thought, until help arrived with supplies and a plan to relocate the masses. God, he could barely remember a time when it was a big deal to let immigrants into your country. Of course, the world did a pretty good job of opening its doors during this crisis as Mickey recalled. He scanned through the images and one thing kept jumping out at him... Holy Christ!

He got on the horn with Andy, his editor, then called United airlines. He packed a bag and took a cab to the office. Andy was waiting for him.

Meet The Nation – NBS News

Walter Safer: *Crime is down, unemployment barely exists, not only is the budget balanced, it's surplus!*

Andy O'Hern: *Mental illness is finally being widely and effectively treated.*

Ira Wainstein: *The American dream is alive and well.*

Andy O'Hern: *So is the Canadian dream, the Australian dream, the Western European dream....*

Ira Wainstein: *But not so much everywhere else.*

Andy O'Hern: *Why can't some of the failing countries make it? What's holding them back?*

Ira Wainstein: *Let's take a look at Castro. Raul blames the Johnsons for the demise of Cuba. Says he just needs more people and he could turn it all around.*

Walter Safer: *Like everything was so perfect before Aqar? Before the Johnson Project?*

Ira Wainstein: *And he has the option of complying with the Johnson's criteria. He can get all the warm bodies he wants if he agrees to equal rights and humanitarian efforts.*

Walter Safer: *Castro claims he shouldn't have to jump through hoops for the Johnsons.*

Ira Wainstein: *How's that working for him?*

Andy O'Hern: *The truth is, he has the same opportunity as everyone else and he's choosing to let Cuba die out rather than comply with some pretty simple requirements. Who's the fool in this picture?*

Walter Safer: *It's not the Cuban people. The ones who wanted out, already left. They're here now living that American dream, or the Canadian dream or the Australian dream or the Western European dream.*

Andy O'Hern: *Some of the Arab countries just can't grasp the idea of equality for women. Some of the Arab women just can't grasp it.*

Ira Wainstein: *But many have gotten out. They're shrugging off those burqas and starting new lives in new countries but at least they'll be able to procreate where they end up. And they'll be equal.*

Walter Safer: *They'll continue to worship as they always have! They can still wear those burqas if they want to. The only difference is, they don't have to.*

Ira Wainstein: *All because of the baby plague.*

Andy O'Hern: *Well, that certainly got the ball rolling, didn't it?*

Chapter 40

"I just need more time, that's all. There's nothing solid but I'm checking on a few things, nothing to write home about yet." Mickey sat before his mystified editor who wasn't buying any of the spiel.

"You came back from that meeting with Penny Johnson a few days ago looking like the cat that ate the canary. Today, you asked me for an airline ticket to Cairo. You think that was easy getting a last minute trip approved with no guarantee or even hint of the story? This is the end of the line, buddy, if you don't produce. My ass is on the line along with yours. We been working together for too long for you to bullshit me like this."

Mickey stood up to leave. "You've known me for years. You're the closest thing I got to a friend. Hell, come to think of it, you're my best friend in the world. I'm asking you to trust me. Will you do that for me, Andy? Can you trust me?"

"I always called you a friend but, swear to God, I don't really know you, Mickey. I never even been to your house. You never been to mine. You barely know my wife and you never met my kids. And you consider *me* to be your closest friend?"

Mickey shrugged. "I'm a loner. Always have been, even when I was a kid. Guess it was my upbringing."

"Will you come up with something I can print by next week?" Andy was begging.

"Sure." Mickey answered.

There was a long moment of silence and careful consideration on both sides of the desk.

Andy caved. "You okay, Mick?"

Mickey sighed deeply. "Yeah. I'm good. It's these god dammed, stupid, fucking ethics that beat the shit out of me."

Andy watched him go, more puzzled than ever. He really was a friend, not his best friend because nobody would ever get that close, still a helluva friend and a damn great investigative reporter. It was gonna be a shitty day if he had to fire him but there was no way he could keep Mickey if he couldn't produce. No way. Godammit.

Chapter 41 - Joey is Three and a Half Years Old

At Friday night dinner, Mary knew it was time to come clean. "There's something I need to tell you about Penny."

"Oh, crap." Nora said. "What'd she steal now?" The others waited.

"When she got into the house the other day, she went into my bedroom."

"She let that jerk into your room?" Lou was furious.

"Did she take your jewelry, Mom?" Audrey asked.

"It's worse than that, I'm afraid." Mary's voice was shaky. For a moment she seemed to forget what she was saying but after a few seconds got her bearings and continued. "Do you kids remember when you were little and you were playing hide and go seek?"

Ted, Rafael and Nora knew exactly where she was going but Lou, Audrey and Lily were in the dark.

"Oh my God." Ted exclaimed.

"She went back to the Mosquito room." Nora whispered.

Ted remembered the game of hide-and-seek back when they were kids. He was probably thirteen, maybe fourteen and Penny was there because her bio mom was

266

in prison or rehab or something. Penny had never been a regular at the house, not that Mary didn't fight for her. The kids tried so hard to include Penny when she was able to live at the Johnson's because they knew her real home life was unstable. They all understood because they'd all been there.

Hide-and-seek at the Johnson estate was awesome. There were eight million places to hide and when mom was at a meeting and the nanny was fixing their lunch, anything could happen. Ted could easily find Rafael because he was usually hiding in the library reading a book. Rafael knew it could take hours to 'seek' out the other kids so he liked to enjoy a good read while he was waiting. Nora usually got creative. She was twelve during this particular game and chose to hide in mom's linen closet, high on a shelf. But that's all it took to end the game. She came running to get her siblings, even pulled Rafael out of the library and told them about a huge surprise upstairs. She took them into the closet and showed them the light switch that was behind the stuff on the top shelf. She hit the switch, the side wall opened and they all went into the secret room in amazement.

It was full of books and binders and some gadgets and gizmos. There was a freezer-looking thing plugged into an outlet. The best part was a bunch of Petri dishes full of bugs! Nora informed her siblings that the bugs were dead mosquitos but they better not touch them. Not like finding a pirate treasure but still pretty cool. They were more fascinated that there was a room in their house that they knew nothing about. There it was behind mom's towels. They poked around for a bit and tried to open the freezer thing but it was locked. They played with the secret door then went back downstairs in case mom came home. Sure, it was awesome but they knew it was probably something they weren't supposed to find so they made a pact never to tell their mom about their snooping. The pact lasted four days.

Rafael couldn't keep a secret from his mom. The guilt was killing him so he tearfully confessed one night before bed. Mary held him close and told him he was not in trouble, she praised Nora for finding the secret room and didn't blame Ted one bit for letting the kids go in. Penny was certainly not to blame as the youngest and the newest in the home. Mary told all the kids that the room was engineered by their father, Oliver Johnson, and that's where he kept his papers and such. She hugged them all, reconfirmed her love and asked them not to go back to the room because it was her special place. Rafael asked her if she called it the Mosquito

Room. She laughed and hugged him close. *Yes, it's the Mosquito Room but we aren't going to discuss it again, okay, punkin?* She truly loved them all, she added. They already knew that and were glad to have come clean and have gingersnaps in the kitchen even though it was bedtime.

None of them ever went back into the Mosquito Room until Penny. In all the years since that game of hide-and-seek, Ted, Nora and Rafael wondered what their mother kept hidden away but would never dare break their word to her or upset her by asking. They respected her wishes to a fault. As adults, they realized that the room was something of a shrine to the late Oliver Johnson and they hoped one day to read through his papers and discover more about the great man. None of them, except Penny, considered visiting the Mosquito Room or even asking about it until their mother was ready.

Mary led them upstairs. It was odd to see the Mosquito Room now as adults instead of wide-eyed children. It was much smaller, to begin with. Still full of papers, notebooks and that Fisher lab-grade refrigerator but now, all three siblings wanted to read the paperwork and learn some more about their 'father' and his work. Mary asked them to wait until another time and they all respectfully agreed. She suggested they retire to the library for further discussion and they obliged. On the way downstairs, it suddenly occurred to Ted that his mother had a *Fisher lab-grade specimen refrigerator* in the Mosquito Room. What the hell? He didn't like where this was going.

"I kept all of your father's research material there," Mary started. She was drinking tea. Her hands shook. Her children were worried for her and nervous for what she was about to say.

"Your father was a genius, so far ahead of his time. I, well, I've lost my train of thought. But, hold on... I'm not sure where to begin but I want you all to know the truth before... while I still can remember it."

Ted was way ahead of his mom and had already anticipated her next revelation but it still nearly killed him. He was the only one who had the slightest inkling of what was to come and he was hoping he was wrong. Dear God, he hoped he was wrong.

"Your father, near the end of his life, was thoroughly disgusted with the state of the world. He saw too much abuse especially of women and children. Back in the seventies, we experienced a surge of unwed mothers and deadbeat fathers. Your father was furious that there was no one to take care of these babies but his anger was directed at the women, in some cases girls, who would willingly give birth to children when they knew good and well that they couldn't take care of them. They also knew good and well that the fathers couldn't take care of them. They got pregnant anyway and society was starting to accept this social plague. His idea was to change the world. He wanted to make it so that women could not so easily become pregnant. He wanted the privilege to become pregnant something that was decided in advance."

Her family leaned in to hear more.

"I know this seems so extreme. Please, hear me out. Your father, created a virus. He called it H1J1-B and wanted to disseminate the virus throughout the world and halt all natural pregnancies."

"It was the Aqar virus?" Rafael gasped.

"Exactly. Of course, he didn't call it that. Oliver had already built the Mosquito Room, back then it was his safe, if you will, and that's where he kept the samples of the virus. In a refrigerator. I didn't agree with his plan, in fact, I realized that he may have suffered some kind of psychiatric break down, it was such an extreme measure, I wanted nothing to do with it. I couldn't stand the thought of a world without children. I hoped he would change his mind. He didn't even have a means of spreading the virus back then so I knew I had time to talk him out of it while he researched the idea of infecting mosquitos and insects and then letting nature take its course. You kids found what was left of the insect experiment. He died before he got very far. The virus samples remained in the Mosquito Room along with all of his notes and I thought it was safe. I went on with my life and had my family. I tried not to think about what he had almost done." Mary broke down as her children comforted her.

"Was there an accident? Oh my God!" Audrey whispered. "Did you try to destroy the samples and accidently let the virus out?"

"Mom, was Aqar the result of a leak from this house? Did someone steal the virus right out of your room?" Lou was incredulous.

"Who the hell would do this? How?" Nora demanded. "Was it one of his colleagues?"

"Darling, your father never told a soul but me about the virus." Mary assured her daughter.

"Please stop calling him our father." Nora said, barely able to keep the anger from her statement.

"You mustn't be angry with Oliver. He thought he was doing something good for all of mankind." Mary reasoned.

Audrey didn't like the vacant responses from Mary or the fact that she seemed to be losing track of the conversation. "Who broke into the Mosquito Room?" Audrey asked gently.

Mary gently wiped her nose with a lacy handkerchief. "Oh, dear. I'm afraid you've all misunderstood. Nobody broke in. I took the virus and made sure it infected every man, woman and child on this planet. I did it. Me."

"Oh, my God. Oh, my God!" Nora buried her head in her hands. Lou put his arm around her.

Rafael stuttered and finally asked the question. "You, you, you... ? You did this on purpose?" Lily took his hand. There were tears in her eyes.

They were all brought to tears. Audrey and Lily wept quietly while Nora cried furious, angry tears. Still, she wasn't angry at her mother. Never. She would never be angry at her mother. It was easier to hate Oliver and she would never call him her father again.

It took a few minutes for everyone to calm down, digest, and accept what they were hearing. Ted was the only one not responding to the news, causing Lily to turn on him and state the obvious. "Oh, my God, Ted. You knew! You must have known!" She burst into a fresh set of tears and wondered how the situation could get any worse. It was Audrey who upped the ante when she made the connection and turned to her husband. "I hope you have an explanation because from where I stand, you're a party to all this." Ted tried to hold her but she wouldn't let him. No one was going to let Ted off the hook. All eyes turned to him for his side of the story.

"I had no idea, you guys. I promise you, I had no idea." Ted was choked up and stared at his mother who was lost in thought, completely unaware and not helping him with an explanation.

"How did you come up with the secret sauce? This can NOT be a coincidence." Nora demanded.

"There is no secret sauce!" Ted yelled back. "There is no secret sauce." He rubbed his forehead, searching for the words to explain. His family stared back in silence.

"I didn't come up with any solution. Mom did. After the outbreak she told me dad, Oliver, had been working on something similar back in the day. She gave me some of his paperwork which brought me to an antiviral drug which temporarily weakens the Aqar virus in women long enough to sustain an IVF procedure."

Ted was met with more blank stares.

Mary piped in as she got herself back on track with the conversation. "When Oliver created the virus, he also created the antiviral. So, I had the formula for both all along. Ted didn't know that I had released the virus, though. I couldn't tell him that. He wouldn't have liked that one bit." Mary assured everyone. Her confession took some of the horror out of the situation.

"Did you actually recreate the antiviral on your own, Ted?" Lily asked hopefully.

Ted shook his head. "I produced it by reading Oliver's papers which in retrospect, should have raised some red flags but I was too excited about finding the cure to connect all the dots. I know that sounds lame, but I swear to God, I was not involved with releasing the virus and I was only able to come up with the antiviral by reading Oliver's notes."

Mary looked up like she was just realizing she was in the same room as her family. "What were we talking about now?" She asked with a genuine confusion.

Ted paced. "She begged me to keep Oliver's name out of it. I thought it was because she wanted me to get all the credit for finding the cure. I was indulging her maternal pride, I thought. Now I see she was laying the groundwork for something bigger."

Lily held her head in her hands and rocked back and forth. "Oh My God. Oh My God. Oh My God." The others shared her sentiment.

"What the fuck was all that secret sauce bullshit?" Nora belted.

"A diversion." Ted admitted. "Mom and I agreed to put the story out there about a natural component in the Petri dish to deflect attention away from the real cure so we wouldn't have to share the antiviral with the FDA. There's nothing in the Petri dishes except the usual stuff. We don't mess around with the fertilization process at all. We acted like the lab procedure was all secret and we kept it locked and guarded but it was just a regular IVF lab. In truth, the antiviral is ingested by our patients weeks before their scheduled implant procedures."

"With the pre-nates and the stimulant." Lily said, without emotion. It was all becoming clear to her how masterfully she and the other doctors had been fooled. How easy it had been with a simple misdirection.

Ted looked ashamed. "The antiviral was mixed in with the stimulant."

"We gave our patients an antiviral, that we knew nothing about, that the patients knew nothing about? And you KNEW this, Ted? You knew?" Lily was horrified.

"I'm sorry, Lily." She looked away from him.

"Did you break any laws?" Nora suddenly wanted to know. "Holy crap, Ted, is that legal?"

Ted looked uncomfortable. "No, but the antiviral ingredients are all natural and very mild. It's not like an antibiotic. When the FDA checked our pre-IVF cocktail, all the ingredients were represented. Every one of them. I'm totally breaking the law, yes, but the patients have never, ever been in danger. I promise."

"How come Charbot hasn't figured it out?" Lou was calming down and accepting this strange revelation.

"Because he wasn't looking for it." Ted answered. "He was so focused on the secret sauce and the egg aspiration and the fertilization that he disregarded the virus itself."

Lily shook her head. "There were teams at Carrel that wanted to focus on an antiviral. Charbot pulled them away from that line of research. Your diversion was brilliant. I suppose."

"It was mom's idea." He said dispassionately. "I thought we reached this decision together but I've come to realize, she had this planned a long time ago. Didn't you, mom?"

Mary nodded absently. "Of course, dear. At least I think so."

Audrey never took her eyes off her husband. She didn't like it but she put herself in his place and wondered what she would have done in his shoes. By studying his face she suddenly realized that her husband was a pawn in this game. And the chess master played him from the day she brought him home from foster care. She could see that everyone was arriving at the same conclusion and the pain in the room was evident by their expressions.

"How'd you do it, Mom?" Ted asked. "How did you spread the virus?"

Mary looked lovingly at her son. "I'm fine, dear. Thank you for asking. I think it's time for bed now."

Ted knelt down on the floor in front of his mother and took her hand. He loved her so much. "Mama. Please tell me how you spread the virus. How on earth did you do it?"

So she told him. She told him and her family all about it like she was relaying an amusing anecdote from the past. What made the situation worse was the serene smile on Mary's face. She had no clue that her announcement was an atomic bomb to her family.

They went back to their respective homes that night burdened with the question of how to handle the future. They agreed to wait twenty-four hours before taking the next step. There would be a lot of soul searching that night and not much sleep.

Chapter 42

Early the next morning, Rafael sent the email, not wanting a reply, he just wanted the articles to speak for him.

Dear Ted, Audrey, Nora, Lou and Lily,

I did a Google search on child abuse for the year 2015 and this is a tiny portion of the available data. I had to stop after the first few pages because I simply couldn't read any more. It hurt too much. I wanted you to see why I believe in the Johnson Project. I want to continue despite all we now know. I hope this helps you in your decision.

I love you,

Rafael

OKLAHOMA CITY (Reuters) - A 3-year-old Oklahoma boy took the wheel of a pickup truck and steered it to safety across a four-lane highway after his drunken mother fell out of the vehicle, police said on Thursday.

CLAYTON, Mo. (AP) — A Missouri woman was jailed Friday after being accused of repeatedly poisoning her 9-year-old son for about a year.

ELIZABETHTOWN, Ky. (AP) — A central Kentucky man who police say was seen driving down a highway beating an infant in a car seat has pleaded not guilty to a murder charge in the death of his 4-month-old son.

ISTANBUL (AFP) - The image of a toddler's lifeless body washed ashore on a Turkish beach after a migrant boat sank sparked horrified reactions Wednesday as the tragedy of Europe's burgeoning refugee crisis hit home. The body of the little boy could be seen lying face down in the sand near Bodrum, one of Turkey's prime tourist resorts, before he was picked up by a police officer in photographs taken by the Dogan news agency.

CHICAGO (AP) — In horrifying detail, prosecutors described how three children, trapped in the back seat of their mother's car, screamed for help before they drowned in 4 ½ feet of water in an Illinois lake while their mother and her boyfriend escaped unharmed.

MUNICH (Germany) (AFP) - German police said Friday they had found the bodies of eight babies in an apartment in the state of Bavaria, in what could be one of the country's worst infanticide cases.

TALLAHASSEE (AN) —The Florida couple accused of murdering their nine-week-old baby boy allegedly let the infant waste away in his crib, and then the closet, for more than a week after his father beat him to death, officials said. After he died, ███ was left to decompose until ███ complained about the smell, the affidavit said.

PORTLAND—███████████████████ don't believe in doctors. Because of this religious conviction, set forth by the cult the couple belongs to, Oregon City's Followers of Christ Church, the ███████ let their premature infant die after being born at home rather than seek medical help.

LONDON (AFP) - The mother of a youth facing beheading for taking part in protests in Saudi Arabia has pleaded with US President Barack Obama to "rescue my son" in an interview published by the British daily the Guardian Thursday.

FLINT (Reuters) - A Michigan woman pleaded guilty on Wednesday to second-degree murder in the death of her newborn son, who was found sealed in a plastic bag at her desk in March, prosecutors said. FRESNO (KFSN)- A South Valley mother was arrested after being accused of letting her baby ride in a car without a car seat -- a decision that allowed the child to fall out of the moving car and into traffic.

KANSAS CITY, Mo (Reuters) - A Missouri woman faces charges of endangering the welfare of her two children, ages 4 and 6, after they were found in a cave, apparently living in a crate among disassembled vehicles, in a suspected illegal "chop shop."

BAGHPAT, Northern India — A petition to save two sisters in India from being raped and publicly humiliated for their brother's actions, a punishment handed down by an unofficial village council, has gathered considerable support for its demand that authorities intervene and stop the "disgusting ruling" from being enforced.

WASHINGTON — When FBI agents and police officers fanned out across the country last month in a weeklong effort to rescue child sex trafficking victims, they pulled minors as young as 11 from hotel rooms, truck stops and homes. Among the 168 juveniles recovered was a population that child welfare advocates say especially concerns them: children who were never reported missing in the first place.

DEAR ABBY: In my family alone, three young women have -- by their own admission -- gotten pregnant on purpose to get their boyfriends to marry and support them. None of these marriages worked out. The horrible relationships were and still are hurtful and damaging, not only to the children, but also to the rest of the family. I'm aware of several other women who have admitted to entrapping their baby daddy by "forgetting to take their pills," so I know this isn't just happening in my family.

Contraceptive measures for boys are limited and fallible, and I am concerned. My nephews' mother entrapped their now-absent father, so I doubt she'll mention this to them. How and when does a relative talk to soon-to-be teen boys about entrapment? -- ANONYMOUS RELATIVE

DEAR RELATIVE: The subject of contraception should be part of an ongoing, age-appropriate conversation about sex and reproduction. Boys and girls mature physically earlier than they did decades ago, and because of the Internet they are often exposed to a wide variety of information.

I do think a warning is in order because of your regrettable family situation. However, you should be aware that no law dictates that a man "has" to marry a woman (or girl) he has gotten pregnant. If a paternity test proves he is the father of the baby, he IS required to support his child until the child is no longer a minor.

BELLEFONTAINE, Ohio (AP) — A woman calmly called 911 to report her baby son wasn't breathing on Tuesday and then hours later confessed to killing him and her two other young sons over the past several months because her husband ignored their daughter, authorities said.

ASUNCION, Paraguay (AP) — An 11-year-old girl who was denied an abortion after being raped gave birth Thursday, the culmination of a case that put a spotlight on child rape in this poor South American nation and drew criticism from human rights groups.

HAGERSTOWN, Md. (AP) — A 9-year-old boy who was fatally beaten over a missing birthday cake had been handcuffed for up to three hours a day for a week before the deadly assault, according to court records released Tuesday in Maryland.

State child services workers visited but had done little for a malnourished 15-year-old boy who weighed 47 pounds when police found him Wednesday covered in bodily fluids and insects inside a dilapidated Baton Rouge residence, the teenager's aunt said.

PITTSBURGH (AP) — The mother of a 2-year-old girl found dead in a ravine has been arrested on charges she asphyxiated the girl after becoming upset that she had to help the toddler clean herself after using the toilet, police said Tuesday.

LOS ANGELES (AP) — A 1-year-old, a wide-eyed, restless ██████████ faces the prospect of deportation to his native Honduras, one of tens of thousands of children who arrived at the U.S.-Mexico border last year. While his teenage mother has been allowed to stay in the U.S. and seek a green card under a federal program for abused, abandoned and neglected children, Joshua has been classified as an enforcement priority by immigration prosecutors, his lawyer said.

DALLAS - Four members of a Texas family have been arrested on suspicion of beating a 14-year-old relative to induce an abortion two years ago after she had been raped by a member of the family, Dallas police said on Wednesday.

UNITED NATIONS - The boys said they approached the ██████ soldiers because they were hungry. Some were so young they didn't quite understand the acts the soldiers demanded in return. One boy, 8 or 9 years old, said he did it several times to the same soldier, "until one day an older kid saw him and told him what he was doing was bad."

FARGO - A 20-year-old woman has been charged with second-degree murder for allegedly kicking her boyfriend's 17-month-old son to death.

DALLAS - A 14-year-old Dallas girl was sentenced by a juvenile court judge on Friday to 40 years in custody, the maximum punishment available, after admitting to drowning an infant in January, court officials said.

ALLENTOWN - A woman gave her 1-year-old son a kiss before shoving him off a bridge into a river and jumping in after him, authorities said Monday as they announced she was being charged with homicide.

BOGOTA - Paraguay's decision to deny a pregnant 10-year-old girl an abortion after she was allegedly raped by her stepfather has sparked a national debate over the country's strict abortion law. Paraguay's health minister recently refused a request from the girl's mother to terminate the pregnancy, but rights groups say the decision could put the girl's health at risk and is "tantamount to torture".

ATHENS, Greece - The body of a 4-year-old girl believed to have been killed by her father will likely never be found due to the gruesome way in which her killer disposed of her remains, Greek police said Tuesday. Regional police chief Christos Papazafiri said the girl was dismembered and her remains were processed and dumped in various trash bins in Athens 'in a way that it was not possible to determine they were body parts.'

EASTON, Pa. – The Pennsylvania father who pleaded guilty after his daughter's teeth were found so rotten her life was endangered now says he didn't neglect his 6-year-old.

PHILADELPHIA - Police have identified and charged a mother who they say left her four children locked inside the basement of their Kensington home for more than 12 hours as a punishment.

DETROIT - A Michigan woman was charged with murder on Friday in the death of her newborn son who was found sealed in a plastic bag and stored in a tote near her desk in March, the Wayne County Prosecutor's Office said.

SALT LAKE CITY - A Utah woman who pleaded guilty to killing six of her newborn babies and storing their bodies in her garage is facing up to life in prison at a sentencing hearing set for Monday.

██████████████, 40, who has three surviving children, told police she was too addicted to methamphetamine to take care of more kids during the decade the babies were born.

GRAND RAPIDS, MI - The brother of a man who videotaped the rape of his own bound 18-month-old daughter photographed the sexual assault of another child, the FBI says in court records.

LAS VEGAS - A 17-year-old taken into custody after her severely malnourished 4-month-old daughter was hospitalized and the corpse of a 3-year-old was found at a North Las Vegas home is a victim and won't face criminal charges, the district attorney in Las Vegas said Monday.

LAGOS, Nigeria - The children's drawings show men with guns, a coffin, a car exploding. One picture has stick-like figures of eight siblings missed by their teenage sister.

The disturbing images come from some of an estimated 800,000 children forced from the homes by Boko Haram extremists, according to a UNICEF report published Monday. It says the number of refugee children has doubled in the past year, making them about half of all the 1.5 million Nigerians made homeless in the Islamic uprising. "Children have become deliberate targets, often subjected to extreme violence - from sexual abuse and forced marriage to kidnappings and brutal killings," the report says. "Children have also become weapons, made to fight alongside armed groups and at times used as human bombs."

PHILADELPHIA (Reuters) - A mother abandoned her quadriplegic son in a wooded area of a Philadelphia park for nearly a week so she could visit her boyfriend in Maryland, police said.

LAS VEGAS (AP) — Two people have been arrested in what authorities describe as a twisted, gruesome case of abuse involving a child's corpse hidden in a broken-down car, a starved baby living on water and a sheltered teenager impregnated by her stepfather.

CLEVELAND - A three-month-old infant was left in an Ohio McDonald's late last week by two parents who didn't feel like looking after the child. According to Fox8, 22-year-old ██████████, the infant's mother, asked her McDonald's co-worker for a ride home. When they walked out of the restaurant, ██████ was approached by the baby's father, 29-year-old Aaron Tate, who had an infant with him in a car seat. When ██████ "refused to take the baby because she had plans" that night and it was supposedly ██████ turn watch the child. The police report notes that ████ then carried the baby into the McDonald's, placed the car seat on the floor, and drove away. ██████ and her co-worker followed him and the two parents got into a fight at a nearby intersection, after which they were both arrested. A McDonald's patron called 911 after seeing the child left alone and now both ██████ and ████ faces charges of child endangering. The baby was unharmed and is now in the care of family members.

GORADZE (Bosnia-Hercegovina) (AFP) - ██████████, abandoned at birth by his Muslim mother who was raped by a Serb soldier during the Bosnian war of the

289

1990s, went on a quest two decades later to find his biological parents.

WASHINGTON D.C. – Two DC parents were arrested over the weekend after police say they left their two toddlers locked in a car while they attended a wine-tasting at a posh restaurant. Cops say they received a call about the kids on Saturday afternoon and found the 22-month-old boy and 2-1/2-year-old girl, who was "crying hysterically," strapped into their car seats with coats but no hats or gloves; the temperature outside was about 35 degrees.

BROOKFIELD, Wis. - A Wisconsin couple is accused of locking their 13-year-old daughter in a cold basement with no toilet or sink, forcing her to wear diapers and refusing to allow her to sit on furniture in the family home, according to criminal charges filed this week. The 41-year-old woman and 47-year-old man — the girl's mother and stepfather — are each charged with one count of child neglect. Court records say the girl continually showed up at school with dried feces on her, and that the stepfather said he was disgusted with the girl and called her "Stink."

<u>Humans of New York</u>

"They would always be in the basement, and I'd think: 'I'm sure it's fine, they're my parents.' But as I grew older, I noticed that a lot of the time, even when we were together, they weren't 'quite there.' And sometimes when I knocked on the bathroom door, I'd hear my mom hurriedly cleaning something up. Then one day I found a crack pipe. I'd say we've probably lived in 20 or 25 states because my dad can't keep a job. We went from houses, to small suburban apartments, to small inner city apartments. They make up for it with how much they care about me, I suppose. They always cook me dinner. They accept who I am. They always tell me they love me. But there's never any money for art supplies, or gas, or college. And every time they tell me they're going to do something, they never do it. They've told me so many times they were going to visit colleges with me. But it's never the right time."

BEIJING - A schoolteacher who gained permission to have an additional child in her hometown in one Chinese province has been ordered to have an abortion because the province where she is teaching has different rules, a family planning officer confirmed Tuesday.

DETROIT — Before the frozen bodies of two children were discovered in a deep freezer at their Detroit apartment, the siblings suffered horrific abuse at the hands of their mother. So did their surviving brother and sister, who knew their siblings were in the freezer.

The oldest child was forced by her mother to place her sibling's body in the freezer after she died, a court document revealed.

ASHTABULA, Ohio - A husband and wife in Ohio pleaded not guilty Wednesday to charges that they kept three of their adopted children locked up 22 hours a day, gave them little to eat and beat them with a paddle that became stained with blood. A judge set bond at $50,000 for each defendant. The parents were indicted last week on charges of kidnapping, felonious assault and child endangering, and the husband was indicted on sexual battery and gross sexual imposition charges. The alleged abuse occurred over a span of at least two years, prosecutors said. A fourth adopted child apparently wasn't abused, and it's not clear why that child was treated differently.

MILLVALE, Pa. - A 9-month-old boy found dead in a Pittsburgh-area apartment is believed to have starved after his mother died of an apparent overdose, leaving no one to care for the child.

GAINSVILLE, Fla. - A 15-year-old north Florida girl who authorities say fatally shot her 16-year-old brother after years of abuse at home pleaded no contest on Thursday to felony burglary and will receive probation and counseling.

CHICAGO, IL - Woman cut baby's throat with power saw in Little Village. Police are investigating the death of a 9-month-old girl whose body was found Monday morning in the 2800-block of South Avers.

SAN DIEGO, CA - Mother Forgets Infant in the Midst of Doughnut Crawl

CONCORD, N.H. - A New Hampshire woman who fled to a Florida amusement park with her boyfriend after allowing him to severely beat her 3-year-old son has been granted parole.

PARIS - Police discovered the bodies of five babies in a house in southwestern France, a source close to the case said, in what appears to be the country's worst incident of infanticide in five years.

Chapter 43

They came together the next day with heavy hearts and agreed to keep the information to themselves at least until they could make sure Mary would be safe. They would conduct business as usual and not offer the antiviral to Charbot or bring the truth to light even though it meant they were committing a crime by not reporting Mary's crime. It was a tough call for all of them professionally and personally; they knew Mary was too frail to face the criminal consequences. They also had to factor in the success of the Johnson Project and its impact on mankind. Did the end justify the means? They needed time. That's all. Just time to think it all through.

While pondering the gigantic decision, they had two other major issues to consider. One was taking care of Mary while preventing her from doing any more harm. Her mental state was deteriorating and they couldn't trust her judgement or let her make any business decisions. They would have to gently make sure she retired from the Johnson Foundation and the Johnson Project while letting her keep her dignity.

The second issue was Penny. If anyone was going to exploit Mary's vulnerability, it would be Penny. With Frank's help. They needed to keep both away from the family and away from Mary.

In Penny's mind, the Mosquito Room was the answer to all of her troubles. Even back when she was a kid, Penny knew that finding that room was a big deal to Mom which meant Mom had something to hide. Too bad her mom didn't try harder when Penny needed her most; back when she was stuck in that horrible life with the drug addict birth mother and her many Johns. Mary was too busy spoiling Ted and Nora and Rafael and flying all over the world to feed little brown babies when all the while, Penny needed her to get off her ass and force the courts to help her. Bitch. When the old lady finally did get custody, it was all rules and school while taking absolutely no responsibility for the fucked up custody bullshit that she, as a child, was forced to endure. Fuck Mary and her self-righteous bullshit. Thank God Frank made it all clear and explained who was really at fault this whole time. Penny was glad she mentioned the Mosquito Room one night to Frank when they were wasted and talking shit. It made him so happy! No easy task, Penny thought. After giving him every detail she could think of, he insisted that they somehow get into the mansion and make things right. He figured out the whole plan by asking her a million questions. He was smart and needed facts to make his plans. So they got into the mansion and Penny proudly took him right up to her mom's bedroom. She remembered that hide-and-seek day very well. She used to have fun with her fake brothers and sister but it always ended up with her being sent home. Thanks a lot, *Mom*! She didn't let herself think about those rare, happy times in her childhood. What was the point? It was enough to know that she made Frank happy by leading him into the Mosquito Room. They didn't immediately realize what all those papers and dead bugs meant but Frank would soon figure out that the information he gathered could be sold to any number of people; press, the WMA, even Pierre Charbot, himself. Penny would use any scrap of information against her mother if necessary. A weapon to wield if all else failed and all else failed after the Petri dish fiasco. Frank was pissed when the payments from Paris stopped just short of the big payout. Frank was hard to live with when he was pissed. How was she to know that the Petri dish didn't have the stupid secret sauce? She needed the Mosquito room to pay off or she would lose Frank forever.

Chapter 44

Mickey called in sick to work so he wouldn't have to face Andy. It was the first time he had ever done so since becoming a reporter. In the past the paper forced him take vacation days which he spent following leads or writing, but he never needed to use a sick day because he never wanted to. He was just back from Egypt, a little jet-lagged but mostly pensive. He had the big appointment this evening and it weighed on him.

He was changing. Something about him was changing and he hated the feeling. He needed a break. He needed to be alone. He needed not to think about what he found in Cairo. He needed Andy to get off his case and he needed to prepare for the meeting tonight but his mind so badly wanted to rest. He couldn't focus on any of the stories he was working on, none of them compared to the big one. None of them mattered. He looked around his apartment for any diversion. He didn't want to read a novel. He sure as hell didn't want to watch television. His eyes settled on the shoe box he was forced to take from that old lady's house. The pitiful journals of an abused woman. That sounded cheery.

He chugged some coffee and opened the box. There were a bunch of notebooks and papers. He scanned a few and saw that once she actually got away for a few days. She mentioned the short-lived escape plan when she took Billy all the way to Indianapolis before turning back to the security of Ron. The devil that she knew. The pages went on and on. The senseless ramblings of a victim who just kept on taking it until the bastard finally killed her. Same old story. At least the kid got out alive. He flipped through a notebook where she talked about how trapped she felt. How she deserved it. Nothing new. He tossed in the notebook and noticed a purse under some of the paperwork. Huh. Well, these were probably her personal effects that the cops gave to the next of kin. He dug to the bottom and found her cell. He doubted the cops had even fired up the phone in the investigation. Why bother? He tried to turn the phone on but it wasn't charged. He took it into his bedroom and plugged it in. The service would be long gone but nowadays, most of the messages and phone calls would be saved in the SIM card. He got some more coffee and came back to see the phone was at two percent. Good enough. He powered up. He didn't care about the day to day babble where she asked her husband what he wanted for dinner and the ass demanded whatever, day after day. Mickey went right to the last few days of phone calls hoping to see she made an emergency 911 call. There was something fascinating and macabre about those last 911 calls. But after thumbing through the list, he saw her last moments were spent texting. Ah, well.

He was about to throw the phone back in the box when he decided to check out the text exchanges between her and Ron on that last fateful day. Her final thoughts and texts were about some guy who was following her and she was scared. Ron texted back that she was a brat looking for attention. She insisted there was a man following her home and she even took his picture. *Here!* She texted. *Here's his picture! He's right outside the door and I'm going to call the police.* Ron texted her to *shut the fuck up and not bring the police into their house ever again! What are you, stupid? The guy is probably a reporter, you idiot! Do NOT call the cops or I'll have to eat their shit. I'm on my way home...* That was the end of the texts. Her last correspondence on earth and the asshole warned her not to call the police so he could come home and beat the shit out of her in private. What a piece of garbage.

Mickey waited for the picture to upload. He wondered if it was a reporter, maybe Mickey knew the guy. Probably a meter reader or a Jehovah's Witness. When the digital picture downloaded, he stared for one second and then dropped the phone. Holy shit. Ron didn't kill her. Jesus H. tap-dancing Christ! There in all its digital glory was the real killer standing on the porch, already armed with a tree branch. God almighty. It was a setup, a frame-job. And no one knew.

Chapter 45

They were on the eleventh floor in Audrey's office. Ted had a break in his appointments and wanted to be with his wife. They had been so remorseful lately, worrying about Mary, questioning their mission. Ted needed Audrey to make it all right. Audrey had made up her mind and she was at peace. Since Mary's revelation, she was more resolute than ever to continue with the Johnson Project. After serious contemplation and Rafael's email, her position about the project had been reinforced. She encouraged her husband. "Look what's it's done here in the States. Every child is wanted and treasured. That Google search Raf did for 2015? You won't get the same Google results in 2019. Parenthood is changing. The world is changing." Audrey reassured Ted.

"We're playing God!" Ted countered.

There was silence while she let him cool down.

"We're trying to figure out what's fair for the rest of the world. Anyone in our position would come to the same conclusion. I can't even think about the old days when today's world is nearing perfection." She finally offered.

"Our position. Our position. I don't want to be in *our position*. How did we get here? Really? How? I can't do this. Let someone else figure it out."

"Like the WMA?"

He thought about it with a deep sigh. "No." He took her hand. "My life was supposed to be simple. All I ever wanted was a great family with a normal life and I got it and it was perfect. I never wanted to make decisions that would hurt people that I don't even know."

"You have the same response when it comes to disciplining Allie and Joey. You struggle with time outs, even that time when Joey ran into the street. Don't you see, honey? Sometimes you have to be the heavy. The buck has to stop somewhere. Someone has to lead the way."

He knew all of this to be true. He kissed his wife's hand. "I know what we have to do. I just don't want to be the one to do it. I don't want to be the bad guy."

"Good thing you're married to me." She said with a grin.

"Because you have the courage to do what's best for the universe?" He said with his smart alec sarcasm.

"That and because I can give Joey a time out when he runs out into the street. Even if it makes him cry."

A sudden change on the television screen prompted Ted to grab the remote and turn off the mute. Both he and Audrey took notice of the famous anchor and the dramatic music. The reporter quickly apologized for interrupting the normally scheduled program. "We take you now to Mexico City where President Carlos Márquez will be making an historic announcement." The shot went to an outdoor stage draped in the colors of the Mexican flag. A huge crowd of reporters and a huger crowd of citizens gathered to hear the leader's announcement. He was speaking in Spanish but a translator closely relayed his words in English.

"...Any government official caught taking a bribe or in any way dealing with the drug cartels will be fired. Assistance from the U.S. and the U.N. has been confirmed. We will start by ensuring the integrity and safety of our judges, then our police force. Drug dealers beware: you are no longer welcome here! Your cars and trucks and ships will be confiscated at every border. You will go to prison. You will not be able to bribe officials anymore. Yes, we admit it has happened in the past, but no more!"

The crowd cheered.

"The Americans are sending an unbiased, unbribable team to Mexico for the next two years. We will take care of our children! If we all work toward this goal, the Johnsons have promised a fertility center here in Mexico City!"

Audrey stood up with a smile and a generous hug for her husband. "You see? Did you ever think we would see *this* in our lifetime?"

Ted smiled and hugged her back. "I know. I know. This is incredible. You're right." They watched the happy scene as President Marquez brought the good news to the Mexican people. Ted relaxed and felt proud of his contribution to a better world and thought briefly about a Cancun vacation one day. Mmm, margaritas and goat cheese quesadillas...

As the president paused for more cheers he looked to the sky and shaded his eyes. Everyone on the platform looked skyward but no one seemed immediately concerned with the helicopter until the first chorus of machine gun fire tore through the group and brought down nine souls within seconds. Live news coverage brought the brutal assassination into millions of homes along with the screams and chaos that ensued. President Marquez was blown to bits. An autopsy would later reveal that his remains were torn into fourteen individual pieces.

Ted and Audrey froze in shock as did most people who happened to be watching the live event. Audrey cried. Ted muttered, "no.... no. No."

Lily and Rafael were relaxing in his office, unaware of the tragic events unfolding. Both were feeling confident about their relationship and the future of the Johnson Project.

"I am finally happy." Rafael kissed her nose. "I know that sounds odd after learning the truth about my mother. We have to move forward and I know we're doing the right thing."

"The rest of the world feels the same way. There is progress everywhere. Even the places we never thought possible." Lily said in wonder.

"It feels good, Lily. Taiwan is working on a policy and rumor has it, so is Israel."

"I understand the Czech Republic is very close."

Rafael holds up his forefinger pinching his thumb. "This close. They'll be in the program in a matter of months."

"I must admit, I was skeptical of mankind, but, now, I am proud. It was your family that pushed for this and won."

"You had a hand in this, Lily. Your contributions have been invaluable."

Lily looked away. "I came late to the party as you say. I can't stand with the Johnsons who have done so much good."

"You are one of us, Lily."

She stared longingly into his eyes. Hoping? "I don't deserve that distinction, Rafael. I will never accomplish the things your mother has done. What you and your siblings have done."

"Not true, Lily. And we're only making headway now because we now have something we never had before."

"What is that?" She asked.

Rafael smiled. "Leverage."

Ted pounded on the office door. Rafael stood as Ted barged in, grabbed the TV remote and turned on the news. Lily and Rafael both stared at the scene in Mexico, quickly gathering the gist of the situation.

"This is not our fault, Ted." Rafael finally uttered still staring at the television.

"Then who do we blame?"

"I don't know, Ted. The drug cartels? The people who don't like the changes in the world?"

Audrey joined the somber group and together they watched the chaos in Mexico City. The raw carnage magnified the ugly consequences that had come out of the Johnson Project. Ugly forces would fight brutally for the chance to get the world back to the Pre-Aqar lifestyle. In this case, the cartels would flex their muscle and kill innocent people to make a point. And it did make a point with the Johnsons who couldn't help but accept the blame for this tragedy. Their emotions were too fragile to discuss it at that moment.

Audrey spoke through her tears. "Let's get through this meeting tonight and figure out how to move forward. We can rise above this."

Chapter 46

Mickey pulled into the circular driveway and stared in awe at the beautiful estate. All these years of covering the Johnsons and he'd never seen her house. So this is where the family convened. The house of Mary Johnson. He rang the chime and couldn't believe it when Mary Johnson opened the door. Didn't she have people for this kind of thing? Mary Johnson was beyond gracious and welcomed him into the palace even though she must know what was about to go down. He mumbled something about her nice home and she gave an appreciative reply as she led him into the family room where they were all waiting for him. Ted and Audrey, Nora and Lou, Rafael and Lily. There were no little kids around so Mickey assumed the three little nuggets were with a nanny. Nobody looked angry. That was good.

Most of the Johnsons had a cup of something or other and offered him a beverage. He accepted a bottle of water while embracing the irony. Maybe he could use it as a prop. Wait, that would suck. He thought he would enjoy this moment of glory but his stomach clenched and he was afraid of his emotions. These people were not monsters.

"Have a seat, Mickey." Ted waved his arm at any number of comfortable choices. Mickey picked an arm chair rather than a loveseat or sofa option. He didn't want to be too close to any of them. Story of his life. He swallowed hard and got ready.

Audrey sat down on an ottoman near him and placed a reassuring hand on his arm. "Please don't stress about this, Mickey. We know why you came and we're good with it."

Great, he thought. They're trying to make this easy on *me*. Were they always kind? Did they ever have bad moods?

"We all knew it could happen at any time." Nora added. "I'm kinda impressed with your detective skills, Mickey." Lou said. "You get props for the legwork. Nicely done."

There they go again. Nice. Mickey looked around the room at the incredible family and hated himself. "I suppose you're wondering how much I know."

Everyone chuckled without humor. They were all curious at how much he was able to uncover because until they knew the extent of his knowledge, they couldn't plan for the fallout.

Mickey at first addressed Mary. "I went to Egypt last week to see your water plant, Mrs. Johnson." Mickey didn't beat around the bush.

Not what they were expecting but nobody responded. They waited for more.

Mickey continued. "Nice operation you got there."

"Please call me Mary." Mary smiled. She didn't seem upset by the revelation. She seemed kind of vacant. Stoned? Something.

"Mary. Water is life, am I right?" Mickey asked the matriarch. He wiggled his water bottle to get a reaction but nobody bit. "I know the official story when you opened the water filtration and bottling factory in Egypt back in the nineties. You wanted access to bottled water close to where the need was the most urgent. You wanted pure water for all of those in need. Because, like I said, water is life."

Mary nodded eagerly and went into her pragmatic mode. "It was more efficient to transport from a central location. It was silly to bring water all the way from the States when most of the need was in Africa and the Middle East. It's very heavy to transport as you can imagine and with the cost of jet fuel, well. I saved millions over the years by opening my own facility."

"You also wanted unfettered access to the purification and bottling of the water. You wanted to own the operation so that you could oversee the production of the water, am I right?"

Mary kept her smile. "It is true, Mickey. Very true. I had far more control of the process than I would have here in the States. The FDA is very fussy."

"So a few years ago, during the Mosul refugee crisis, you stepped up production and sent an unprecedented amount of bottled water to those in need. You made sure your water was the first to arrive at every refugee camp in Iraq."

"All true." Mary agreed.

"As we all know, those refugees were finally let loose on the world. Forced to migrate to anywhere that would take them. In fact several countries stepped up and hosted the Iraqi refugees. Europe started the trend by laying out the welcome mat but eventually they were spread out far and wide and welcomed all over the world. Even the United States took their share of refugees. And all those migrants came fully hydrated with Johnson water. Some of them were holding Johnson water bottles as they deplaned in their new countries. Remember?"

Everyone nodded. Mary continued to smile. "I was happy to be of service."

"What we didn't know, Mary, is that every single drop of Johnson water was contaminated with the Aqar virus. Millions of tainted water bottles were given to thirsty refugees who unknowingly ingested the microorganisms then carried the virus to dozens of host countries, all within a matter of weeks. The pathogen was initially disseminated in water bottles but quickly mutated and became airborne within days. The planet was successfully infected and every woman became barren. And no one figured out it was you. No one connected the Mosul crisis to Aqar even though the timing of both events should have been noticed. Well played."

Nobody responded but nobody looked panicked either. Mickey thought that was weird. Well, this was not new information to them, he realized. They were prepared for the worst and they would handle it well.

"I felt the need to do something drastic." Mary said, conversationally. "My husband, Oliver, created the virus back in the seventies but the time wasn't right. After he died, I adopted my children and planned for their future. I tried to help the suffering children with the Johnson Foundation but I couldn't even make a dent. I knew years ago I had to lay the groundwork for an extreme solution and I came to realize my late husband was correct. None of my kids knew what I was doing until recently. They were as shocked as you about the Aqar plague and how it started. They all jumped aboard the Johnson Project not knowing that I had intentionally created the need for responsible reproduction."

Mickey was truly astounded at Mary's cavalier attitude. "You seem so matter-of-fact about the whole thing. You secretly infected three and a half billion women with a virus and changed the course of history. Don't you think you've overstepped your bounds?"

Her children and their spouses did not like Mickey's tone and their faces reflected it. Mary held up a hand before any of them could respond. "I know what I've done and I have slept peacefully every night since. I will sleep peacefully tonight. I've had my regrets but overall, I did what needed to be done. My own children have questioned my choices and I understand their concern. I do. But at my age, having seen what I've seen in this world, I did the right thing. I regret nothing."

Mickey could tell by the looks on their faces that many a debate had been had over this topic. He sympathized with this family, he really did. Mary led her children down a primrose path without telling them where they were headed. It was really her husband, Oliver Johnson, who started the journey but she finished it and brought her kids along for the ride. God in heaven, this story would go down in history and Mickey would be the one to write it. He could finally have his moment; the biggest achievement of his life. His mother always told him not to get his hopes up because disappointment and regret would soon follow. She was wrong. He would never be disappointed or regret what he was about to do.

"When will the story come out, Mickey?" Rafael asked.

Mickey didn't want to look at the sad face of Rafael. Poor kid, he always liked the guy. "I gotta break it soon or someone else will do it first. I figured this all out by talking to Penny and Frank. They know about the antiviral and they know your mom is responsible. The thing is, they think it was spread through infected insects. The story could come out but the experts will squash the theory about the bugs but it might get people asking questions. It seems Penny and Frank will sell the story to the highest bidder even if the story is not quite true."

Silence.

"I guess they saw some paperwork in some secret lab closet room place. I didn't totally believe her about the mosquitos since all along that notion has been debunked even when Charbot was throwing it out there. But I did believe that Mary might just be behind all this. That didn't seem crazy to me. Frank even showed me some credible paperwork written by Oliver Johnson claiming to have the technology to make the world barren. But why would anyone do that?" Mickey paused for dramatic effect. "Maybe old Oliver was nuts because what would anyone gain by making the world infertile and then it came to me out of the blue. Mary Johnson. She's our bright and shiny philanthropist with the heart of gold but she's also brilliant, although frustrated with her fruitless efforts to end suffering, her inability to ultimately champion human rights. She was trying to empty the ocean one spoonful at a time and it was getting her nowhere. She figured she'd had enough and maybe Oliver had the right idea. She knew she could get the virus out there pretty easily. She knew the uncertainty that would follow but she also knew she was practically guaranteed a spot on Task Force 200. But then she had years to position herself to be asked. She's had years to work out every detail. She's been planning this a long time, haven't you, Mary?"

Mary smiled. "Well, yes. Oliver started the plan. But I added to it. I made it better with the financial recovery and I knew we could end the wars. Most of all, I wanted to make it so children would be loved. Oliver wanted to punish the world. I just wanted to fix it." She was lost in thought for a moment. "I didn't want the virus to stay forever. I wanted to bring reproduction back but I wanted it done with more thought. I wanted to make happy families."

Her family members were frozen in place, barely breathing.

Mickey looked kindly at Mary. Batshit crazy but her logic was kind of interesting. He needed to put this family at peace. They were dumbstruck shocked right now and it was about to get worse. They clearly knew about the Mosul crisis and maybe hoped the story would be contained, now they were wondering how to handle this spectacularly incredible situation. Nora finally spoke. "Do you have hard evidence from the water factory in Cairo? Do you have witnesses? This story will seem farfetched to authorities."

"Nora, things aren't looking good in Egypt these days so it wasn't hard to find a few locals who were happy to talk for a couple a pounds." He turned to Mary. "They mentioned you and Burke getting involved in the 'purification' a few years ago just as the Mosul crisis was getting attention. According to my sources you and

Burke were in the bottling warehouse every day for a week, in fact, the workers found it unusual but distinctly remember that week because you brought treats each day and spent a great deal of time chatting up the work force. Wow, they must have loved you. A rich white woman hanging out with the worker bees, patting everyone on the back. Just another Mary Johnson philanthropic endeavor. Those workers cherished the days you spent with them so much that many captured the moment with selfies. And they proudly showed me those selfies. Those selfies with the time stamp bearing the date; May 10, 2017, seven weeks before the world realized every woman on the planet was barren. Those locals didn't put it together with the Aqar outbreak. But I did."

"Burke helped you, Mom?" Lou asked. He couldn't believe Burke knew the whole time. But it made sense. There were some logistics she would have needed help with. Damn that Burke.

"I think so." Mary said. "Yes, Burke." But her blank stare belied her lack of comprehension.

"Anyway," Mickey added. "Frank told me I would get the exclusive but we all know how much we can trust Frank. This will be horrible for your family but... I may as well be the one to break the news. I'm gonna get fired this week if I don't come up with a story."

"We understand, Mickey." It was all Ted could offer. He was lost in the inevitable crash of their world as were the others. Mickey felt horrible for them. He honestly felt a strong emotion for this family and the consequences that were about to befall them.

Then Mickey cursed his own weakness and made a pitch. "But, I was thinking... Maybe Penny and Frank have a price. Maybe you guys could pay them off." He raised an eyebrow, wondering how they would respond. "I suppose they just want the money, right?" Ted reasoned. "We might be able to buy their silence."

Nora paced. "Yeah. We could pay them off but it means we'll *always* be paying them off. Well, at least if we're paying her we can keep an eye on her. Make sure she takes care of herself."

Lou considered. "We could keep a handle on it. They won't want to stop the money train so if we pace the payments, we should be okay."

It was not a bad idea.

Audrey looked intently at Mickey. "But you'll still know."

"Nah. I'm not gonna write this one." Mickey said.

Rafael finally said. "Are you saying that if we can contain Penny and Frank, you don't plan to publish your findings, Mickey?"

Mickey had already made up his mind and this decision would never cause him disappointment or regret, he was certain. "No. I don't plan to tell anyone. That's what's killing me. I got the story of the century and it will never be told. At least not by me." He felt the rush of relief from the room.

"That would make us very happy, Mickey." Mary said but she seemed confused about what was happening.

Mickey went on. "I get what you guys are doing. I didn't like it at first. I didn't like the whole situation but seeing what you've done with the world, am I supposed to be the one to ruin it?"

"It's a quandary we all struggle with, Mickey." Audrey admitted.

"I will take this information to the grave. My notes will be destroyed and I'll tell my editor the story is dead. I can assure you that I am committed to your choices; in fact, I thank you for what you have done for mankind."

Everyone smiled. "We appreciate your discretion. We really do." Ted said, meaning it.

It was a relief for everyone. They still had to work with Penny and Frank but maybe they could turn their cooperation into a healing process for everyone.

"It's just that...," Mickey had to continue. "There's more to the story, isn't there, Mary?" He hated the looks on their faces as they turned suddenly to look at him.

Mary shook her head. "I'm not sure what you mean, Mickey."

"I'm guessing you haven't told your kids the full story." He didn't mean to sound menacing but it came out that way. Mary didn't respond but continued to smile as if she hadn't heard Mickey.

Mickey shouldered on. "I went to Cleveland to visit with Mrs. Timmons. You all remember Billy's other grandmother, right?" As Mickey looked around at Mary's children, he knew they were unaware of his next revelation. Nora and Lou looked terrified. Damn this was going to be a tough one. Mary sat politely poised, waiting for the story.

"Mrs. Timmons told me all you had done for her." He assured the family. "She's at peace with Billy's placement and the whole arrangement."

"Where are you going with this?" Nora demanded.

"What, what...?" She looked to her husband.

Mickey held his hands up in a sign of peace. "Please let me continue. I'll be brief but it's time you all knew the truth. Mary, would you like to tell them or shall I?"

Mary tried to remember but couldn't. "Why don't you tell the story? I can't recall the details and you'll tell it much better." She settled in for a good yarn. Rafael moved to sit next to his mother and hold her hand. He was holding his emotions in check. Audrey sat on the other side of Mary with her arm around her mother-in-law.

Mickey almost gave up but he realized that these people needed to know so they could prepare. "I can see that your mom is... not well. I can see that she may not have been acting with a sound mind."

"Get on with it." Nora demanded.

"Billy's bio mom wasn't murdered by her husband, Ron, and he didn't kill himself." Mickey hesitated. "They were both murdered in cold blood by Burke. Your mom ordered the hit. She told Burke to make it look like a murder-suicide."

Mary continued to smile and stare absently into space. Her family absorbed the news and didn't speak. They were in shock but Lou nodded like he remembered something wasn't right about the investigation. Still, he wasn't expecting this. He kept shaking his head like he could reboot the truth to a normal explanation but it wasn't working.

"It's true," Mary said conversationally. "I knew the only way to get Billy into our family was to get rid of his mother and that horrible man. I did it. I asked Burke to help me and he did. He's always done what I asked of him. Well, you must know about the sad situation of his upbringing. Burke has done far worse I'm afraid, before I met him I think..."

Ted was the first to cry but the others soon followed. Rafael hugged his mother and cried on her shoulder. Mickey stood awkwardly. "I guess I better be going. I can't tell you all how sorry I am." He paused. "Seems kind of a stupid thing to say at this point. I just hope you can get a handle on Penny and Frank. Just know that I'm on your side." He stood to leave.

Mary patted Rafael to comfort him. "Don't cry, little punkin.' It will all be okay. Now I must get to bed. I'm so tired." She stood and addressed her family. "Good night my darlings. I love you all so much." She headed for the doorway but stopped and turned to Mickey. "Oh, and don't worry about Penny and Frank. That's all taken care of. It was so nice to see you again, Mickey. Sweet dreams everyone!"

"What's that mean, mom? What do you mean about Penny?" Nora asked frantically as she ran to her mother's side.

Mary turned again when she got to the doorway. "She's dead. Burke killed her just this afternoon. My daughter is dead. Burke killed Frank, too, and he made it all seem like they were drunk or something. Penny was never going to get better and she broke into the Mosquito Room and she found out about the virus. I had to do something or the rest of you would have been in very bad trouble..." Mary paused and wondered why everyone seemed so upset when all she did was take care of the problem. Suddenly she remembered something else. "Oh, and Burke has retired. It was time, he said, and now he's gone to an island to live with a different name. He wouldn't tell me his new name so I said good-bye forever. It was just before he left to kill Penny. I'll miss Burke. Well, goodnight, sweethearts." She blew kisses from the archway.

Nora gripped Mary's hand. "I'll help you up, Mama." She brushed her tears aside and helped her mother upstairs.

As the family dealt with their shock and grief, Mickey wondered about the protocol of one being stuck in the same room as a group of adults who had just learned that their mother was a homicidal maniac and, by the way, their wayward sister was lying dead somewhere. See ya. The reporter in him instinctively wanted to take notes. The new and improved human side of Mickey was struggling with how to gracefully exit and leave this destroyed family to their sorrow. If there were societal dictates for this situation, he had no idea what they were.

Rafael leaned against the mantle and stared into the fire. Lou went and poured a drink and seemed focused on that task. Audrey and Ted held each other. Lily quietly wept and then joined Rafael by the fireplace.

Ted broke the silence. "What do we do, Lou? How do we...?"

"I don't know." Lou interrupted. "I don't know. We gotta think this through. My initial thought is to check on Penny. Maybe your mom is just confused. I'm gonna call Burke." He had his phone out while he spoke. After listening for a few seconds he tapped the screen and reported back. "Burke's phone is out of service. Does anyone have Penny's number?" He was grasping for procedures so that he wouldn't have to think about this. But there weren't any procedures.

"I do." Mickey offered. He had made his way toward the door and was close to a departure until he offered to make the call. He pulled out his phone and tried her number but it went right to voicemail. He looked up in shock. "Shit. If she is dead, the cops are gonna see that I called her. I've talked to her a few times this week, goddammit. My number's on her phone."

"No more calls. I'm going over to her house." Lou announced.

"I'm coming with you," Ted and Rafael said simultaneously.

Lou shook his head. "No. I have no idea what to expect and I sure as hell don't want you guys... finding... her."

They hadn't thought about *finding her* and the image brought a fresh wave of horror. Lou started thinking about the consequences they were all about to face. He thought about the implications of being spotted at the crime scene, if there even was one. But he knew the hard side of Burke and somehow the crazy story seemed probable. There was always something about Burke that wasn't right. "Maybe I shouldn't be going to Penny's house. Maybe we just need to work this out. I don't want to betray my oath as a peace officer..."

"What the hell?" Ted said grimly. "I betrayed my oath as a doctor. I did harm. My ethics are in serious question."

"Mine, too." Lily admitted while she absently rubbed Rafael's back. "Also, Rafael's and Nora's."

"We all took shortcuts in our ethics." Rafael tried to rationalize. "We all tried to justify the means but it didn't seem horrible until now. We thought we were responding to a natural disaster. We didn't come clean when we found out the truth about the spread of the virus. Now we know Mom's a murderer. We can't... I don't know..."

"Listen," Lou started. "If Burke handled this double homicide like he did the last one, he covered all his bases. The police will come. They'll rule it a murder/suicide/overdose or whatever and it's over. Maybe we should consider that. Let this go."

They did for a few minutes then Nora's scream from upstairs brought them all running up the grand staircase and into Mary's bedroom suite. Mary was face down on the floor. Nora was trying to roll her over as Ted took over and checked Mary's vitals. "What happened?" Lily asked.

Nora could barely speak. "She was fine, talking like sweet, nice mom. She was going into the bathroom and started talking about 'Burke got this for me. I asked him to help me and he did' and I saw her reach into a cabinet and take out a bottle. It looked like there were only a couple of pills in it. She popped them both in her mouth and then collapsed to the ground clutching her chest.

Her eyes were rolling back in her head, then I screamed for you guys and she looked me in the eye and she said, 'Your father didn't die from a heart attack. I killed him.' Then she closed her eyes and..."

Ted interrupted. "She's gone." He was choked up. "I think it was poison." He rubbed her cheek and wept.

Chapter 47

Condolences came from around the globe. The president made a statement from the rose garden and most news reports led with the news of Mary Johnson's passing. She was featured on the cover of every major newspaper and news feed. Calls, emails and letters poured in to the family who were still struggling with the ugly side of Mary Johnson while accepting the kind words from others. They were not surprised to learn just how many lives she touched and how much her largesse meant to an untold number of recipients. The dichotomy was overwhelming to her children as they tried to cope with the loss and the revelation of the real Mary Johnson. Maybe the dementia kicked in earlier than they thought. The emotional toll became more difficult after a visit from the police to inform them of Penny's 'accidental' overdose. The press couldn't believe the family had to grieve another one of their own and were kind with the memory of Penny Johnson under the circumstances. The doctors and staff from the Johnson Project and Johnson Foundation were on hand to offer sympathy and express their remembrances of Mary. Sybil took the news very hard. She had always been especially fond of Mary, but she kept the center going while the family took time to mourn. Only a few people questioned Burke's absence and most assumed he was grieving his mentor and would retire anyway, now that she was gone. He had no real friends and no family that they knew of.

The days between her death and the funeral were a blur for the family. Because her heart gave out, the manner of death was ruled natural causes and no one questioned or contested the issue. The family was prepared to acknowledge her suicide but they never had to. The world would never know that she took her own life and she would be forever remembered as a sainted woman who died a natural death in the presence of her beloved children. It appeared that Mary would be laid to rest with the world unaware of her greatest crimes. She would be laid to rest next to the man she murdered years ago.

Each day leading up to the funeral got a little better for Mary's family and they hoped that the worst was behind them. The service was well attended and included memories of her many accomplishments. The family shook hands and hugged throughout the day and thanked everyone for coming.

Chapter 48

They wanted to be together after the funeral and Mary's house was the obvious gathering place. In her life, Mary loved having her children together, under her roof, where she could simply enjoy their company. It seemed a fitting tribute to end the dreadful day in a place where they'd always been loved and felt secure. The staff was on paid leave except for the security detail that had been recently fortified. They were alone in the huge house feeling the loss even more so now that the flurry of events were through. They discussed the funeral as they sipped red wine and wondered how they didn't see the real Mary Johnson.

"I still believe she loved Oliver with all of her heart." Audrey offered.

"I don't doubt it," Rafael agreed. "In her mind she was doing the right thing. She had to stop him and I guess she thought killing him was the only way to go."

"I was thinking during the funeral that if she hadn't killed Oliver, then we might never have been born. Any of us." Ted surmised. "She protected us before she even knew us. Maybe that's when she became our mother." It made everyone stop and think.

Lou nodded. "I guess you're right. Wow. I never thought of that."

Lily looked up suddenly. "You are correct. My goodness. She was such a good woman, so admired by millions, it is hard to swallow that the goodness was not real." Everyone turned to Lily for further explanation because they didn't all see it that way but Rafael diffused the statement in her defense. "I think you mean that her rationale was subject to some scrutiny but her goals were always the same but with a different course to get there."

Lily grasped Rafael's arm to show her appreciation for the clarification. "Yes. I think what I mean is that humility covered up an incredible mind. What we thought were acts of kindness may have just been part of the plan. I mean no disrespect to your mother, Rafael. I am still trying to understand how I underestimated her brilliance."

"She was excellent at skirting accolades." Nora offered.

Rafael nodded. "Mom would automatically deflect praise of her business acumen. She religiously credited her success to others in the organization but I always knew she was the heart and soul of the Johnson Foundation and then the Johnson Project."

"She was so humble!" Audrey added.

"True. Her modesty covered up all of the crazy." Ted frowned. "I mean, she made it look like other people were making the decisions but I've come to believe that she had complete control the whole time, every step of the way."

"Like a fox, am I right?" Lou asked.

"Until she knew the dementia would take over." Nora said. "As the lucid moments came less and less frequently, she fixed the whole situation so that we wouldn't have to suffer the consequences. I truly believe that. I also believe she intended to take her own life during a time when she was still capable of making the decision."

"Burke knew." Rafael said. "He got the poison for her and knew about her plan. He may have even instructed her on how to do it. I have tried to hate him but I can't. He would have given his life for mom and when she asked for his help, he never hesitated. Even if it meant murder."

Audrey shook her head. "I still can't believe it."

Everyone paused. It had been a long day of reflection and they were only now able to put the last few years into perspective."

"Where do we go from here?" Audrey asked.

"I can tell you where we go from here." Rafael said with his arm around Lily. "We plan to get married and have a baby." The couple smiled and accepted the congratulations although Lily was troubled by the timing of the announcement. In any case, there was finally a reason to celebrate. Hugs and handshakes went round and glasses were raised in a toast to the happy couple. Rafael was radiant in his happiness even with the recent tragedies. He hoped their happy news would help the family move forward.

"It's a bit odd to announce it on the day of mom's funeral." Rafael started. "But I know she would be happy for us and we all could use some good news. I just wish she were here, the old mom, I mean, I wish she were here to toast us."

"She is." Audrey confirmed, raising her glass. "And she's all better now and loving her kids like crazy."

The toast ended with the sound of a buzzer coming from the front hall. Nora went to respond to the guardhouse, a little puzzled that they were being disturbed although it may be a late flower delivery or something funeral related. She came back to the great room quickly with all heads turning to see about the interruption. "Arturo says we have a visitor. It's Pierre Charbot and he insists on seeing us. All of us."

"He's here?" Ted asked. "Here at the gate? Charbot?"

Nora nodded. "Yeah. Arturo says he won't leave. Huh." She paused to consider the Frenchman's motive.

"Completely inappropriate," Audrey started. "On the day of your mother's funeral..."

"What the hell does he want?" Lou was curious.

"Maybe he just wants to offer condolences." Rafael suggested. He looked at Lily, worried that a visit from Charbot might be uncomfortable under the circumstances. She did seem unsettled. "I think he can wait."

"I kinda want to see what he's up to." Ted said. "Maybe he's had a breakthrough or something. What could it hurt?"

"Well, I don't care one way or another." Nora said. "Should I tell Arturo to send him up?"

There were shrugs of nonchalance. Rafael studied Lily who wasn't responding one way or another. He was certain she would have voiced an objection if she weren't up to it.

"I'll go tell Arturo." Nora said and was off.

"You think he found the antiviral or whatever you call it?" Lou asked the room.

"I dunno." Ted answered. "But I have to know what made him leave his high horse in Paris and come here, on the night of Mom's funeral to see us. Without calling first. Rude."

"I don't like it." Audrey said, watching Lily protectively. They heard the front doorbell and Nora led Mssr. Charbot into the great room where he immediately spoke. "I think we can skip the introductions, no? They will not be necessary."

"Nice to see you, too, Pierre. How are things?" Ted asked.

"I have never liked you, Ted, so my purpose for coming this evening will bring me great pleasure."

Lou stood and took a protective stance. "Say what you have to say."

Charbot smirked. "I shall do that. You Johnsons and your spouses sit here in this grand house while you dictate morals to the whole world. I have come to tell you that your reign is over. You are about to find out what it feels like to be the losers. You are about to be humiliated and shunned by the entire world. I am about to bring you down and I will enjoy every minute of it."

He chuckled and looked at the expectant and worried faces. He was in his glory.

"Go ahead, Pierre." Ted said with an exaggerated yawn. "We're kinda tired, can you get on with it?"

"You will not be so glib when I tell you that I know all about your mother spreading the virus through her water bottles and refugees. I know about the fake secret sauce. I know all about the antiviral and I will be reporting your conduct to the WMA and the AMA. I doubt you will be a doctor for much longer, Ted. And I know for certain, you will go to prison." Which did wipe the smile off of Ted's face.

"Do what you have to do." Nora interjected angrily but she was scared. Her voice gave her away.

"Oh, but there's more, Mrs. Berger. You knew about this, you are acting counsel for the Johnson Project and you have covered up an enormous crime. I doubt the American Bar Association will want you after all of your deceit comes to light."

"Get out of here." Lou growled and moved toward the doctor.

"You, too, may face criminal charges, Mr. Berger. As will Rafael. You all played a part in this mass murder of the human race. You are all looking at prison and it makes me extremely happy!"

Nobody wanted to respond with any statement that could fan the flames of the accusations but everyone was trying to figure out how he had this information and how best to defend themselves. Or if they even should.

Rafael had the pragmatic approach. "Dr. Charbot, may we please discuss this as professionals?"

Charbot smirked. "If only we could but I am alone in that distinction. You and your family are nothing but common criminals who will soon know the feel of an entire universe hating your guts."

"I think you misunderstand the meaning of criminal behavior," Audrey said without conviction. Still hoping to reason with him.

"I do not think so, Mrs. Johnson. I do not think so. You are all a party to murder, you see. Not just the murder of all the children who will never be born because of your *project*, but your complicity in the murders of four innocents whose only crime were getting in the way of your plans. You all knew, my Lord, your own *sister*, and yet you kept quiet and let others take the blame. Burke will be found, your mother will be outed as her true criminal self and all of you will pay the price in prison. I plan to announce my antiviral breakthrough immediately and start bringing children into this world. I will be the hero and the world will thank me."

No one moved a muscle, in fact, they were frozen in place, except for the rapid rise and fall of their chests. Lou's forehead immediately showed beads of sweat. Lily released a sob and walked away from the seating area with her back to the scene.

Mickey Bruce. They were all thinking it.

"Oh, Ted, no more funny retorts, eh? You don't have something funny to say to me now?" Pierre laughed loudly.

"I take full responsibility for every act you've mentioned, Charbot. None of the people in this room know anything about what you're saying." Ted was firm and resolute. "I am the only one with this knowledge so go ahead and report me but there's no reason to drag the whole family..."

"Shut up." Pierre interrupted. "You are pathetic. You are all involved and I have irrefutable proof. I just wanted to see your faces when I told you. You can try and run. Leave the country. But your life here is over. The whole world will be looking for you so there is nowhere to hide. You think the president of Mexico considered himself safe? You are through and I am so pleased to be the one to bring you down." He laughed from his belly and took in the looks on their faces. The picture would last him a lifetime.

Lou was the first to react by taking his phone out of his pocket and tapping the number for Arturo. "Yeah, Arturo, can you have Ricky cover and come up here. We have someone who needs an escort out." He tapped off.

"No need for escorts, Mr. Berger. I will be on my way. I'm sure you've thought of killing me, or having your man, Burke do it, but as you all realize, the guards have seen me come in and now they will escort me out. My phone records will clearly show my visit to this house. You can't keep killing people who find out about your plan for world domination. Your federal agents will know the whole story very soon."

"Was it Mickey?" Nora had to ask. "Did you pay off Mickey Bruce? Is he your witness? How much did that cost you if you don't mind my asking?"

"Mr. Bruce was not at all helpful. I have a much closer spy who was able to infiltrate your family with such precision, you will be shocked to find out just how stupid you are. How trusting you are. My irrefutable witness is Lily Simone and she is prepared to testify against all of you."

Lily turned to Rafael. "I'm so sorry Rafael." She truly seemed distraught but nothing compared to the anguish on Rafael's face as the realization dawned on him. "I really cared for you..." Rafael's face lost all expression.

She had the decency to look away. "I would never fit in with you or this family. I'm not like you. I'll never be like you. Uncle Pierre convinced me to come back."

Rafael mechanically asked, "This is your uncle? The one that...?"

"Enough!" Pierre shouted. He crossed the room and took Lily's hand roughly. She kept her gaze on Rafael who had stopped breathing momentarily. The rest of the family slowly caught on and responded with gasps and rancor.

"You. Bitch." Nora said coldly.

"Lily..." Ted whispered. He couldn't fathom the betrayal. "What has he done to you?"

"He opened my eyes to a family who I thought was so saintly. You are all guilty, most of all your mother. I looked up to her. I wanted to be like her but Uncle made me see she is like all the rest of the world. Maybe I thought joining you would make me a better person but all it has done is show me that horrible people can hide behind altruistic intentions. With Uncle Pierre, I don't have to pretend. At least he is honest about what he wants."

Pierre smirked, enjoying the victory. "She has also learned to abandon a sinking ship. The Johnson Project is over and the Charbot reign will triumph. Lily knows how to survive and her only hope now is to cling to me. Of course she will first pay the price for her defection to your camp." Lily looked dejected as she accepted the blame for her family betrayal. But she turned to Rafael as Pierre led her to the archway. Nora wanted to strike but used her words instead. "You are just as culpable as the rest of us. You're going down with us."

"Not so, Mrs. Berger." Pierre pulled Lily to his side. "Lily was coerced and bought into this syndicate known as the Johnson family. She will be vindicated by your justice system when she confesses everything she has recently learned about the Johnson Project. She will be punished in private for her betrayal to me but she should expect that. She has nowhere else to go but with me."

They all heard the front door open and assumed Arturo had arrived. Lou was the only one who could move or think. "Get these fuckers out of here!" He bellowed to Arturo. "And call in some reinforcement for tonight, please. We got rats getting through the perimeter." Arturo tried to take Charbot's arm but it was not necessary. He and Lily walked out the front door and into his waiting car. Lily never looked back. Lou made sure the front door was bolted shut and he returned to the agony in the great room.

"We can contain this." Ted assured everyone as he ran his hand through his hair for the hundredth time and paced. "I can take the fall for everyone and you'll all be okay."

Nora was with Rafael who sat stone faced and unmoving. Nora put her arms around her brother but he didn't seem to realize it. Audrey sat on the other side of him but stood to address her husband. "You can't, Ted. Please think of the children." She cried.

"I am thinking of the children, Audrey." He replied gently. "They need you and I have to keep you out of this."

Nora shook her head. "We *all* knew about Mary's crime and none of us reported it..."

"You never knew!" Lou bellowed. "You never knew about it, Nora. You gotta keep saying that. But I did and I'm the one who didn't report it. I was the closest to Burke and the police will buy it. You need to deny everything and stay out of this for Billy's sake. Do you understand?"

Ted turned to Lou. "How much time have we got?"

Lou shrugged. "We got until at least tomorrow. Those two have a long story to tell but the cops or the feds will need to verify their stories and get warrants. We have all night to get our shit together and most of tomorrow. We

343

have to make plans for their future. We have to keep Nora and Audrey out of prison, Ted. That's the best we can hope for. Lily knows everything..."

Rafael sobbed. "How could she do this?"

"I hate her so much right now." Nora said with vengeance.

"I don't understand this... Why?" Audrey asked no one in particular.

"I have no idea. I don't know." Lou said. "But one meeting with the feds and we are through. They won't go to the local cops, no way. They'll get with the feds, report the four murders, now bolstered with the Burke involvement, they will find cause. This is far worse than what Mickey Bruce would have done."

Ted sank into a chair. "Lily can easily produce the antiviral for Charbot and the WMA. They can start mass reproducing within days. She'll tell the FDA we had the antiviral all along. We'll be shut down immediately and I'll be arrested. Although I suspect I'll be arrested immediately for not reporting Mom and Burke. I can't get around that. Guys, it's over. We have to keep the damage to a minimum. Please don't argue with me. I can take the fall for this if you will all please point the finger at me and play along. *PLEASE!*" Ted rested his weary head in his hands. Audrey joined him on the couch and they held each other and cried.

Nora's mind was racing for all of the legal consequences. "We're all toast, Ted. Maybe we can keep Audrey out of this but the rest of us are in for the long haul. We have a lot of fallout to consider. We have a whole lot of doctors on staff who are about to be fired. We have a building full of people about to lose their jobs. They're all going to feel duped. Used. The lawsuits are going to crush us."

"We won't be safe. None of us." Lou said grimly. "We can't stay here."

Ted looked up. "I'll have tomorrow with the kids, right?" He looked to Lou then Audrey. "I can spend tomorrow with the kids all day before...." He sobbed.

Everyone cried. Rafael was destroyed. "I'm so sorry." He managed to choke out. "I had no idea she would do this to us."

"Why don't we bail?" Nora said through her tears and seemed almost hopeful. "Let's get the kids and get on Mom's plane tonight. We can find some country..." She stopped speaking as she realized there was nowhere to go. There was no country that would harbor them.

"We need to face up to what we've done." Audrey said firmly. "And you know what? I'm not ashamed. And I won't be ashamed. We can stand up to this and admit we made some errors in judgement but we have no reason to hide. Every step we took was done with the best of intentions."

They all considered her words but it didn't cheer anyone up. It was the end of their family and the life that they loved. The grief was physically painful on top of a week of devastating revelation and loss.

Before they went back to their own homes that night, they hugged, especially Rafael, and spoke of their love for one another. They all agreed to meet back at Mary's house the next morning since it was the most secure location and they could hopefully spend the day together and finalize their strategy. They all knew it would be their last day together.

Chapter 49

Audrey hit the grocery store early and planned a day full of meals including everyone's favorites. When she thought back on favorite family memories, she realized that most were at the table eating good food and today would be no different. It was surreal to push a cart down the grocery store aisle where she'd been a million times knowing what was to come. She saw people she knew, even said a cheery good morning to some friends but the pit of her stomach burned and her nerves were in shreds.

Ted brought the kids to Mary's home and told them it would be a day of fun with dad. He told them that he loved them and each time he thought his heart would burst out of his chest. Rafael never left Mary's house the night before. He didn't feel he could drive or function and he didn't want to face the coach house with Lily not in it. Nora and Lou came last bringing Billy and Tuffy. They had a family breakfast together with Ted trying to eat and hold both of his kids in his lap during the meal. It was intensely difficult for everyone to keep a happy face on for the children but they managed.

The guard had been told that they were not seeing any visitors but if any law enforcement showed up, they were to be escorted in without question. Ted did not plan to resist arrest or even avoid arrest, he would go quietly. The others weren't sure if they were going to be arrested immediately or after further investigation but Nora thought everyone but Ted would probably be allowed bail so it was just a matter of having the bail money on hand for when it was needed. It would take time for Pierre and Lily to make the official report and even more time for the feds to prepare the charges. The family didn't expect anything official until at least the afternoon but they didn't know for sure. The waiting was miserable.

They drank coffee in the kitchen after breakfast and the kids left to play. Nora brought up a topic they hadn't thought about. "I think we can expect the government to seize mom's assets and the house. They'll find the Mosquito Room, I'm sure Lily will tell them about it. They'll have a lot to work with." She advised. "She knows the whole story."

"I've been thinking, Audrey, you may need to move some money around. Dump as much as you can into checking for now." Ted suggested, wanting to change the subject. "They may freeze our accounts but they can't take away living expenses for you. The kids don't need to feel the pinch, although things are about to change for them."

"I was just thinking that poor ol' Mickey Bruce might be in a heap of trouble if it comes to light that he knew about this. His editor knows he went to see Mrs. Timmons, he must know about Egypt. Mickey might be in a world of hurt."

"Yeah." Lou agreed. "Maybe we should give him a heads up. He did us a solid. I got no problem repaying the favor."

"You know, maybe he could help us." Ted said. "As long as the story is going to break, why not let him get the credit. At least we can explain ourselves."

"Call him, Lou." Audrey said. "Give him a chance to save himself. See if he wants to come over."

They all pondered it for a minute while Lou stepped into the butler's pantry to call Mickey.

"As long as he can do it without incriminating himself." Nora said.

"I don't want him painting Mom in a bad light." Rafael mumbled. "But, well..." Rafael couldn't finish the thought. The others contemplated the raw facts of the story and it was a subject nobody wanted to ponder so they left it alone.

Audrey had her arm wrapped around Ted as she addressed Nora. "I'll need to pull Allie out of school for a bit. Are you thinking the same for Billy?"

Nora nodded. "Definitely. Just until we can figure out how much they're going to hear from other kids. We also have to consider that the press might follow you to school or cause a distraction around town. We have to lay low. They might not be able to go back, now that I think of it. My poor little Billy, he doesn't deserve this." Nora held back her tears. Lou came back into the room and put his arms around her.

"I've been playing it in my mind." Ted said. "When they know mom spread the Aqar virus, they're going to assume we were all in on it. We can deny it, but that's going to be the first reason they hate us."

"I think we're legally off the hook." Nora said. "We can prove we didn't know about it. Even Lily will have to back us on that." She sneered while she said it and then looked at apologetically at Rafael.

Lou agreed. "Now consider that shocker along with the implication that we had Billy's parents killed. They're gonna find Mrs. Timmons and they're going bring up Billy every chance they get. I'm gonna lose it on somebody if they splash my boy all over the news. They can't use his picture, right?"

350

Nora shook her head. "Oh my God, Lou, they can take him away from us while they investigate!"

"NO!" Audrey cried. "That's just not possible, is it?"

Lou took Nora's hand. "They might. Legally, Mrs. Timmons has no claim, nor is she healthy enough, but the court may try to find a more suitable guardian for him in the interim. We're going to beg them to make you the guardian, Audrey. If it comes to that."

"Of course." She whispered. "But will I even be considered?"

"Not if I'm in jail." Ted answered. "Not when there are a million capable foster parents out there to choose from."

"Jesus." Was all Lou could say.

Nora chose to ignore the topic because the possibilities were unthinkable. "Are you going to call Khan? And Sybil?"

Ted looked even more miserable. "I'm working up the courage. Khan's in Belgium this week but I'll try to get him home. This will devastate them but I can't keep them out of it. There will be a cloud of suspicion over their heads for the rest of their lives but at least they won't go to jail." A fresh wave of despair took hold of the group as they thought about the friends and colleagues who were about to have their worlds torn apart. Would any of them understand the course of events that led to the downfall of the Johnson Project?

"The feds are gonna go looking for Burke." Lou said, grimly. "Hell, Interpol will be looking for Burke. The WMA will be looking for Burke. The CIA, FBI, Homeland, and every stinking news station and reporter on the planet will be looking for Burke. He knows way more than we do. I hope he figured out a good place to hide." Lou paused like a thought just occurred to him. "Good God, is the guy a sociopath and we never noticed?"

Ted answered. "Mom told me once about his childhood. It was horrible. He never had anyone in his corner until she found him in a halfway house. She gave him a leg up and he stuck to her like glue. In a way, he was like her son."

Audrey let tears fall down her cheeks. "She only wanted to help people. I know, now, that she was a little unstable but, I still admire her. I do. I still love her. And I'm devastated for what's about to happen to our family, truly, I will never recover from this loss. But what I fear the most for the future is all the good that is happening in the world will be undone and all of our mistakes will be for nothing."

Ted stood up, thoroughly spent but trying hard. "I promised Allie a game of Pretty, Pretty Princess and I intend to let her win. Excuse me."

Rafael watched his brother leave the kitchen. "Lily didn't have it easy as a child. Sometimes when we were all here having dinner I could see she would look around the table in wonder. She enjoyed the camaraderie but she never fully understood it. She never felt like she could be a part of it."

"Mom would have gotten her to be a part of us." Audrey said. "I know what you mean about her feeling left out. I always thought that would change once you two were married..." Her face fell as she realized her faux pas.

"It's okay, Audrey." Rafael said kindly. "I see now that it never would have worked. Never.

Like you said, none of us will be the same again. But as for Lily, I feel sorry for her more than anything else. The things Charbot did to her as a child... how could she go back to him?"

Nora sneered. "I hate her guts more than anything else. A little more every single minute."

Rafael looked almost vacant. "We have to move on..."

Everyone gave him understanding looks of empathy.

His eyes were red from crying all night and the pain was weighing heavily on him. "I can't bear the thought of Ted going to prison. We have to do something. I wish I could take his place."

Lou took a call from the guard house and gave instructions to let the visitor through. "Mickey Bruce is here."

They gathered in the great room. Nora set the kids up with a Disney movie in the playroom while they waited for Mickey to drive up to the house. It would be good to talk to him about his article and answer any questions he might have while they still had the freedom to speak. At this point, they were all ready to come clean. Oddly, they trusted him.

When Audrey let him in he came bustling into the great room with a smile. A bit odd, they all thought, under the circumstances, but maybe he was excited about the inevitable bylines. He didn't bother to sit. "I got some news for you all. I came as soon as I confirmed the details." Mickey said.

Nora wasn't having it. "We're not exactly feeling chatty right now, Mickey."

"Lou told me what you guys are going through and I know it must be hell for you. I'm real sorry, Rafael, about Lily. God, I didn't see that one coming. It sucks and you deserved better."

"Thank you, Mickey. I mean it." Rafael replied with automatic manners.

"You're probably thinking jail time and financial ruin and devastation for your family and the world, huh?" Mickey asked.

"Nailed it." Ted said without humor.

Mickey looked into the faces of the Johnsons. "I just got a tip that Pierre Charbot was flying his Cessna Citation Encore early this morning en route to D.C. with one passenger on board, Miss Lily Simone."

Lou nodded. "Yeah, I figured they would go right to the feds with the story. I'm sure they have an appointment with the biggies at Langley."

Mickey waited for it. "Well, they didn't make it. The plane went down over Lake Michigan shortly after take-off." He had the good manners to frown as he said, "There were no survivors."

None of them responded at first. None of them even changed expressions for a good fifteen seconds.

Mickey calmly said, "You guys don't have to worry anymore. The whole story went down with the plane."

It took a few minutes to absorb the information. Once they did, they turned to Rafael to comfort him even though she had just sucked the life right out of him, Lily was a huge part of his existence, and theirs, if they had to admit it. They were not naïve enough to believe that they were completely absolved. There might be written records, evidence, possibly digital proof of all that they were guilty of, but to lose both the whistle blower and the eyewitness before there were sworn statements would certainly dull the impact. The immediate pressure was off for now. There would be no arrests or even questioning for the moment. There were no other humans on the planet who knew about the antiviral. The relief was exhilarating and exhausting.

The first few weeks were iffy but when nothing came to light, the family was able to step back and breathe. The kids went back to school, the adults went back to work. If they seemed unsettled or distraught over the next few months, coworkers chalked it up to the recent loss of their mother, sister and, of course, Rafael's love, Lily. Most of the world empathized with the Johnson family. The family wondered what would be discovered in the wreckage, but even that outcome ruled in their favor. It took months, but the FAA recovered only enough of the aircraft to determine that the plane was brought down by a stroke of lightening so intense that most of the fuselage was destroyed before it hit the water. It was odd that there had been no forecast of lightening on the morning of the incident and only light rain. Still, bursts of unexpected weather were not uncommon on the Great Lakes and the FAA unofficially ruled it a freak occurrence. They found no human remains and the hunks of metal that were recovered were melted into blobs of unidentifiable matter. Mother Nature had taken down the craft and made sure there was nothing left of it.

The Johnson Project continued and thrived and for a long time, there was peace on earth.

18340605R00211

Printed in Great Britain
by Amazon